The Greatest Bastard

Zoe Morelli

ISBN: 978-1-5356-1755-0

DEDICATION

*Alfred Lee Glass Jr. – Your Wings Were Ready, My Heart Was Not
1990-2016*

*To my husband Christian who has always supported all of my
crazy dreams and carried me through the toughest times of my life.
I will love you always.*

*To my children & grandchildren: Staci, Kelsea, Trey, Avery, Adri-
an, Messiyah, Juelz, Azaiah, Raeia, Skyler, Carlton III, Jullius - my
loves, my life, my inspiration*

Contents

Everything has a Price

*"Lilith, you know necromancy is an eternal sin!
Our entire coven will pay for this with our eternal souls!"*

"Mary, do not make an enemy of me!" Lilith shouted as the thunder rumbled like the voice of an infuriated god in the distant skies. Mary retreated and took her place alongside the rest of the group. The static in the air made her skin feel alive. Goosebumps and fine hairs rose from her flesh.

Lilith was the leader of the coven. An elder, the most powerful sorceress in the New World, maybe even beyond the new world. The coven knew very well the cost of necromancy. Universal laws had to be followed. Balance would need to be restored. Resurrecting one person would require the death of another. Lilith was willing to pay that price for her only child.

But was the rest of the coven? Lilith did not ask, she didn't care. Her focus was singular, deeply rooted in her grief. There would be no reasoning with her. The rest of the witches were either onboard or took the risk of becoming the life sacrificed so the dead could once again live. They had little choice but to participate. What this meant for their souls, that was another matter that Lilith did not concern herself with. Although the spell was not fully understood by the lesser witches, it was well known that lifeforce manipulation involved the sacrifice of a dark angel.

Lilith had prepared the alter and was ready for the ritual. They were in a stunning room, gold from the walls to the floors, the hanging chandelier to the gold-trimmed ceilings. It was insufferably sophisticated, a testament to the wealth and power of the upper class, immaculately elegant, formal, and cold. Just standing inside the room made Mary feel out of place, like she was unworthy of the privilege. In contrast to the golden room, Lilith's dead son had been laid out before them on the grand dining table. He was pale, as death makes all, yet, there was a darkness about him. He didn't look like a sleeping man. His eyes were sunken behind closed lids, his jaw slack. He was still and cold, but even death could not rob him of his beauty. A room like this was becoming of him. He fit, even in death.

What lay on the table was but an empty shell of a once vivacious young man with dark curls and a perfect smile. His demise was a crushing heartbreak for them all. They had watched the boy grow into a man, and they had all loved him like family. Tonight, they stood around his body, unsettled, terrified of what they were about to do.

The French doors rattled, taking their stance against the gale force winds that swept in from the distance. Candles flickered, surrounded by herbs and potions. Precious stones were laid out in meaningful patterns. The storm that was brewing was an unexpected but welcome addition of power. It moved quickly; loud, angry waves battered the coastline. The sky was full of tumultuous, dark and rugged clouds, churning angrily. Lightning flashed in sheets across the sky, eerily illuminating the scene.

Lilith seemed to glow, charged with the energy of the storm.

She took Mary's hand. In turn, each caster took the hand of the one beside her until they formed an uninterrupted circle around the dead man's body. It was quickly approaching the witching hour. Lilith broke the silence with a chant.

"Mortui estis Consepulti sumus cum ilio per baptismum in mortem, ut, quomodo Hugr krellr náttúra hefja nú. surrexit a mortuis per gloriam Patris, ita et nos in novitate vitae ambulemus"

The trance began to spread, one witch after the other began to chant. *"Ressurrexit a mortuis, suscitare de veritate. surrexit a mortuis per gloriam Patris, ita et nos in novitate vitae ambulemus"*

Once the trance was induced, there was no breaking it; except with the spell's success or the grand witch's acceptance of failure. They all knew that Lilith would never accept failure.

During incantations, time meant nothing. They were no longer physical beings. It was a state of weightlessness. To be one with the rest of the coven was a gift. The act of chanting was spiritual, as close to being one with the universe as a human possibly could in their physical body. It was difficult to focus on anything else, but Mary tried. Mary distracted herself with attempts to pray. She prayed for success, she prayed for failure. She just wanted this madness to end. No matter how hard she tried to pull away, the power drew her back in. She could feel her brow crease into a frown as she took in a deep breath and surrendered to the force, like being sucked into a black hole of nothingness. It was just too powerful to resist. Mary succumbed to the witches' chant.

The hours passed agonizingly slow as she resisted, but once she yielded, time slipped by quickly like wind ripping through a storm. Eventually Mary's eyes flickered open, and reality poured in as her senses were gradually restored. She always came out of chants a bit disoriented. It took her several long seconds before she regained her composure. Mary concentrated intently on the here and now. Everything was slowly coming together. There was always so much to take in as she 'woke' from a trance.

The windows in the room were now ajar, and the smell of ozone filled the air. Mary breathed in the earthy scent. The storm produced a sweet pungent zing in her nostrils as it mixed with the salty ocean humidity. A strong breeze blew through the room, whipping the curtains like a flag in a storm. Daylight cut through the darkness as the drapes were snapped violently away from the glass panes. The sunlight stung Mary's eyes, causing her pupils to constrict rapidly. It was the morning sun. Mary's vision slowly came into focus, the young man's body laying rigid in front of her, his chestnut hair glistened in the light, his porcelain skin was flawless, the once pale full lips were now a soft rose color.

Lilith was first to break the circle as she stepped toward her son and reached for his hand. Tears streaked her pale, beautiful face. A proud motherly smile curved her lips as she brushed a stray curl from her child's forehead.

He was motionless. Lilith's eyes seemed to stare blankly through the mask of death piercing her dead son's soul. She was fidgeting with her nails, and that said as much as any words could. She was uneasy.

Time held no relevance as they stood patiently through the rising dawn that had now fully pierced the night sky. The night was witches' domain. Mary willed the sun to vault itself higher over the horizon; like an instigator, it crept inch by painful inch. The world moved silently around them, as if taunting her.

Mary thought she glimpsed movement. Yes, his finger had moved. Her eyes were still adjusting, maybe it was just shadows moving around the room with each whip of the drapes as they danced in the post-storm breeze. Then again, she saw movement! Dark eyelashes flickered ever so slightly. Mary's heart leapt. Suddenly, a deep breath caught in the once still chest. The pounding that was the boy's heart continued to accelerate, becoming a staccato, rapid and furious. The man's eyes abruptly opened. Startled brown eyes stared up into the face of a beloved mother.

The witches all stepped back to give Lilith and her son privacy. Part of Mary felt painfully excited to see the young man alive again, awakened from darkness. Another part of Mary's subconscious felt the cold through her chest as she listened to his human heartbeats. She knew he was no longer the boy they had laid to rest. She felt an awful omen of blackness wash over her as she realized she was listening to the very last of his humanity being vanquished. She was filled with dread and selfish anticipation of things to come. This was Lilith's choice, Mary told herself, Lilith's choice alone. But Mary knew that she too was culpable for the coven's actions.

In her insanity, in her grief, Lilith had used a spell that was forbidden to her kind. A spell to bring her child back to life. A spell that would leave a curse on the world. A curse no caster could ever reverse. The price, Lilith would lose her soul and be consumed by darkness forever. That was likely the fate of the entire coven. Nevertheless, the spell had worked.

The young man stretched out his arm and took Lilith's hand into his. It was ice cold. He squeezed her hand in reassurance. "There's no need to worry any longer. Everything's going to be alright," he said with a flash of the most perfect smile Mary had ever seen.

Lilith had loved her son so thoroughly in life. A perfect love. In the past there had been so much goodness within Lilith, but that was gone now. The love between a mother and her child, so pure, so perfect, had been replaced with darkness. Lilith knew that death was not the end, so why she had evoked evil and darkness to bring her beloved back to this realm was unexplainable, pure madness. In that kind of madness, a person loses sight of reason. Only power prevails. And power always has a price. But everything has a price. It just depends if you are willing to pay it.

Chapter One

Chloe

Today I would be free of all worldly possessions, today was the bank closing on my family home.

I stared into the mirror attempting to tame my long, curly hair into two braids. From the outside, my reflection resembled many other twenty-one-year-old women. The outside did not echo the pain and torture that was constantly gnawing at my insides. I can barely look at myself. The nightmare that has shadowed every day of the past year has taken its toll on me.

I slammed the brush onto the dresser. Why had I even bothered to look in the mirror? Frustrated, I finished taming my hair into braids without the aid of brush or mirror. I could care less if I ever looked at my reflection again. Everyone always called me an attractive girl, but I had never really fit in. I was too edgy, too intellectual for most teenagers. I always felt that people my age were intimidated by me. Never really trying to get to know me, which was fine, I liked solitude and felt most comfortable alone.

I preferred sleeping in, reading a book or watching movies. I hated television, especially reality TV which was all the rave with people my age. I never found a niche, I always expected too much of my peers. There were so many barriers to forming a lasting friendship, like the fact that I hated pop culture, preferred Indy and classic music and always felt as if empty conversation was worthless and a waste of time.

Mom always called me a closet intellectual, a beautiful geek. "I'm not really in the closet about it Mom," I would answer back. My greatest problem before last March was the fact that I never really related to anyone. I sometimes wondered if I see the world differently than everybody else. I considered that I may have a type of autism that prevented me from connecting with people. My sister, Mia, was the only one who ever actually understood me. The bond between sisters was a beautiful thing, a true gift. But Mia was dead now.

From my mother, I inherited a sense of adventure. Even as a small child I loved the solace of backpacking. The further away from civilization, the better. The outdoors was the one place that I could always count on to make me happy, bring me peace. I had hiked a lot lately, counting on it to still my mind. At times my life was literally hanging in the balance when I went off on a backpacking trip.

Since the loss of my family, despite counseling and medication, depression and anxiety loomed like a dark cloud of doom, ready to consume me at any moment. I was numb, lost, and alone.

I stray tear ran down my cheek as I took in all sights of my childhood home, the only home I had ever lived in. Every square foot held a memory. I could see my mother experimenting with recipes in the kitchen. My father sitting in his recliner watching the Dallas Cowboys, cheering or yelling profanities at the television depending on how the game was playing out.

I concentrated on the memory of my mother. "There is so much I don't know about you," I whispered running my fingers along the granite countertop. "I can't even remember your favorite movie." Standing there, I focused, willing the memories to appear. "What was the name of that stupid perfume you wore?

The one we gave you every Christmas, birthday, and Mother's Day. Why can't I fucking remember? " I could see the shape of the bottle, smell the scent, a rosy, clean musk, but the name was just out of my reach. I balled my fist up tightly, my chest aching. I was already losing my mother.

I was jarred back to my senses by a rapid succession of *KNOCK, KNOCK, KNOCK.* "Chloe Jamison?" a man's voice called out from the other side of the door.

The unexpected knocking had sent my heart racing. It didn't take much to do that lately. The car service had arrived.

"I'll be out in a minute," I responded, and immediately began to race around the living room gathering the few belongings I had left.

A black sedan was idling in the driveway. As I opened the front door, an elderly man popped out from behind the wheel. He was wearing khaki pants and a red polo with the car service logo embroidered on the chest. He sported a grandfatherly smile. He was way too chipper for my current mood. He opened the trunk, and I followed his lead placing my suitcase and duffle bag into the space provided. He used both of his fleshy hands to reposition the bags before slamming the lid closed. We drove in silence, but I noticed him glancing back at me through the rear-view mirror. I was happy he didn't engage me in conversation, I didn't like small talk but especially today. The quiet lull of the car ride gave me time to think.

My thoughts picked up where they had left off, my lost family. My loneliness was reaffirmation that over the past twenty-one years I had never felt unloved, until now. My parents had loved me completely, perfectly. Just thinking about them was comforting yet so painful.

The time with my parents was a blessing, like a long perfect summer day that lasted for twenty-one years. Then it all ended abruptly. Now I was wealthy but lacked any joy. Money didn't buy happiness. Nothing materialistic would ever take away my pain. Riches beyond belief would never restore what I had lost. It couldn't buy back the three lives that were ripped prematurely off the earth, so what value was money if it would never make me whole again?

The gentle movement of the car abruptly stopped, snapping me back into the present. The car door creaked opened then slammed shut, the driver seeming hesitant as he opened my door for me. "Sir, I'll be here for only a few minutes to sign some papers then I'll be ready to head to the airport."

He nodded in agreement. Stepping out of the warm car, I glanced around. The title company was in the city centre of the town I had grown up in. Once I left, I would have no reason to ever return. One last time my eyes skimmed over the modern shops and manicured sidewalks and streets. I experienced a fleeting moment of nostalgia.

I turned and headed into the building where the papers and check were waiting on me. I signed and dated without even reading one word that was in front of me. It took less than ten minutes to rid myself of the last invisible string that kept me tethered to my past life.

On the way to the airport the driver detoured to allow me to deposit the check into the bank. The balance on my checking account receipt was exorbitant. I actually couldn't help but laugh every time I saw it. There was nothing, not one thing, that I wanted to buy other than the ticket out of this state, which was purchased as soon as I knew the date the house was closing.

After the bank we were off to catch my plane. This chapter of my life was over. I was uncertain where the next chapter would take me, but I felt just the slightest bit of excitement, an emotion that I had not experienced in a very long time.

Chapter Two

Goodbye Life

I had no idea what I was going to do other than fly to Boston. The Northeast called to me like a lost lover. After the death of my family I had made the decision to drop out of college. I had always wanted to be a writer. I also knew that I was amongst a dwindling minority of youth who still preferred reading a book to watching a movie, so instead, I had opted to become a teacher. I had never really wanted to be a teacher, which made it an easy decision to not return to school.

I would never have to work unless I became financially reckless or I chose to. I however wasn't reckless, and at this point, I didn't choose to work. I would try my hand at writing. The first step toward any dream was believing I could do it. Writing was never a choice for me, it was a calling.

The real question was where I would live? The world was my proverbial oyster. My home would be in a quiet location, with four seasons, a place that inspired me. The ocean inspired, so did the mountains. Seclusion was important, no crowded cities or big towns. For now, I would explore the northeast.

Since the loss of my family my brain never seemed to shut off. I missed my mother, ached for her. My mother would have loved this adventure. She would have, but she was never coming back. I would never again walk a trail with her, never again feel her arms around me. There was no one left that cared if I lived or died. No one to remember my birthday. No one to be proud of me. Hell, no one to even remember that I existed. It was at this moment that I began to realize how unimportant humans really were in the whole scheme of things, how quickly people can fade away, completely out of existence.

After those who are bound by blood are gone, no one cares. Horrible thoughts began to flood my head. I realized that I couldn't remember my great grandmother's name. My mother's grandmother had already faded out of existence. Dead less than fifteen years, and no one remembered that she had ever lived. What wretched, selfish creatures' people are. It was incredible the depths to which a person's mind would sink when confused and at an emotional low. Fighting to push those thoughts from my mind, I pushed my duffle bag into the overhead bin and took my seat next to the window.

Why won't they stop? I popped a Valium in my mouth and chased it with some water, praying for it to kick in quickly. As I dissolved into my seat memories continued to play inside my head, like small film clips I couldn't turn off.

My father's face, handsome and smiling tenderly as he peeked through the opening of my bedroom door. He rarely entered my room, fully respecting my privacy.

"Trouble sleeping?" he questioned. I was home from college for Christmas break.

"Nope," I answered, barely looking up from my book.

"You sure?" He ineffectively attempted to mask his fatherly concern.

"Mm-hmm." I continued reading, wishing him away.

"Burning the midnight oil?" He lingered.

"Yeah." I sighed loudly to punctuate my annoyance at the intrusion.

"Okay." He returned the sigh. "Goodnight, love."

"Yeah, you too," I responded dismissively.

My father hesitated. "By the way, I came across some University of Texas tickets at work. Want to come along?" I was a huge UT fan growing up, and my father would always take me to the home football and basketball games. My room, thanks to my dad, sported a great deal of UT memorabilia.

"Dad, I don't think so. But thanks for offering." I was openly aggravated by his persistent interruption of my reading. I don't know why I acted like that. At the time I just wanted to be left alone to finish my book in peace. I guess you should be careful what you wish for.

"Okay. Don't worry about it. Get some sleep." He didn't even try to hide his disappointment.

"Okay," I said as impersonal as I could so to drive home the point that this conversation was unwelcome. Dad finally left, closing the door behind him.

What a bitch. Looking back, it was evident that he was longing for conversation with his daughter, bonding time. Of course, I couldn't be bothered with him. I shook away the memory.

During the plane ride I had lots of time to think, and I believed that all true revelations were conceived in silent meditation. Think, I did, my mind ambling randomly through the years of memories. My thoughts were vivid, lucid, real.

For some reason my father's dry cleaning came to mind. He always dropped his clothes off on Thursday and picked them up on the following Thursday. Did he have suits hanging at the dry cleaner right now, never to be retrieved? I don't know why the thought of that bothered me so much.

I began to doze off as I dreamed of Mia's funeral. Mia's service was much harder than my parents'. It was decided, by whom I was still unsure, that Mia would have a separate memorial service.

This would give Mia's many friends the chance to say goodbye and pay tribute to her. Everyone had loved Mia.

Following the accident, friends of my parents had made sincere attempts to look after me. They wanted to let me know that I was not alone in this world. But with time the efforts faded, and I was grateful. I didn't want people's pity. I especially did not want people lingering around. I liked being alone, took comfort in my state of depression. The pain was the only thing that made me feel alive. To feel anything but numb was an improvement. If my heart stopped beating, I would welcome it because at least the pain would finally be gone.

However, my heart continued to beat. And the reality was and would always be that my family was killed by a truck driver who was on the job. The insurance company settled with a check. A check that amounted to a sum they figured my mother, father, and sixteen-year-old sister's lives were worth.

For a month I couldn't bear to even look at the check. I barely even left my room. Both of my parents had substantial life insurance policies through their work as well. Those policies doubled because their death was an accident. None of that mattered to me, those checks sat on the table in the entryway, unopened for weeks.

Then one day my mother's best friend dropped by. She talked me into seeing a counselor. She also set an appointment to speak with an estate attorney. Nikki was sweet and kind. She was also suffering from the loss of my mother. I loved her for the help that she provided me in my hour of need and cherished the way Nikki loved and missed my mother. However, in the end I took her help then pushed her away. The separation started after meeting with the estate attorney. That was the day that I announced I wanted to sell everything.

Nikki looked at me eyes wide, jaw slack and said, "Maybe this is too soon, I'm not sure that you've thought this out, sweetheart."

I wanted to say, 'mind your own business,' but instead said, "It hurts too much to live here, surrounded by their things. If I am going to survive this, I am going to need to make a fresh start. I've been thinking about this for a while, and this is something that I need to do!"

I could see the hurt on Nikki's face. I could see the understanding in the attorney's demeanor. It didn't matter though; I didn't care what either of them thought. I needed to be free of this misery. A few days later there was a 'for sale' sign in the yard. The house sold quickly, for a bargain price, and the attorney set up an auction. I removed a few sentimental belongings, photos, other keepsakes and had those items taken to storage. As per the agreement, the estate attorney paid the storage bill for two years. The rest of the family's belongings were sold to the highest bidder. As I packed my bags in preparation for the new owners to take possession of my childhood home, I felt nothing but relief.

The attorney had set up accounts for me and deposited the checks, for a modest fee, of course. Whatever he charged was worth it. After the auction, I relieved him of his duties. He seemed surprised and talked about investments and my future. He told me that this might seem like a lot of money, but it wasn't enough to last a lifetime. I thanked him and hung up the phone. Shortly after the first meeting with the attorney was when I decided to move away from Texas. I never felt the need to tell anyone. Nikki called frequently, but I didn't pick up. The calls continued until the house phone was shut off just before the home sale was final. Nikki was sweet, but I had no intentions of carrying on a relationship with her.

I thought about D-day at the university. The police and school counselor appeared at my dorm to tell me that my beloved family had died. I pushed that memory away. That one hurt way too much to re-live.

It's funny how in death you tend to forget a person's faults and only remember the good things about them. I thought about the decision I had made during my parent's funeral to not return to college. I imagined how disappointed they would be. Then I thought, 'no they won't dummy, they are dead'. It almost made me laugh out loud right there in the church during the service. It is odd the gamut of emotions that suddenly appear during the deepest moments of grief.

My father always said that I had an odd sense of humor. "To know you is to love you," he would say with a laugh.

As my mind continued to wander, I was taken back to my last breakfast at home before returning to school. This memory was important. Little did I know it would be the very last time I would ever sit down to a meal with my parents.

"Morning," Mom said cheerfully. My mom was always a morning person. An attribute I did not inherit from her.

"Morning," I grumbled in response.

"Did you sleep?" she asked.

"What's the deal with everyone asking me if I slept?" I snapped back, then caught myself and answered, "Yeah. I slept."

"Hungry?" Mom ignored the inexcusable behavior.

"Uh... Hungry, uh. No," I stammered as mom slid a piece of French toast onto my plate.

I pushed the plate away.

"Chloe!" Dad exclaimed. "It's French toast. It's your favorite."

"Uh... I'm not hungry. I don't typically eat breakfast much anymore. Usually just coffee." I shook my head. "Anyway, I need to leave soon."

"Breakfast, hun, remember? Energy! Most important meal of the day."

I shook my head and continued reading. Mom, irritated, took the plate away.

"Chloe, your mother got up this morning just to make you breakfast, and you thank her by saying you're not hungry?" Mom looked dejected and began to clean up.

Dad stopped her, took the plate of French toast back, placing it in front of me. "Wait a minute, love, hang on. Chloe's gonna eat it. Come on. Right, Chloe, it's French toast. Your favorite." Dad glanced from me to my mom, raising his eyebrows and softly jerking his head toward his wife. It was painfully obvious that he was indicating to me that my behavior was hurting my mother's feeling. I sighed, giving in to the charade.

"Sure, Mom, I'd love some French toast." I stubbornly tossed my book across the table and glared at Dad as I pulled the plate closer and dramatically began to eat. It was delicious. It was the last meal my mother ever made for me, and I didn't even thank her, much less tell her how wonderful it was and how much I enjoyed it.

After returning to school that day I opened my backpack to find fresh fruit packed neatly into Tupperware containers. A small note from my mom in loopy handwriting, 'Stay healthy. I packed some fruit for you to snack on while you study. I love you to infinity! XO. Mom'

A tear ran down my cheek as I looked out at the clouds. All I wanted was to sleep. I sat listening to the thrum of the plane engines. I focused on the slight bouncy vibration that ran through the plane. I ran my toes through the carpet beneath my feet as I tried to clear my mind. I must have finally fallen asleep.

At some point later, I awoke to a woman speaking overhead, "The captain has started his final descent into Boston. Please make sure your overlap table is upright and secure, your bags are either in the overhead bins or tucked all the way beneath the seat and your seatbelts are securely fastened; we should be landing in Boston in five minutes."

I glanced at my watch; it was nearly five PM. Tonight I would check into the hotel, have room service and get some sleep. Tomorrow I had decisions to be made. I was excited, I felt like a reader whose emotions were at the mercy of the author. A reader staying up all night to get through the next thrilling plot twist during a moment of elevated drama. However, what I realized at that moment was that the pen was in my hand. I was the author.

Chapter Three

A Place to Call Home

I had just checked out at Barnes & Noble. As I stepped outside the heat was so intense that I couldn't finish my coffee, and I loved my coffee. I sadly dropped the cup in the waste can by the door. Just as I turned the corner, a man wearing a wrinkled sport jacket and holding an armful of papers came rushing by. He slammed directly into me, and the contents of both our arms flew everywhere. He shook his head and blinked, disoriented, behind wire-rimmed glasses.

"I'm sorry. I am late for a meeting." He rushed around sorting through the mess of magazines, books, and papers, attempting to organize them into a his and her pile.

"It's okay." I bent down to assist him.

Underneath his beard he bit his bottom lip nervously. He rambled off some additional apologies and shoved an untidy stack of books and papers in my direction. There was just a second of equivocation before he flashed a quick smiled that bordered on creepy. It seemed fake. "Sorry again, ma'am." He nodded as I accepted the stack of my once neatly organized belongings. I watched in amazement as he scampered off down the sidewalk. What an odd gentleman, I thought.

It took me a moment to get over the shock of this encounter, but I slipped the jumbled mess of books into my bag, and soon I was on my way again. Fifteen minutes later I was at a park in the middle of the city. I didn't know how big the park was, but I could hear the freeway nearby. Finding a bench overlooking a wooded area, I took a seat, soaking in the scenery. The trees had likely been around for hundreds of years. The city's downtown had built itself up around this parcel of land. The city got bigger and sprawled wider, but this little piece of history remained.

One of my sharpest childhood memories was when I was six or seven and my family took an outing at a park very similar to the one I was sitting in now. It was the last summer with all my grandparents. Nana passed that fall, and Grandma passed a few years later. Neither of my parents had siblings. There were no aunts, uncles or cousins. As far as I knew, none of her grandparents had siblings either. We never knew our grandfathers, as they had passed away prior to Mia or my births.

It was during the first days of summer vacation. All students and teachers alike were exhausted and ready for three months of sleeping in, wandering in indolence, and discovery. The grass was green, thick, and soft under our bare feet. The air lambent, and everyone ached to be outside, longing for the warmth of sun on their skin.

Mia and I were lying on a blanket watching the roiling sky. Their dad tilted his chin upward screening the sky, "I hope it doesn't rain," between bites of barbecue and balancing a paper plate on his lap. During mealtimes, Dad always became quite the jovial storyteller. Along with the juicy hamburgers and charred hot dogs he was serving up, there was always a cheesy joke as a side. He would recount stories from his younger years, or sometimes those of the grandparents' or his wife. No matter what the story, there was always a punch line, which would generally draw an exasperated sigh from Mom, indicating that perhaps this story was somewhat embellished for comedic effect.

A gust of wind blew the ball cap off Daddy's head. He grinned and wiped a dribble of sauce from his chin, smearing it on his forearm all the while Mom scolded him, handing him a napkin. Mom sat, legs crisscrossed, with a cup of lemonade wedged between her foot and calf. In perfect balance to her father's delicious BBQ and cheerful chatter, Mom served up macaroni and cheese along with a verbal bulletin of the comings and goings of neighbors and friends. Birthdays, upcoming celebrations for new babies or marriages, and recent accomplishments at the hospital were all shared among the gathering. There were also the more scandalous tidbits of information that she would hear through the grapevine. I couldn't remember the specific conversations they had that particular day, whether it was music or gossip or politics, but she knew that they all actually talked to each other about something, and it was comforting and memorable.

As the day continued the wind grew stronger. Huge raindrops spattered onto Grandma's potato salad. Nana smiled and gnawed on her ear of corn. Contagious giggles echoed in the air from Mia and I. We weren't even sure what we were laughing about, but we could barely contain ourselves. Dad said something that made Nana snort and spew iced tea from her nose and mouth. The adults howled, clutching their ribs as she went into a coughing fit that eventually led her to sneeze her dentures out of her mouth and directly onto the banana pudding.

Just then the wind began snatching napkins and plates off the picnic table, scattering them over the park. Paper cups waffled across the neatly kept grass, making their way into the parking lot. The gale of amusement must have been too much for the storm, and the dark clouds quickly danced away, revealing the sun accompanied by a beautiful full-arched rainbow.

I had fallen asleep on the car ride home. My last memory of

the day was Daddy carrying me inside the house, tucking me into bed and kissing me softly on the forehead. I sighed at the memory and began to organize the books, papers, and magazines that sat on her lap.

In the jumbled pile of reading materials, I came across a travel brochure for Maine. It must have belonged to the man that ran into me earlier, I had never seen it before. I flipped through the pages. The pamphlet had big bold letters that read ***MAINE, BE INSPIRED***. On the first page was a beautiful image of a quaint oceanside community with clapboard houses and a tiny white church with the steeple poking up high above the richly colored autumn leaves. They say a picture's worth a thousand words, and as I looked at the photo, I could actually envision myself there. Editors always put a strong selling message into brochures, along with pretty pictures. Entice them without telling the whole story. Give them enough sizzle, without the whole steak. This brochure was on point, and I longed to be there.

The next day I bought a plane ticket to Portland, Maine. I felt as if it were destiny in some hypnotic way. It didn't disappoint. Maine was the most beautiful place I had ever been. The landscape seemed untouched, dramatic, and soul stirring. The air smelled like brine, pine needles, moss, and ocean.

There was lots of good food, like a food revolution! As I strolled around downtown Portland savoring a blueberry with lemon glaze Holy Donut for breakfast, taking in the street art and local farmers market, I felt at peace. A few hours later I found my hands wrapped around a New England split-top bun griddled in butter and golden brown, overflowing with luscious, sweet, freshly caught Maine lobster. There was something magical that happened when a warm, soft on the inside, crispy on the outside bun contrasted with the cool sweetness of lobster. The chemistry between those elements became sinfully good. There was also something about feeling the warm sun and the spray of the ocean on my face while watching the lobster boats go by as I perched myself on a giant slab of granite overlooking the ocean while enjoying my second lobster roll. This moment satisfied just about every mental image I ever had of a Maine summer. I was feeling inspired, empowered, and astonished. I wished I could start writing down how all the dots were connecting in my head at this moment. It seemed to me that if I continued to explore this path, something weirdly magical would come out of it. Once you draw enough dots, some of them are destined to line up. Right?

I had been living out of a suitcase, and one very handsome-looking carry-on bag ever since the estate sale. I didn't want to drag around a lot of stuff, but I did want to feel equipped for any situation I might encounter. Having a streamlined wardrobe of basics made getting dressed easy in a way that I long craved. Generally, I felt more confident in what I was wearing, too, because I was rarely trying to pull off something new. It had been relatively simple, everything I owned had to match perfectly together. Every piece of clothing had to be interchangeable with everything else. I chose fabrics that were versatile, light enough for summer but easily layered for winter, like viscose and neoprene. Nothing I owned needed to be dry cleaned. I had running shoes, flip flops, and a pair of black flats. One day I may need more, for now it was perfect.

There's no such a thing as a routine when you don't have a home or job. I couldn't live in a hotel forever, though. I needed to make a home somewhere, and I needed a vehicle. Maine was rugged and beautiful, and I wanted to explore it and see everything it had to offer. A Jeep seemed to fit the bill perfectly. Iconic appearance, terrain-conquering capabilities, and its open-air spirit won my heart.

My next stop was LL Bean. I purchased Bean boots and a

couple of fisherman's sweaters. They were chic, and strangely well-suited for ever-changing weather: a crisp sunny day, a sleet storm, a light drizzle, or a blizzard. From what I could tell, it wasn't uncommon for three of the four conditions to occur on the same day in Maine.

I ended up spending several months driving around the state until one Saturday afternoon I had a gnawing feeling to drive down a specific secluded country road, at the end of which was a stunning country estate that sported a red and white for sale sign at the end of the drive. WOW! I knew immediately that I had to learn more about this home. I wrote down the number on the sign and called the realtor when I returned to the hotel.

The next day I was at the estate for a tour. The price tag set me back a bit, but money was the one thing I had lots of, and what else was I going to spend it on? This home was circa 1737. To own a historic home in Maine would be everything I ever dreamed of. The antique home had maintained its historic physical integrity, and it was rich in history. The period details of this grand home had been lovingly maintained throughout the years, including a curved grand foyer staircase, gorgeous crown molding, wrap-around porch, and multiple fireplaces. The expansive yard included an inground saltwater pool, and the front yard overlooked the length of Winter Harbor. The original home had been extended, preserving its original character and enhancing its presence on the land. Two additional structures, a large boat barn/workshop and an oversized garage were styled to blend seamlessly with the house. There were orchards and gardens, gardening sheds, and an additional smaller three-bay garage. I soaked in the breezes blowing up the bay as I descended the stairs that cut through the rock-faced cliff to the waterfront dock. It was all ageless ambiance that blended with the charm of the old with the conveniences of new.

As I strolled in and out of the twelve rooms, which include six bedrooms and four and a half baths, I knew I needed to look no further. The home showcased multiple fireplaces, wood floors, paneling, detailed molding and stained-glass windows. The attached garage had a finished, heated second floor currently set up as an office. The home was known to be the second oldest residence in the county. One of the outbuildings was built in 1758 and used as the original post office. Many antique details were preserved in the fully renovated and updated residence, from rough-hewn beams to charming fireplaces and carved doors. Overlooking a quiet saltwater cove, the historic residence and large barn were surrounded by significant plantings, and well-insulated from the road. It was the perfect blend of historic integrity with all the modern amenities needed. State of the art chef's kitchen, large dining room, garden room, sunroom, and most rooms had fireplaces. Bucolic setting of 56+ acres of luscious fields, mature gardens, stone walls, heirloom orchard that backed up to mountainous state land. The home had been lovingly cared for, and it showed.

"Such a rare offering comes along once in a lifetime," the realtor bragged. "The open area to the left of the home is a prime example of a gorgeous family farmland passed down through the generations and is now protected by an agricultural conservation easement. This ensures acres will always be available for its traditional use as productive cropland, open fields, and woods. No builders, so no neighbors. For centuries, the farm has transformed based on need, and has served as a beef/cattle farm, dairy farm & creamery, produced endless veggies, strawberries, pumpkins, uncountable bales of hay, and most recently a vineyard." The realtor looked up from her listing paper. "The barn has a brick chimney and wood stove hearth, a three-season bath and a meditation room, as well as a forced hot water heating system. Do you want to go see it?"

I shook my head. "No," and continued confidently "I want to make an offer."

"Do you have financing set up?" the realtor questioned.

"No, I will be paying cash."

"Ok," she answered skeptically. I could tell she wanted more information, but I didn't offer, so the woman, who was very much a professional, let it go. "Well let's do this."

I offered 10% less than what the property was listed at, the owner accepted since it was a cash offer. I demanded a closing within two weeks, I would transfer the entire agreed upon price to the real estate attorney, and I would take immediate occupancy. The deal was signed.

A few days later I drove up the country road speckled with old farmhouses to my new home, a content feeling washing over me. Having a place to call home felt good. It smelled green, like farms and flowers and newly cut grass. As I got closer to Old Foundry Road, there was a fresh salty smell in the air from the ocean. I made the turn onto the tree-lined gravel driveway, and the smell of pine overtook me. The sun was warm and bright, the grass green, the ocean blue, and I was home. My home.

Chapter Four

Caleb

On the first night in my new home, darkness fell early over the fall sky. Emptiness settled in where joy should have been. Living here was my first step toward independence and transformation into my new life. I laid quietly on the pallet by the fireplace, looking outside at the bright stars against the inky dark sky. The vast beauty of it renewed my belief in the possibility of heaven. Later that night I awoke to a low burning ember on the fire. There was the constant whooshing sound of rain and wind outside of the window. It wasn't cold enough for a fire, but I wanted one anyhow. I pulled the comforter over my head, but it still took what seemed like hours to fall back to sleep. When the rain finally settled into a quieter thrumming, my eyes grew heavy and sleep overcame me.

The furniture started arriving early the next morning and continued throughout the week. The movers came from Texas the first week of September to deliver my belongings from the storage unit. Boxes began to be unpacked, and the house started to feel like home. It was my home, not my parents' home, not a collage of old memories that dragged me down and kept me in a constant state of melancholia. The feeling of a new beginning started to creep in. An old photo album from my former life sat in the bottom of a box. I was afraid to touch it for fear of opening a Pandora's box of sadness and pain that would again take hold, ripping away the fragile layer of optimism that had crept into my soul. Eventually, I confronted my fears, found a place for the photo album on a bookshelf, still unopened, my happiness was safe, for now.

After several long nights of unpacking, I awoke to a beautiful, brisk fall morning. I couldn't help but to explore the property. Cliffs or mountains? The choice made me smile. I still had unpacking to do, and didn't have proper hiking attire, so I opted to explore the cliffs. My former hiking gear had all been auctioned off back in Texas. I did have my running shoes and yoga pants, and that was enough for a small adventure out on the trail.

I could take in ocean views throughout my home—the cliff line was an easy stroll, approximately fifty yards straight out the front door. As I approached the cliffs, I was amazed at the sharp drop down to the rocky edge where the ocean met the boulders. It had to be forty feet down. The disappointment was quickly re-affirmed at the lack of access to the water. No beach, only a dock and boat house. I began to follow the cliff further east into the thick tree coverage. My land was adjunct to state land, so it was public access. The walk through the dense trees was beautiful, occasionally opening to views of the ocean and cliffs, the sound of waves breaking below ever present. The trees were full of color, and the ground crunched beneath my feet. The sun was bright, but the air was brisk and made me feel alive. It was quiet except for the sounds of the ocean and nature that surrounded me. I found comfort in this.

About forty minutes into the hike I came upon a cliff that jetted out over the water. I climbed over a few fallen trees into the clearing and sat at the edge of the bluff, watching the water. In the distance I could see a waterspout from a whale. I finished an apple and sipped on an energy drink, losing track of time as my thoughts wandered. Mom would have loved it here. I felt very connected to my mom at that moment, more than I had felt since her death. Every time I hiked; I felt a connection to her. Mom so loved the outdoors. I had naturally come to feel joined with nature through my mother, so it made sense that I felt her mother's presence in this beautiful, secluded spot.

I watched as a seagull plunged down to the water's edge, retrieving its prey, then gracefully swooping back up into the clouds. It made me remember the robin's eggs that Mia found by the garage one spring. Mia brought them inside and gently placed them under her desk lamp. Yes, I remembered. I remembered how silly I thought Mia was for trying to hatch those stupid eggs. That was the closest we had ever come to having a pet. Mia was so devastated when they didn't hatch.

What Mia really wanted was a golden retriever. The neighbors down the road once had puppies for sale. That's what she wanted. A retriever. Despite Mia's constant and relentless pleading, Mom refused, and Mia was heartbroken. It was the little things I missed the most.

I swallowed hard and fought tears, a voice startled me back into reality. I was so alarmed that my heart skipped a beat before speeding up. I turned toward the sound but could only make out the outline of a person standing in line with the late morning sun. The shape continued to approach, the sun partially blocking the figure before my eyes came into focus.

I stood up to face him. A young man with dark, tousled hair, dark eyes, and tan skin that almost seemed to glow. He had the kind of straight, bright smile that lit up a room. He could have been in a toothpaste commercial as perfect as his smile was. He was devastatingly beautiful, a palpable sexiness like no one I had ever seen outside of the movies. I stared at him. At some point he started to laugh.

"Are you alright?" he asked.

I immediately nodded through a flush of embarrassment and quickly dropped my eyes to the ground.

"Umm, yes, I was just startled. I thought I was alone out here," I answered, a bit defensively.

"Ditto. It is a perfect place to be alone." The man had pouty lips and thick black eyelashes. "I haven't crossed paths with any-one out here for years."

I awkwardly glanced away in an over exaggerated attempt to show disinterest. God knows I was interested.

"My name is Caleb." He extended his free arm in greeting.

I accepted the stranger's steady hand as it enclosed mine.

"Chloe." I smiled uncomfortably. "I'll share my seat if you would like." I pointed to the tree trunk.

Caleb accepted and the conversation flowed quite effortless-ly. Conversations with strangers rarely came easily for me, I was quite the opposite of verbose. Since the death of my family, people seemed to be nervous around me, treating me like a fragile piece of delicate china. Out here, no one knew me. No one knew my history. No one felt bad for me or uneasy to offend by saying the wrong thing.

Usually, the minute a stranger sparked up a conversation my posture stiffened, and I began to overthink every word that es-caped my lips. The more I tried to relax, the more self-conscious I would become. This morning felt different. I felt completely relaxed in this beautiful stranger's presence. Maybe I had been alone for too long. I had always been alone, just not this isolated. In the past I had the safety net of my sister or parents if I needed to talk to someone, needed advice, or needed anything for that matter. This morning I welcomed the company and feared for its end. We talked for several hours. Eventually, Caleb rose to his feet. He seemed taller than I remembered.

"Well, it has absolutely been my pleasure meeting a kindred spirit out here in the middle of nowhere. Could I expect another chance meeting say, tomorrow around ten? Weather permitting." The words rolled off his tongue followed by a toothy smile, which automatically caused me to grin.

"Ok, it's a date," I answered, kicking myself the minute the words rolled off my tongue. Before I could correct myself, Caleb winked and disappeared into the trees. I felt faintly nauseated over the stupid date comment, insinuating that Caleb wanted a date, rather than just being friendly.

On my way to the house, the rain moved back in and the wind picked up, making the temperature drop significantly. I zipped my jacket and wrapped my arms around myself. The rain continued throughout the night and into the next day.

During the night the cliff drew me like a lover. Calling my name; I stood at the edge and yelled, "Caleb?" The shrill echo knocked down the chasm causing rocks to crash below into hard stone. My ears rang and my face shone with a glowing paleness through the wrapping fog. The chittering of night birds gusted toward me. It oddly felt like home, as if the winds wrapped me in my mother's arms. Warm and inviting me into its depth, desiring to enfold me forever. Part of me wanted to jump into the chasm and feel the full embrace.

I leapt from the cliff and my breath caught in my throat and I sat up from sleep dripping wet, sweat covered my body. As I pulled the covers over my feet, I noticed a brown leaf stuck to my heel. Hmm must have picked it up off the floor somewhere. Sleep did not return easily.

When the alarm went off at eight AM I was still exhausted but excitement pushed me along. The first thing I did was step out onto the porch to check the weather. The wind struck my body with the force of a rogue wave hitting an unsuspecting swimmer. It was bone chilling. The rain pelted me like shards of ice. I couldn't make the trail in this weather, so instead I sat at home sulking about my missed "date" with Caleb. The rain continued another miserable two days. It finally began to back off and the sun peeked out from behind the clouds.

It was still cold, but I was determined to complete the journey I had set out on days earlier. My destination a two-mile round trip. When I finally got to the opening on the cliff, it seemed like a sanctuary. The rain had stopped, and a beam of sun broke through the clouds, cutting through the trees and providing much-welcomed warmth. As I stood there, waiting, the realization set in that Caleb was not going to come. There was no way for him to know that I would be here. My mood dampened swiftly to sadness. I found a semi-dry rock and sat down, staring blankly out over the ocean, until it became so cold that I began to tremble. I had to head back to the house, fighting back tears the entire way. I ridiculed myself for being so disappointed. I felt stupid. As I entered the foyer, I removed my outerwear and pulled my damp hair up into a ponytail. I deciding to start writing in my journal. I wrote about the disappointment I felt, wrote about Caleb, and soon I was four pages in and felt much better.

That night the dreams began. It was the same dream every night for months. I could never see a face, but I knew him like I had known him my entire life. I was walking toward him. It felt like something terrible was going to happen when I finally reached him. At the same time, I wasn't scared at all. I wanted him, needed him. No matter what happened. In the dream, I never got to him. Then I died. At first the dreams scared me, I thought I was losing my mind, until I decided that it would be no great loss, as for my insanity was inevitable. What was worse than waking up every night, wanting someone I had never met, was loving a man who didn't exist.

I made it a habit to jog the two-mile trail to the cliff where I had met Caleb. Each morning I jogged there at the same time of day. The same time they first met there. I would sit on the cliff for at least an hour, and then run home. It was good exercise, and the hope of running into Caleb again was great motivation. October turned to November, and the trees turned from yellow to red to brown, eventually losing their leaves altogether, the bare limbs adding a spooky element to the wooded pathway. I loved my time on the trail, genuinely, even after giving up hope of running into Caleb ever again. I eventually began to expand my running territory to include different pathways, deeper into the forest or a further stretch along the cliffs. I continued my runs because it gave me an opportunity to clear my mind, and it certainly helped ease the depression.

October came, along with the first snow, a light dusting. I couldn't wait to see what wonderland awaited me on the beautiful trail. It was not disappointing. The woods were transformed under the layer of fresh snow. I could see my breath in puffs of white clouds as the crisp winter air immediately froze my cheeks. Everything looked brighter with the snow. I took the trail slower, not being used to traversing snow-covered terrain. Texas rarely got snow. In fact, winter lasted little more than a month most years. Snow was like a fairytale. It reminded me of Christmas, my favorite holiday. As I approached my cliff, my heart began to speed up. I could make out the shape of a person standing in the opening between the bare trees. I immediately knew it was Caleb as I burst through the trees into the clearing.

Caleb turned, and again I was mesmerized by his gorgeous face. Dark eyes under thick black lashes peered back at her. His pale face sported slightly rosy cheeks, chaffed from the chilling wind, his windswept mane kept in place under a black knit hat. His dark eyes sparkled as a smile spread across his face.

"Hey, stranger, you're a little late for our date." He laughed. I instantly felt embarrassed again by the date comment long ago. If he only knew that I had been here practically every day since our encounter, hoping to see him.

Conversation picked up as if they were old friends. They sat on the fallen trees and quickly became lost in discussion. Several hours had flown by when Caleb stood up, swiftly and gracefully. I was desperate to hang on to the moment, afraid that Caleb would slip away forever.

Frantic to not lose him again, I blurted, "Would you like to come over for dinner this weekend?" Immediately I felt my cheeks heat up with embarrassment. I tried to remember if he had mentioned a girlfriend, but I knew he hadn't. A lump rose in my throat, and I felt like I was going to faint right there in front of him.

Caleb shot a smile and a simple, "Ok."

Relief at once washed over me, easing the tightness in my chest and opening up the lump in my throat. "Saturday? Say six o'clock?" I confirmed, but without allowing an answer, began to tell him my address. "I live at..."

Caleb interrupted and in his low attractive voice said, "I know where you live." Then he winked. "Welcome to small-town Maine." Again, he smiled. I wondered what I had gotten myself into. I had no idea how to entertain a man alone at my house.

I floated back home with the knowledge that I was turning the page to the next chapter in a new life. I wasn't sure how Caleb had managed to come into my life. Sometimes people must accept certain things that cannot be explained. I knew I was at risk of falling for him. I was not doing anything intentionally, but even so, it was happening. It was like being caught in a riptide and carried out to sea. Instead of fighting the riptide and being pulled under to my certain death, I had chosen to ride it out. So here I was floating in the tide, peacefully and willingly being pulled out to sea. This riptide could eventually save my life and bring me back to shore, or it could pull me so far out to sea that I might never manage to make it back to land. My future was now in the hands of a Riptide called Caleb, with soft eyes and the most beautiful smile I had ever seen. For the first time in two years, I truly hoped I would not drown.

CHAPTER FIVE

Riptide

Friday night was tough. The house was clean and put together, although still quite bare. The table was set. An easy yet suitable first date meal of stuffed chicken breast was pre-prepared in the refrigerator. I didn't like chicken, but most people did, and I didn't want Caleb to think I was odd, so I would eat a little for show. I was also making an attractive green salad that would hold me over. I had bought an excellent white wine that the clerk at the liquor store had recommended. Just in case, I also had sparkling water and beer on hand. I wasn't a huge fan of wine, but it seemed expected, especially at social events, so it was reasonable to include.

I took melatonin to help me sleep, but it had been nearly two hours, and I was still wide awake. Plagued with anxiety, tossing and turning, I finally rolled over and looked at the clock, two AM. I had to get some sleep! Then I remembered the Ambien in the bathroom medicine cabinet. Okay, desperate times, desperate measures. I swallowed the little beige sleeping pill and fell back into bed. Sleep still did not come easily. I continued to toss and turn until the medication took over and pushed me through the wake-sleep veil until I was finally out.

I always had vivid dreams, but Ambien seemed to make them worse.

I was sitting in Dr. Laura's office. It was my first appointment. Nikki waited outside as I endured my first session with the psychiatrist. At the end of the session, Dr. Laura asked, "How's Tuesdays and Thursdays? Same time."

"Twice a week?" I grumbled, unable to disguise my frustration with the entire situation. "Well, the death of your family, that's a tough one. I think it would be for the best."

"I've got yoga Tuesdays and Thursday night. It really helps me." I lied.

"Well. That's a problem. How do we solve that?" Dr. Laura asked patiently.

"Guess I'll have to change my yoga days and come here." I shrugged, obviously put off by the intrusion.

"Well. It's up to you," Dr. Laura offered.

"Honestly, I don't like being here. I'll admit, I don't like being here at all," Chloe said, irritated by the entire situation. I needed to sleep. I needed sleeping pills. I did not need to sit in a doctor's office twice a week answering questions that made me sad. Talking didn't change anything. I just needed the pills.

I went for a few more sessions. The next time Dr Laura was more straight forward.

"Mm-mmm." Dr. Laura nodded. "Now, this is what I see. I see you yawning, I see you coming in late to your appointments. I don't see you having any fun in life anymore. I don't see you getting enough sleep." Dr. Laura was stating the obvious like she was some kind of genius for figuring this out. "Well, am I correct?"

"Fun?" I answered as insulted as I could sound. "Am I supposed to be having any fun in life less than a year after my entire family was wiped off the face of the earth?!"

"Well, there's no point in life if there's no fun, right? At least getting some enjoyment out of life."

"Hmm, yep, I believe you've figured it all out for me, Dr. Laura.

I'll book a trip right now," I said in an irritating, upbeat and obviously fake tone dripping with sarcasm. "What about Christmas in Aspen? That's fun, right? Maybe I'll forget all about my family if I take a holiday in Aspen, throw on some skis, huh, Dr. Laura? That could change everything!"

"I don't think going away is the answer, Chloe. Happiness comes from inside, not from geography."

I nodded, shrugged, and took the prescriptions Dr. Laura gave me. Dr. Laura was apparently unimpressed with my wit and sarcasm. Nonetheless, I returned for my twice-weekly appointments with the doctor. I didn't try to let Dr. Laura help me, and if someone doesn't try, then counseling is a moot point.

My alarm went off at eight. I always set the alarm. I could have easily fallen back into being lazy and sleeping all day, giving into the gloom that had nearly choked the life out of me the last few years. Dr. Laura suggested that I set a schedule and stick to it. It did help. I snoozed the alarm a couple of times but begrudgingly succumb to the morning and rose out of bed to face the day.

The rest of the day went by very slowly. Around four o'clock I showered and dressed for dinner. I rarely dressed in anything more than sweatpants and a tee-shirt. Tonight, Caleb would see me at least casually cute. I fixed my hair into loose, playful curls and picked out a flirty, yet simple black dress and flats. I wore flats most of the time because I was nearly five foot eight and I didn't need to emphasize my height. Caleb was around 6'2", so if the need ever arose I could get away with wearing heels around him.

The fireplace was burning, and soft music was barely audible in the background. It was full on dark around four-thirty these days. I flipped the front porch light on and sat down to wait. I poured myself a glass of wine and sipped on it, affirming that I still did not care much for it. I was just hoping it would calm my nerves, and it definitely gave a better impression than drinking a beer. As I swallowed the last of the wine, I did feel a bit calmer, bordering on giddy. I wasn't sure if that was the effect I was hoping for.

A few minutes before six the doorbell rang. I flung the door open, more excitedly than I had intended. Caleb stood there smiling. In his hand he held a small bouquet of giant yellow sunflowers accented with Texas bluebonnets.

"Hi, beautiful." He smiled and handed me the flowers. He looked delicious in a V-neck navy-blue sweater under a brown leather jacket, his hair unruly as always. However, that look fit him. He had a sexy dark shadow beard and mustache that supported his strong chin. It was messy yet well-shaped, looking a little scruffier than the typical five o'clock shadow. He pulled his facial hair off without a flaw, looking like a man who just had too much testosterone coursing through his veins to ever get a decent shave.

"Beautiful," I said, not clarifying whether I was speaking about the flowers or Caleb—I was actually talking about both. It was very thoughtful to have brought flowers. I loved sunflowers, and bluebonnets. "Come in." I stepped aside, clearing a path for him. After Caleb was comfortable on the couch, I offered him a glass of wine, then excused myself to the kitchen where I put the flowers in a mason jar and started the chicken cooking. Afterward, I joined Caleb. We chatted about the area, the trails, the mountains, and the ocean. Caleb was a lifelong resident of the area, and he seemed to have detailed knowledge about the best places to explore. He was also a world traveler and a historian, so conversation was always easy with him. Before I knew it, the food was ready, and they moved the conversation to the dinner table. I brought out a bottle of sparkling water and poured each of them another glass of wine. The wine was helping to facilitate conversation, at least on my behalf.

We sat at the dinner table long after we finished eating, continuing to talk. After the meal the conversation turned more serious. I had never spoken of my family to anyone. As we sat with candles flickering and lights low, wine and conversation flowed easily. I asked Caleb about his home and family. Caleb's face took on a solemn tone as he told me that he was the sole living member of his immediate family. He was an only child, and his parents had died several years ago, his mother in an accident and his father of an illness. He might have some distant relatives around, but he had no contact with them. The wine and conversation were making me tired, but I was exhilarated at the same time.

Eventually, we moved back to the couch. It was very comfortable sitting in front of the fire listening to Caleb talk. At one point he slid his arm around me. It provided me a coziness that I hadn't felt for many years. When I was young, my parents would wrap their arms around me in a gesture of comfort—that's how it felt. I could feel the warmth of his arm spreading across my neck and shoulders. His voice lulled me into the soft fringes of unconsciousness. Along with it came waves of the most delightful drowsiness, and before I knew it, I fell blissfully asleep against his shoulder.

I awoke to the sun beaming down on my face. I was laid out carefully on the couch with a throw blanket laid across me. I smiled and covered my face with my hands, not believing I had fallen asleep. The restless night before had caught up with me. Caleb had left at some point during the night. I was sad for that, but I still felt good about my evening with him. I sat up to see that my shoes were neatly placed together at the edge of the couch. There was a piece of paper on the coffee table. I picked it up.

Chloe, I had a great time last night, especially the part where I got to watch you sleep :) You do that so beautifully. Any-

way, I eventually got tired myself and headed home. I was hoping it would be okay if I brought dinner by this evening around 5:00. Hopefully this isn't too presumptuous, you did say you didn't know anyone else in Maine. Respectfully, Caleb

Caleb had beautiful handwriting. It looked like calligraphy. Glancing at the clock, I saw it was nearly ten in the morning. I sprung up, refreshed. After tidying up, I sat down to update my journal. It was too cold to run—or maybe I was making excuses. I decided a nice pair of yoga pants and university sweatshirt were appropriate for a takeout food second date. I did fix my hair and put on a bit of mascara; I didn't want to downplay it too much.

The doorbell rang at five. Caleb stood there wearing jeans, a V-neck sweater, and his erotic brown leather jacket. Okay, the jacket might not have been erotic, but jeez, it looked terrific on him. His cheeks were pink tinged from the cold weather, and he was holding a pizza box in front of him.

"You hungry, babe? Cause I'm starved." Then that beautiful smile flashed across his face. "I got a veggie pie—it doesn't seem like you're much of a meat eater."

I stepped aside, attempting to avoid swooning at Caleb calling me babe. We sat on the rug in front of the fireplace with glasses of wine and pizza, again talking late into the night. The pizza long gone, lying in front of the dying fire, facing one another, our eyes growing heavy. I shed my sweatshirt, opting for a t-shirt. Caleb lifted his hand and ran his fingertips up my arm, up the side of my neck, his thumb gently rubbing the lobe of my ear. He scooted closer. A tickle grew in my stomach, and gooseflesh covered my arms. Caleb's other hand found its way to the small of my back and pulled me gently towards him. I could feel his breath on my neck ever so lightly as he kissed me. The warmth of his breath traveled down the neck of my shirt.

"Is this ok?" Caleb asked, sounding slightly out of breath as he continued to gently kiss my neck, moving up toward my lips.

"Yes," I whispered, winded. I wasn't sure yet if she wanted this to lead to full on love making, but the kisses, caresses, and cuddling felt alluringly perfect. I felt safe with Caleb. His hand found its way to the hem of my t-shirt, and I could feel his bare palm against the curve of my waist. His touch was soft and warm and lingered there. He moved slowly, as if a sudden movement might startle me away. His kisses found my lips. His breath tasted sweet, and the light probing of his tongue was welcomed. His hips pressed against mine. I wanted this to continue, but the rational side of me took over, and I slowly began to come to my senses.

"Caleb, I'm sorry." I gushed breathlessly. Caleb immediately stopped and pulled away.

"No, I'm sorry. I guess I got carried away." He sat up, pulling his hair back out of his face with his right hand. He looked younger, more vulnerable in the pale light of the fire. He gently took my hand and kissed it. "Should I leave?" he asked, almost pleading for me to say no.

"Please don't," I quickly responded. "Don't go."

"Ok." He smiled—that smile always melted my heart. Caleb laid down beside me, draping one arm around my waist, resting his head on the other.

"I've never done this before?" I said softly, my cheeks flushed with embarrassment.

"Done what?" Caleb asked. *Oh. My. Gosh!* Was he going to make me say it? Did he not know, or was he messing with me?

"Oh!" he said suddenly, "That!" A crooked grin spread across his face.

"Well, that presents a problem," Caleb said, sitting back up, rubbing his chin. A wrinkle suddenly appeared between his eyebrows. My stomach dropped with disappointment. His grin was still there though. "I was hoping one of us would know what to do if the opportunity presented itself," Caleb said softly with a huge grin on his face. I wasn't sure if he was making fun of me or joking to lighten the mood. Maybe it was a serious comment.

He positioned himself behind me and slid his arms around me. We lay cuddling in front of the fire. I laid my head on his chest. I felt so comfortable and safe in this position, but I hated not being able to see his face. My mind was reeling from his statement. Could what he said be true? Was he a virgin? No way, he was way too handsome, too smooth, every woman's dream. I lay there debating to myself whether he was teasing. We continued to talk, but not about that.

His voice was gentle. Caleb had a way of making me feel special. He provoked me to talk and share my feelings, my past. I even found myself talking about my family with him, without the usual pain. Eventually we fell asleep.

Later that night I woke up and couldn't help myself. I kissed him deeply as a pulled him to me. Kisses like that begged for more. He gently responded and we made love. The fireplace was warm and inviting, and Caleb was patient, kind, and gentle. It wasn't clumsy or awkward like I had expected. It was beautiful.

The next morning, I woke in his arms. We had coffee, walked along the cliffs, taking in a vast view of the autumn coastline ebbing and flowing. Caleb told stories of the many days and nights he had spent fishing, crabbing, and trapping lobster. The ocean was Maine's livelihood, the way most Mainers made their living. Church always seemed to be the center of family life.

"Growing up here there were 18 churches just in this tiny county," Caleb explained as they settled back onto the couch. "With all those churches you would think Mainers would be friendly, welcoming, open-hearted." He had a boyish, whimsy look with a sense of irony in his voice. "Being negative is a lot more work than being positive."

"So, you've been here all your life?" I quizzed.

"Most of it. I've traveled a lot." I could see the outline of his face in the firelight. His perfect teeth seemed to glow against the darkness. He was beautiful.

"Do you like staying in one place?" I couldn't stop myself.

"There's a lot to be said for being settled." He responded.

"Ten years. Where you going to be?" I questioned.

Without hesitation, "If I have any choice in the matter, right here with you."

"Man, you are good at this." I exhaled with a smile and a flush of the cheeks.

We finished our coffee and gently kisses turned into more lovemaking.

Over the next few weeks the relationship moved quickly from friendship to much more. On the weekends we hiked nearby trails and explored the mountains that were still winter accessible by snow shoeing.

Early November we decided to take a week and backpack the Appalachian trail. Our first day on the trail and we had walked until the sun began to drop below the tree line. I didn't have a watch and didn't truly care about the time. I didn't know how many miles we had covered or how many we had to go. Caleb was never out of breath or tired. I on the other hand was struggling immensely.

As the dark crept in I fumbled through the steps of starting the camp stove while Caleb set up the tent. When it was done, we sat down to make dinner. Meals Ready to Eat—otherwise known as MREs. I read the package labeling aloud as I poured hot water into the silver pouch. Tofu Pad Thai appeared as if by magic. It was edible—no, it was good—and I was famished. I was also exhausted. When I finished dinner, I told Caleb I was ready for bed. We snuggled together in our large down sleeping bag that felt like heaven, and I fell asleep quickly.

I awoke aching from my forehead to the tips of my toes. It hurt to move, to breathe, to think. I crawled out of the tent on all fours, finding it difficult to stand. My bladder was full, and necessity forced me to push past the agony my body was experiencing. I found an obscure tree and squatted to pee, literally thinking I might pass out from the pain that shot like lightning bolts down my thighs. Standing upright afterwards was equally painful.

As I walked back to camp, I found myself contemplating the options. However, there was only one. Keep walking. We were in the middle of nowhere. No one was around. No helicopter was going to swoop in and airlift us out of this beautiful hell. Although I did enjoy entertaining that scenario as I slowly began to help Caleb load up the campsite.

Three hours later we were beginning to meet some serious elevation. I trekked about two hundred yards up the third peak and stopped. Eyes wide, breathing hard, heart pounding. A little late in the game to realize that I was hopelessly out of shape for this kind of thing. My pack weighed excessively too much. Every step was a struggle. The hardest part was coming to terms with the constant discovery that there were always more mountain peaks in front of us.

At one point we came to a clearing at the top of a mountain and could see nothing but bright blue sky and a canopy of alpine trees below us. I knew we had made it to the crest. I sat in my triumphant glory, eating lunch, internally congratulating myself and thinking about the decline that would be in my near future. I smiled victoriously, because I had conquered the summit that had nearly brought me to my knees.

After our meal we packed up and optimistically headed on our way, only to find that the mountain had once again deceived me. The elusive summit continued to loom in front of us as we pressed forward, breathlessly up more elevation. The end felt unattainable. I carried on, because what other choice did I have? Finally, after hours of torturous and treacherous uphill battles, we actually did reach the top. It was absolutely the summit. The air was chilly, brisk, thin, and clean. The pines smelled strong, and my head was light with a vague hint of dizziness. Hypoxia. The thin air at the higher altitudes caused it. I dropped back onto a large boulder, allowing it to carry the weight of my pack. I laid there, soaking up the sun and the accomplishment. It was spiritual. Even more so because I was with Caleb.

How many miles had we walked? The concept of distance changes entirely when you take the world by foot. A mile is much further, five miles unthinkable for most people, twenty miles stretch the very limits of conception. The world is vaster, I now realize how enormous it is in a way only fellow hikers could understand. Life on the trail is simple, time has no meaning. When it's dark you go to bed, when it's light you get up, and everything in between is simplistic. There is no point in rushing, because you have nowhere to be.

I plodded along, always in the same place—in the woods, in the mountains, yesterday, today, tomorrow. Everything was the same, one boundless singularity. Every turn indistinguishable from the other. For all I knew I could be walking in pointless circles, and I would be no more the wise. The funny thing is it wouldn't even matter.

Another summit, another resting point. Caleb was like a goddammed mountain goat. He never even looked winded. I let my pack fall to the ground and took in the vista. It could have been heaven. I hoped it was. Mom and Mia would be happy if heaven was anything like this. There was snow in the distance on north-facing slopes and in shadowy ravines, exposing a range carpeted in an amalgam of bog, birch thickets, and veins of scrawny spruce. I stood at the peak of the 3000-foot butte overlooking the vast wilderness below, and I couldn't help beaming with satisfaction.

I ate a tuna pack, taking in the grandeur of the mountain, I could not imagine a better afternoon. This moment was the first time I had allowed myself to be truly happy in months. There was a sense of harmony deep within me. I didn't know where I was, didn't know what time it was, didn't know where I would sleep tonight, but I was at peace.

We lost track of time staring out at the views from the summit, listening to Caleb talk of his travels. He was so easy to listen to. It was effortless to be in his presence. As the sun began to shift to the west, we begrudgingly left the mountaintop vista and set out to find camp. The weather was clear and dry. The trail would be at least partially downhill. I departed feeling contented. It seemed like the hard part was over. However, I was wrong. It was hell.

At one point during the descent, the stones were sharp, and my toes hurt so badly they eventually became numb. We came across a small shelter and I decided to reevaluate the items in my backpack, analyzing each one of my belongings and weighing its importance. Slowly a large pile of supplies emerged on the bench in front of us, justifying the discarded belongings as a type of kindness to the next hiker to come along. The last item I laid down was a cell phone and unused solar charger. I didn't need it. I had no one to call, and no one would call me. When I left the shelter, my pack was significantly lighter. Good riddance. I was purged of several "comfort" items that were unnecessary for this journey. I walked away from the mound of material things that once would have been significant to me, without a second thought.

I wasn't as tired as I had been the first few nights. Tonight, I laid in Caleb's arms, listening to the evenness of his breathing. The campfire crackling and popping in the background. Twigs snapping under an animal's foot and the wind whistling between the trees all brough back memories of my family. I had always loved the hikes with my mother, but I was never one for suffering hardships. I didn't like to be cold, and certainly was not one of those people who wanted to risk stumbling out of the wilderness with a mountain lion attached to a much-valued extremity. I liked the solitude and beauty of being surrounded by nature and being away from civilization. I also had loved modern comforts and conveniences.

One March, my mother had dragged the family to Oregon on a camping trip. It was frigid, and it was bear country. I refused to sleep in the tent with my mom and sister, instead opting to sleep in the SUV with the bear spray tightly clutched in my hand. The thought of that made me laugh. "Mom would be proud now…" Then I further contemplated, "Wouldn't she?"

My thoughts darted between memories to even darker times. Back to the funerals, during which I was in complete denial. My parents were in their mid-forties, the prime of their lives. How were they dead? People don't die at that age. My sister's death was by far the worst. By accepting her death at sixteen, I had to face the possibility of my own mortality, had to accept the fact that humans die young. Life was fragile and imbalanced. My parents never got to retire, never got to travel. Mia never even got to graduate high school or have a serious boyfriend. Life was unfair. As far as I knew, Mia was still a virgin. So was I for that matter, until Caleb. Not that I hadn't had the opportunity, but no boy ever kept my interest long enough. Now, who would ever love me? Who would care about me? Who would worry about me? Was I investing too much in Caleb too soon? These questions floated around in my head until I finally drifted off into a restless sleep.

The next morning, we awoke early to a vast, snow-blanketed wilderness that sat beneath the icy summits of the Mountain Range. A new day had begun. I took a deep breath, the air, clean, crisp, and cold, stung my lungs and nasal passages. I imagined that if green had a scent it would smell like this very moment. The earthy dirt, evergreen trees, and dampness with a faint whiff of fungi—it was delicious.

Darkness was slowly ascending beneath the western vista as the eastern horizon was filled with passionate colors that exploded in the heavens, as if the sky was painted with warmth like a basket of fresh fruit: pink grapefruit, lemons, blood oranges, and cherries. It was like a work of art with a spectrum of colors that all merged beautifully with one another.

I slowly took it all in. There was a plunge waterfall in the distance, crystal cold water jetting off the side of a mountain with white riffs and deafening roars on its vertical journey into the depths of the forest, disappearing from the line of vision behind the dense evergreen coverage, water spray reverberating just above the branches.

Caleb often offered to trade packs with me as I struggled to get my heavy pack hoisted up onto my back. I would politely refuse his offers, but Caleb insisted and gently lifted the bag off my shoulder, quickly hoisting it onto his. His pack was extremely light, as he was better versed at packing for section hikes. My neck and shoulders would cry out in thanks each time. I forewarned him that I was a slow hiker before we even began the trail.

He laughed. "It's the journey that we are here for, not the destination."

Caleb was funny and had a way of putting me at ease. I had liked him immediately. Liked him even more with every minute I spent with him. He was not only beautiful to look at, he was strong, helpful, and comforting to be around. He had an internal fortitude of strength, a firmly planted I know who I am strength. There was nothing sexier to me than a man who was grounded without a hint of arrogance. Caleb seemed to have nothing to prove. He didn't work at being something he wasn't. He had depth of feeling, intellect, and humor. His brand of humor synced up nicely with mine. His easy laugh was disarming in the best sense of the word.

We talked about books we had read or wanted to read and places we would like to visit. Caleb was very interested in history. I loved hearing the historical facts and stories that he shared as we strolled along the trail. The way he brought to life the smallest of details; it was as if he had personally experienced them. His ability to vividly describe the people and places made me feel as if I too were a part of a living story.

Walking for hours and miles had become as automatic and ordinary as breathing, by day four. At the end of each day I never thought about the twenty miles we had trekked that day any more than I thought about the 18 breaths per minute we took. It's just what we did.

As the last day ended, we looked for a place to set up camp. I stared out over a beautiful vista at the top of a cascade waterfall. Surprisingly, parts of the A.T. were well-marked with a wide variety of trail signs. Some very formal, "National Park-like" wood panels with carved recessed letters—others considerably less so, some as informal as a torn piece of paper in a zip-lock bag pinned to a tree. This was a well-marked area. *No camping at waterfall. No fires.*

"That's a bummer." I frowned. "This spot is beautiful."

"So, lets camp here," Caleb shrugged.

I lamely pointed at the sign. Caleb bowed to the sign, detached my pack, lowering it to the ground, and then peeled off his jacket, which he tossed over the sign, completely obscuring it.

"Signs, signs, everywhere a sign. Fuckin' up the scenery, breakin' my mind." He flashed a knee-weakening smiled as he continued to sing the classic rock tune Signs as he walked toward me. "Do this, don't do that, can't you read the sign?" He finished the verse drawing out the last word as he removed his pack off my back. "What sign?" Caleb said glancing around with a quizzical look.

We set up a shared camp, afterward sitting around the fire extending Caleb's tales, talking and laughing late into the night. Caleb had enriched my spirit in the short time I had known him. It was the last night and we were holding on for dear life, talking well into the early hours of the morning. I was exhausted by the time the last burning log collapsed into the campfire, reduced to glowing embers. We said our goodnights and snuggled together into the sleeping bag. My dreams were peaceful and full of hope.

We awoke the next morning well after sunrise. I fluttered into awareness and then bolted upright in a state of panic noticing Caleb was gone. However, I found that he had renewed the fire and made breakfast. Most of the campsite was packed up and ready to go. He offered me breakfast and packed up the rest of the site while I ate. As I had breakfast I took in the views, to the east are the mountains we crossed, whitecapped and foreboding, and I wondered how Caleb ever convinced me to go into them. Maybe it was just that I was too naive to realize how hard the passage would be. It was a great adventure and I was happy I had experienced this with him.

He was such a gentleman. I thought to myself that I could get used to him being around, then I flushed with embarrassment. With every step and switchback, as the trials of the trails tested and deepened our relationship, we fell more in more in love with each other.

After the section hike, we spent all our spare time together. This became the routine. Caleb could talk about philosophy, religion, history, culture, literature—or anything really—and I loved the fact that I didn't have to carry the conversations. He was blessed with intelligence and outstanding looks. I was falling completely and irrevocably in love with Caleb. He had filled an emptiness in my heart. He provided something that had been missing, taken away the loneliness that the death of my family had left. He had given me purpose, something to look forward to, a reason to look forward to life.

December crept in; Christmas was beautiful, romantic. Caleb surprised me by putting strings of tiny white solar powered Christmas lights up on the trees that lined the trail in front of my home. We cut down a Christmas tree and dragged it back to the house on a sled. I pulled out old family decorations and placed them on the tree. I baked and played Christmas music and awaited Caleb's arrival each evening.

Saturdays often started with breakfast in bed. It didn't matter what we did it was just a backdrop for us to be together. For Christmas Caleb gifted me a magnificent telescope. The card read.

Chloe, I count my lucky stars every time I gaze at the face of my angel. The only thing I could think of that rivals the beauty and magnificence of my girl, the solar system itself. The heavens are surely jealous of you. Love, Caleb

It was a very clear night as we gazed at the surface of the moon. I was in awe. There were eight other planets that were visible that night. Only three of them were close enough to get any detail. We could see clouds and a dust storm on Mars and cloud bands on Jupiter. Jupiter also had four easily observable moons rotating around it. Caleb pointed out several visible moons around Saturn as well. Neptune and Uranus were small, featureless, bluish green disks. Pluto was not visible. The Milky Way was fantastic.

"Saturn is stunning."

"There are thousands of rings around Saturn made of floating ice and debris from a moon that broke apart. Sometimes it's comforting to me when I can spend time just scanning the heavens."

"Looking for intelligent life?" I joked.

"Looking for something. Do you believe you will ever see your parents again?" He asked with a thoughtful tone.

"I hope so." I shrugged. "Maybe they see me now."

Our eyes met. I glanced quickly away, my eyes shining with tears.

Caleb quickly changed the subject. "The Greek gods and goddess were jealous of mortals and each other. Sometimes the Greek goddesses would punish a mortal because they dared to have beauty or skills that rivaled their own." Caleb loved Greek mythology. It was often a topic of discussion. "You know if all humans died off right now, Earth would not suffer in the slightest. However, if ants or bees disappeared it would be catastrophic."

"Wow, that's profound." I responded honestly as I continued searching through the night skies. "This gift is lovely. It's like I am able to gaze into another world."

"World of the dead?" He hugged me tightly from behind.

"Maybe?" I shrugged. "I was hoping to live long enough to see Haley's comet when it comes back around, but it's not likely that I will be around that long."

"Hmm, yeah, that's like seven decades away, and tomorrow isn't promised-" He broke off, realizing that he was putting a damper on the mood.

"Do you ever wonder why things happen like they do? Do you think there is a plan? A Point? Is everything predestined?" I turned to face him.

"There is no point. You live. You die. The end. There is no plan or destiny." He said it with certainty.

"Hmm," I nodded, not necessarily in agreement but in contemplation. "Caleb, this is the best gift anyone has ever given me. Thank you." I changed the subject with a smile.

"You can thank me by cuddling by the fire," Caleb said with a scandalous grin.

Cuddling led to lovemaking. Afterward, I lay there looking at the luminosity of Caleb's skin in the fireplace light, my hands softly drifting to my lips as I remembered the feel of his kiss. A smile that I couldn't contain came from within. I thought about his kisses exploring my body, his touch lingering in places that made my spine tingle. I could almost still feel him, hands on my hips, my back, on the inside of my thigh. I lay back on the pillow, feeling content in life. Was this happiness? Somehow, I had managed to climb out of the depths of despair to this. I closed my eyes and drifted off to sleep, not a care in the world.

Chapter Six

Awakening

We grew close over the months. We talked a lot; made plans for the future. Made love frequently and passionately and life began to come together. I was writing again and dared to be hopeful. I had never been someone whose life was defined by anything other than my own accomplishments. I didn't need anyone else to give my life meaning. That was a past life, this was my reality now and maybe it wasn't the boyfriend aspect of things at all, but Caleb did give me a reason to go on.

Once again, I had a human connection with the world. Someone to care about me, and for me to care about. As much as I wanted to make those changes on my own, I couldn't. I would make progress only to be sucked back down into the dark grip of depression once again. Yes, I still missed them. I cried less, a lot less. I even thought a few times about putting out photos of them but hadn't taken that step yet. I wasn't sure if I was quite ready for a daily reminder of my painful past.

At times I vaguely noticed that Caleb had a way of evading conversations about himself. I usually realized this in retrospect. I decided that the next time they were together I would just ask more direct questions about his family, his farm, maybe even ask to visit his home. Months together and I had never been to his house. I felt like I knew him completely, but I was missing some vital pieces of the puzzle. The problem was that those pieces never seemed to matter when we were together.

Then one cool spring day everything changed. I woke up ill, tired and nauseated. I had slept until 1:00pm. Later in the day, the illness had subsided, and I was ravenous. Still physically exhausted by the time that Caleb arrived, nevertheless, I had dragged myself out and driven into town for pizza. I loved being in the country, but one disadvantage was that my house was too far out for delivery.

I told Caleb about the virus I must have caught. How I had been ill for most of the day. Caleb smiled, "Maybe you are pregnant."

"What!" Why hadn't I thought of that. "Don't joke like that!"

"Why? Would it be such a bad thing, to have my baby?"

"No Caleb. It's just that we should plan it out, there's an order to how these things go."

"Says who?" He grinned.

"I don't know. I'm better now so it was probably nothing anyway."

That night after lounging around the house watching movies and talking, I fell asleep in Caleb's arms. In the morning I woke up alone, as per the typical routine. I was still vaguely ill. I wished Caleb were there to comfort me, care for me. I remembered how my parents always took care of each other when one of them fell ill. They loved each other completely, unconditionally.

It was then that I decided to speak with Caleb about possibly moving in together. Caleb was going out of town for a few days to purchase some farm equipment but when he returned, I would breach the topic.

Caleb spent that night with me, he woke me early the next

morning to say goodbye. We made love in the pale morning light, afterward Caleb held me tightly, for a very long time. Laying face to face. I took in the scent of him; it was clean and manly, with a vague hint of sweat and nature. Caleb touched my cheek, looked deep into my eyes and said, "I love you Chloe. You know that don't you."

I smiled and whispered a confident, "Yes."

I got the sense that Caleb didn't want to leave. I loved that. He was going away and he was going to miss me. I could see it in his eyes. Read the pain in his face as he got up from their bed. The way he lingered at the bedside kissing me goodbye one more time before walking out the door said volumes about the way he felt. He did love me. Somehow, I had this beautiful kind soul in my life and he loved me. Truly and deeply he loved me. The feeling of contentment rose inside my belly and warmed my soul. It was overwhelming, almost to the point of a physical reaction. I sat up on the side of the bed with a smile. Immediately becoming nauseated I ran to the bathroom, barely making it to the commode before vomiting.

The illness lingered and after another day of being ill I decided to go to the local Doctor. There was only one clinic in town, with a Medical Doctor and Nurse Practitioner. They were able to work me in for an appointment that afternoon. The doctor asked some routine questions about allergies and health history. Then after discussing the current illness, he asked if I could possibly be pregnant. I had always been able to answer that question with an absolute 'no' but this time it was different. I hadn't even thought of pregnancy before Caleb brought it up. A few minutes later, the nurse brought in a cup and requested a urine sample. Within ten minutes, the doctor was back in the room, announcing that I was pregnant.

I sat in shock. The room was closing in around me. I closed

my eyes to ward off the syncope that was creeping in. When I opened my eyes, the room seemed brighter, blinding, sterile. The scent of disinfectant crept into my nostrils prodding the back of my throat, evoking a gag reflex. A sour taste rose, burning my esophagus. My tongue began to stiffen and tingle. Tears filled my eyes. I fought it, but I was going to be sick. I jumped up in a dash for the trashcan and barely made it. The nurse and doctor stood back quietly until I was finished. The nurse handed me some tissues and a plastic cup of tap water.

Before I left the office, the doctor gave me a prescription for an antiemetic and a prenatal vitamin. I couldn't imagine taking a vitamin right now. Multivitamins tended to make me nauseous even when I wasn't pregnant. I didn't plan on taking the antiemetic either. I didn't typically like taking medication and certainly didn't want to take something that wasn't absolutely necessary and risk finding out ten years later that it caused babies to be born infertile or with three arms or something even worse. Growing up with a mother who was a nurse, most ailments were solved with hydration and ibuprofen. Now even the ibuprofen was off limits.

How could I have been so stupid and careless?

I made it home but barely remembered the drive. Shock had set in. Tears streamed down my face as I fell into bed and curled up into a ball. All I could think about was how was I going to tell Caleb? Somehow, I felt like this was a betrayal, as if it were solely my fault. I was unable to lie any of the blame on him.

I spent the next day pacing the floors with a knot weighing heavily in my stomach. Caleb was supposed to return the next evening and for the first time ever I was dreading the reunion. I wasn't sure how I felt when Caleb didn't return, possibly relief. I missed him greatly, but I didn't know what I was going to say when I finally seen him and had to confirm his suspicions.

As I got ready for bed I thought about Caleb. Maybe he had

arrived late and went home instead of coming to my house? I was a little concerned but not overwhelmingly so. I had never bothered getting another cell phone after leaving it on the trail. Who would I call? My cable subscription had come with a landline. I had connected a phone but quickly realized there was no need? When the phone did occasionally ring it was always a salesperson. The ring would rip through the silence scaring the living shit out of me each and every time. Moreover, since Caleb didn't have a phone, I unplugged it and never connected it again.

Caleb didn't show up the next day either. I had quickly moved from relief to borderline panic when Saturday rolled around and there was still no Caleb. We had never officially declared ourselves a couple, but things had evolved into what I assumed was a serious relationship. Yet I had no idea how to reach him; no idea where he lived, it was close enough to walk to, but in which direction? What would I tell the police if I were to call them? My friend was missing. My boyfriend? I knew his name but not an address, not a license plate number; not even where he had gone to purchase the equipment, just somewhere in Portland.

Finally, Sunday night I drove to the local police station and asked to speak with someone about a missing person. The station was small and old and resembled a scene out of an Andy Griffin sitcom, minus Barney Fife. The police officer was genuinely warm and friendly. He had apparently lived in this county his entire life, as did a large percentage of the county's population. People who weren't born here were PFA's, people from away. There was a bias or at the very least a skepticism when it came to the local folk's view of PFA's. This made it even more uncomfortable going to the sheriff for help.

"Sir, I know this sounds strange, but I am here to report a friend of mine missing." I swallowed hard, choosing my words carefully in an attempt to avoid sounding certifiably crazy. He nodded, a signal for me to continue. "I moved here a few months ago and since then I have become very dear friends with Caleb Frasier. He was supposed to be out of town for a few days but returning Thursday. I expected him to stop by when he returned but it is now Sunday and I haven't heard from him. I am very concerned"

"Frasier huh? Where does Caleb live?" The Sheriff seemed to be taking my concern seriously, at least for now.

"Well sheriff we hike together along the cliffs out by my house and he walks to meet me there, so it has to be walking distance from my home which is on Old Foundry Rd." I stammered. The Sheriff smiled at me kindly, and nodded again, he was well aware as to where I resided.

"Does Caleb have a phone?" He asked.

"No." I quickly added, "But neither do I." I felt the need to explain that not all people had phones and I wasn't just some off the rocker out of towner stirring up trouble.

"Yep, a lot of folks in this part of the state don't necessarily have phones, but the young'un's usually do." The sheriff nodded to himself, deep in thought. He had lived in this county a long time, as did his family for generations. There were no Frasier's in these parts, at least not anymore. "Well, Miss Chloe, I don't reckon I know a Caleb Frasier and I know most the folks in these parts. I even knew about you." He paused briefly, then continued. "I haven't gotten any reports of major accidents with fatalities on the highways this week." The Sheriff got up and yelled into the next room, "Charlie, you know any Frasier's that live up around Old Foundry Road?" The sheriff knew Charlie's answer, but the girl seemed sincerely and genuinely concerned about her friend.

"There's that old Frasier property up off County Road 28 but I don't think anyone lives there. As far as I know, it's been abandoned for as long as I can remember. Some type of probate situation. There's a caretaker that lives out back of the property though." Charlie answered back.

"Well, Miss Chloe, I'll do some checking around and if I find anything, I will let you know." He shoved his arm out to me. I took his hand and shook it firmly, doubting that anything would come out of this visit. I felt hopeless. The sheriff walked me to the door. He would check around, but he reckoned that some young fella from a neighboring county was playing games with this young lady and has now grown tired of her. Shame, she was quite pretty and seemed sweet.

That night I fell into a restless sleep. In the middle of the night I awoke to Caleb sitting on the bed next to me. I bolted upright and hugged him tightly. Tears were streaming down my face.

"I'm sorry," he said simply without any further explanation. "Please forgive me." I felt him trembling. "We will talk in the morning," He said climbing into bed, wrapping his arms around me. "I'm exhausted."

Caleb was back home again, and I felt safe. Nevertheless, there was still a vague sense of injury and restraint on my part; things were far from healed between us. I forgave him, of course, out of relief for his safety, but the memory of his disappearance and the lies and stories still hung tight in my memory, not to be easily forgotten. For the time being, I would enjoy the warmth of his body and the safety of his arms around me, knowing he was alive. Tomorrow there would be time for explanations.

Chapter Seven

Without a Trace

My alarm went off at 8:00 AM. I could smell Caleb on the pillow next to mine, could still feel the warmth of his arms around my waist. I opened my eyes slowly only to find an empty bed. I sat up trying to clear my head. Was I dreaming, or had Caleb been here during the night? I concentrated on the memory.

Of course, he was here, I told myself, tears running down my cheeks. An uneasy resonating feeling in my stomach that told me Caleb had not been here at all, it had been a sick, twisted dream. The hollow feeling in my gut turned to nausea, and I followed my daily routine of running to the bathroom to vomit.

A bit later as I recovered from the nausea and was able to take some tea and toast to settle my stomach. I always felt better by the afternoon, so I decided to drive out to County Road 28 where the deputy had said there was a Frasier property.

I slowly maneuvered the country roads where old farmhouses dotted the fields. It was hard to tell if they were occupied or abandoned. They were all old, weathered, and showed their age. I had no idea what I was thinking coming out here.

A farmer was driving his tractor along a recently harvested field. I thought about asking him about the Frasier property, but didn't want to disturb his work. Besides, what would he think if a crazy woman came running across his field attempting to flag him down in his tractor? I shook my head at the absurdity of the idea and continued driving slowly along the gravel road, passing several mailboxes. I scanned the names as I passed. I noticed an elderly man in overalls walking up one of the driveways toward the road and decided to stop and ask him if he knew the Frasier's.

I pulled my Jeep across the street from his residence and stepped out. "Excuse me, sir," I said, feeling a little uneasy about approaching a stranger. "I was wondering if you knew where the Frasier farm is?"

"Frasier farm?" he repeated, squinting his eyes slightly, looking faintly confused.

"Yes sir, I am looking for Caleb Frasier."

The old man raised his eyebrows, his eyes shooting up briefly to the left as if he were attempting to retrieve a vague memory that was just about to disappear. He then proceeded to draw in a deep breath as if considering the answer thoroughly before speaking. "Well," he began slowly, "there is a Frasier property that has been under some kind of probate for about a hundred years." He pointed further down the road. "No one lives there, but I've heard that the lawyers pay for the upkeep. It's about four miles down. End of the road backs up to the ocean." He pursed his lips and leisurely nodded his head. "Beautiful piece of property. One of these days some family member is gone get rich off it. That's 'iffin they can't ever get it out of the lawyer's hands. Lawyers, they can be real bloodsuckers iff'in you're on the wrong side of 'em."

"Do you know the family or how I can get into contact with them?" I asked, almost pleading.

He shook his head. "Naw, that's the trouble. They can't find no family. The last of 'em died off 'round the turn of the century. I guess the lawyers keepin' it in trust until someone comes forward or the money runs out. Old Ernie Griffin is the caretaker though. I guess he knows the most about the state of affairs with that place than anyone. He lives in the house out back, 'bout a mile down the private driveway past the main house. He's prolly around if you wanna go speak to him. He's a nice enough fella. Been workin' that job since birth, I s'pose. His daddy had the caretaker position before him. Prolly his granddaddy before that too."

"Ok thank you, sir. I appreciate your time." I waved goodbye as I crawled up into my Jeep. Anxious to check out the lead, I planned on making a beeline to visit old Ernie Griffin and the Frasier property.

I followed the road to the end and found the house. It was more like an estate. Beautiful, but a bit weathered. The lawn was tidy, and you could tell that someone was caring for the place. From the location, it looked like the cliffs by my home would eventually lead to this property if you followed them far enough. I had never followed them that far but thought I might check it out some time. I drove up the driveway and parked at the edge of the sidewalk that led to the front porch. There was an older model pickup truck out back, but no other vehicles. I walked up to the front door of the main house and knocked. Waiting for what seemed like forever, but there was no answer, so I knocked again. Damn, still no reply. I was on my way down the front steps to inquire at the caretaker's quarters when the front door slowly screeched open. Startled, I swung around. A man was standing in the door, holding the screen open.

"May I help you?" His voice was deep, his speech deliberate. His skin was weathered with deep wrinkles. He was wearing a John Deere ball cap and a paint-splattered plaid shirt, the top button undone, exposing a crisp white undershirt. His Wrangler brand carpenter jeans were faded and sported a hammer hanging in the denim loop on the right thigh. At that moment, I realized I had never seen that loop used for a practical purpose.

"Hello sir," I stammered, "I, um, I was looking for Caleb Frasier." I had given up on anyone answering the door at this point, so I had not prepared myself to explain what I was doing here, standing on this stranger's front stoop.

The old man looked me up and down, skeptically.

"I spoke to one of the neighbors down the road. H-he said I would find you here. Are you Mr. Griffin?" I asked hopefully.

He slowly nodded his head. "Yep that's me, but just Ernie's fine."

"I'm Chloe Jamison. I recently moved into a home over on Old Foundry Rd. I was just wondering if this is where Caleb Frasier lives?"

"Caleb Frasier, hmmm?" Ernie removed his ball cap, exposing a crease across his forehead where the cap had rested. His hair was pure white. I thought he must be at least eighty years old, maybe older. He produced a handkerchief from his pocket and used it to wipe the sweat from his brow, then placed the cap back onto his head. I nodded, looking intensely at Ernie, willing this man to tell me something, anything. "Well, ma'am, there's nobody lives here. I'm the caretaker, I live out back thar." Ernie pointed towards the back of the house. "Caleb is a Frasier family name, but that line's done run its course."

"Are you sure, sir? This is extremely important. I saw Caleb just a week ago, and he said he lived over this way. I don't know exactly where, but I know it was walking distance to my house. I really need to find Caleb, sir." I knew I was coming off as desperate, but I was desperate.

"Ma'am, those fancy attorneys down in Portland been lookin' for a Frasier blood kin for as long as I 'kin 'member, and I may be old, but I still got a good memory." Ernie smiled broadly, exposing a beautiful set of white teeth that contrasted with his dark skin.

"There's no other Frasier line 'round these parts that I know of. My pappy and grandpappy were both caretakers for the Frasier's, so I think I'd know if there were any Frasier's runnin' round here." He rubbed his chin as if he were contemplating some great mystery. "I was just a bit confused thou' cause you called out the name Caleb, and that was a Frasier family name, like I tol' ya before."

I started to cry. I couldn't help it. Maybe the stress and the hormones had caught up to me, but there was no holding back the tears.

"I'm sorry, ma'am, I didn't mean to go upsettin' ya. Maybe sum'un playin' games wit' ya?" Ernie looked concerned. "Come inside, I'll give ya a drink o' cold water. I got some Poland Spring bottles on ice in the cooler for when I'm workin.'"

I followed him inside. He moved swiftly and with ease, making me think that maybe he was younger than I initially thought?

"Thank you, sir. I'm sorry I broke down like that. I'm just really worried about my friend. He's been missing almost a week now." He handed me a plastic bottle of cold water from a small igloo cooler. The label was loose and slid off into my hand as I took the bottle. I was thirsty, so I twisted the cap off with a crack of the seal and took a deep drink. "This is a lovely home," I complimented, looking around at the well-kept interior. There was striking crown molding everywhere. The inside of the home was immaculate, both in upkeep and décor.

"They call it Georgian architecture. The attorney's put money into it each year. I guess that's what the trust tells 'em to do, so they do it. They also keep payin' me to do the upkeep 'round here. Guess they'll keep doin' that 'til the money runs out," he said, looking around the room in admiration. "I think that'll be awhile though. The Frasier's always had a grip of money from what pappy tol' me."

"Since I'm here, do you mind showing me around? It's such a

beautiful place." I could tell Ernie took tremendous pride in his work, so I figured he wouldn't mind showing it off. We walked through each room slowly, Ernie pointing out the art, furniture, floors, and décor. Everything seemed to be original time-period pieces. It was like strolling through a museum. Countless family portraits were hanging on the walls, lovely people, all with serious faces, dark-haired, dark-eyed, fair-skinned. We turned left down a long hallway which led to a grand staircase. On the top step I froze. I was face to face with Caleb.

"Ma'am, you okay? Your colors done left your face!" I felt Ernie's strong, callused hands grab my shoulders to offer support. "Ma'am?"

"Who is that?" I gasped, pointing to an exquisitely framed portrait of a young man. He was striking in what appeared to be a riding suit from a time long past. He had fair skin and dark eyes that peered out from under thick black lashes. The man wore a very familiar perfect smile, the kind you might see in a modern-day toothpaste commercial.

Next to the painting of the young man was the portrait of a stunning young woman in a flowing dress with flowers in her hair. She wore an amulet on a chain around her neck. She looked serene, very different from all the other serious women's portraits throughout the estate.

"Well, ma'am, that's the thing. You were askin' bout a Caleb Frasier, that's the only Caleb Frasier I be knowin' of. That's his momma there next to him and his pappy next to her, he was also called Caleb." Ernie looked at me with genuine concern. "But this young man here died in his youth, so the namesake died with him I'm pretty sure. Old man Caleb didn't have no other chil'rens the way I understand it. To hear the story told, old man Caleb's wife was a witch. When she los' her only child, she went crazy, lost her mind right along with her boy. They say that's part of the reason the family's gone barren and can't have no more chil'rens. That's why this house sits empty to this day. That woman put some kinda hex on 'em. I dunno, but that's what my pappy and grandpappy tol' me. Thoughts of her used to give me nightmares as a chil'," Ernie said, shaking off what appeared to be a shiver. "This place is haunted to this day."

I moved in for a closer look at the portrait. "My God," A gasp escaped my lips. This could be Caleb, my Caleb! He was the spitting image minus the facial hair. My Caleb had to be related to these people. "Sir, I don't mean to question what you told me, but this Caleb looks exactly like my Caleb, the one I'm looking for. They have to be related. Are you sure there is no other family in the area?"

Ernie was shaking his head. "Nope. No, ma'am, I'd know'd it if thar' was."

I didn't know what else to say. I continued to scrutinize the portrait to the point of Ernie once again becoming concerned about me. I couldn't take my eyes away from it. Finally, I surrendered to the fact that the portrait wasn't going to help me find my Caleb, and I forced myself to move on. "Ernie, when did this Caleb die, do you know?"

"Well yes...um, kind of. I don't rightly recall the exact date, but I know where to find it. I see it all the time when I'm out back carin' for the lawn. It's etched on the tombstone in the family plot. I do recollect it's in the late 1700's. He was a young fella. I 'member that too." Ernie was forthcoming in answering my questions. He didn't seem to care, and he wasn't rushing me. He probably didn't get many visitors, and maybe he didn't mind the company. Whatever the reason, he was incredibly kind.

"Do you mind if I visit the grave, just for a few minutes. It's more out of curiosity now that I've seen the house. I promise I won't keep you much longer," I asked in a pleading voice, but I didn't think it was necessary to plead, as Ernie eagerly agreed to show me the Frasier family plot.

Ernie was quite the historian himself, at least when it came to Maine history. "Eastern Cemetery ov'r in Portland is the oldest cemetery in the state. It came bout in 1668, with the first burial on record bein' in 1718, and that's jus' cause they didn't keep good records back then. It's on the National Register of Historic Places. But there's gravestones here old'r then that, so I'm guessin' they don't know 'bout this place."

It was a lot of land sectioned off, much larger than I thought it would be. Ernie pointed out Caleb's headstone. Caleb Michael Frasier Born October 10, 1740, Laid to Rest October 2, 1763. There was a very faded inscription that looked like it may have been written in another language, I couldn't make it out. I stood frozen. How could these two men who look so much alike share the same exact full name and day and month of birth two hundred and fifty years apart?

"Is sumthin' wrong, ma'am?" Ernie broke my trance. His eyebrows creased, and he looked at me with unease. I had lost track of time and had been standing there longer than I realized.

"No. No, sir. I won't take any more of your day. Thank you very much for showing me around." I extended my arm and took his hand in an offer of thanks. My head was spinning. "You've been very kind," I said, then I turned away and rushed toward my Jeep.

I felt as if I might faint, and I certainly didn't want to trouble this old man any more than I already had. I walked without delay to the passenger side of my vehicle and vomited violently. I was thankful for the water Ernie had given me. The water was warm now, but it was nice to be able to rinse my mouth out. I felt better once I was able to sit in the Jeep for a few minutes with the air conditioner blowing into my face. I wasn't sure what had happened or why I had such a violent reaction to the portrait and the grave. It obviously wasn't the Caleb I was looking for, but it was extremely odd how much they resembled each other. Then to see the shared name and birthday must have pushed me over the edge. It was just too much of a coincidence.

The tension had taken its toll on me, and I badly needed a nap. I drove back to my house, brushed my teeth, and lay down to rest. My body was on downtime, but my mind just would not shut off. I wasn't sure what else I could do at this point. I had searched the county records and found nothing. I had been to the sheriff. I had even driven around looking for Caleb's home, stalking the locals in a last-ditch effort to gain information. It's likely that by now the entire community thought I was insane.

I stood in my master on-suite. Panic rose into my chest, and I felt as if I couldn't breathe. The strain of the day had caught up with me. I rubbed a wet washcloth over my face, still feeling faint and dizzy. My knees trembled, and I clutched the edge of the sink for balance. Slowly I lowered myself onto the tile floor and sat cross-legged on the cool tiles trying to get my bearings. I felt the same despair I had relentlessly battled against for the past two years slowly creep into my chest to rear its ugly head. I sat wondering if I had the will to fight this battle yet again. I felt numb from exhaustion and the shock of recent events. How stupid I had been to have believed that it might be conceivable for me to look at the world with new possibilities. I was a fool, and once again I was alone.

Chapter Eight

Something Wicked this Way Comes

I shivered in the cold wind, hugging myself as I gazed out over the open ocean. I tried to force all emotion from my thoughts and use reason to reflect upon the past year. Rationality did not seem to be helping much. Historically I took the easy route of denying my emotions, but not this time. This time I chose to step up to the task of reconstructing the details of my time with Caleb. I knew that the only possible outcome of this would leave me shattered with a full-on emotional break. Nothing would change that—all avenues would lead me to the same finale. Tears formed icy trails down my cheeks. I had no more understanding of what was happening than I did when I started my amateur sleuthing.

I stood reflecting upon the past, remembering several pivotal events in my life. Events that resulted of my own choices, and events that just happened that were no one's doing, they just were, fate per say. Everything came together to create the tapestry of my life, good, bad, and indifferent. I was here because I was supposed to be here. That's the only way this made sense to me.

The sky had grown darker. As the evening stars began to glow behind the black pine branches, I concluded that I was cursed. It was the one explanation that made sense. There was no logic to any of this. I could tear myself to shreds trying to make sense of the events of my life, but I had other things to worry about right now, more pressing issues to consider. At last, my tears were entirely spent. I tore myself away from the cold ocean breeze and put myself to bed, where I lay exhausted and unable to sleep.

I had vacillated between ambivalence and desire for the child in my womb for nearly a month. There had been so much loss in my life, how could I willingly and purposefully open the door to more loss. I supposed it was never really a choice. The baby was mine, part of my legacy. It was the only legacy my family would ever have.

That night as I lay in bed, feeling lost in despair and loneliness, I suddenly realized that I wasn't alone. I would never be alone again. I had found my answer, my hope. The key to the future was inside of me all along, I had just been too caught up in my grief to grasp it. At that very moment, I understood how much I would love this baby.

I awoke the next morning, and each morning after, greeted by a stout wave of nausea that came on strong and swift. My pregnancy progressed, and I embraced it with all its nuances. When I was hit with certain smells, I felt a catch in my throat and fought off waves of queasiness. My breasts became heavy and began to swell. This little one wanted to make itself known, announcing it loudly, with no sense of foul play. The symptoms of its presence were very prominent. Moreover, as the symptoms of pregnancy strengthened, my love grew. Every cramp sent my anxiety into overdrive. Then around twelve weeks into my pregnancy I woke up and felt normal. No nausea, no sprint to the bathroom to vomit. Relief washed over me. I had been positive there was something wrong with the baby because of the fierce waves of nausea and vomiting that I had suffered through each morning. That was gone. Over the next few weeks I had a few isolated episodes of queasiness when I caught whiffs of certain foods—fish being the most offensive—but that was it, the morning sickness had ceased.

A few weeks after my first doctor's appointment, the office had called to offer a referral for prenatal care, which I accepted. They provided me with the name of a local midwife, Betty Sessions. I hadn't called right away, but eventually got around to it. My first obstetric appointment was quickly approaching. Apparently, it was the first day of the second trimester of pregnancy. Betty was kind and gentle. She educated me about my pregnancy the entire time that she was examining me, taking away some of the embarrassment I felt. Based on my exam, sonogram, and last period, Betty estimated the date of conception to be approximately the first week in April. It was possible as there were not many nights that we had abstained. Any break in love making was usually the four days during the month that I was menstruating. She estimated the baby's due date to be December twenty-sixth.

Betty explained the sonogram and then removed the gel from the warmer and squirted it on my abdomen. The probe tickled as she used it to spread the gel around my still nearly flat stomach. "I may have to push a bit on your belly to find the heartbeat because the baby is so tiny right now. Let me know if you become too uncomfortable." I nodded.

I squinted at the screen, moving closer toward the monitor as Betty slid the probe across my abdomen. "Here it is sweetheart. Meet your baby." I beamed brightly as Betty pointed out the heartbeat and the little sac that encircled the fetus. It didn't look like a baby to me, but there was definitely a heartbeat, I could see it clearly as it thumped away. Seeing the heartbeat truly brought the miracle of pregnancy to life. There was a baby, another human life growing inside of me. The reality was overwhelming, and a tear trickled down my cheek. When the ultrasound was over, Betty handed me a grainy black and white picture of the baby to take home. It looked like someone used chalk to draw a tiny snowman surrounded by a black balloon with random static. That photo was the most precious item I owned.

That night I felt hopeful and fell into a deep, peaceful sleep. Dreams always came. I often dreamt of Caleb. Sometimes I dreamt of the child. Rarely it would be a girl, in most dreams it was a boy.

This night, the moonlight fell in floods through the tall windows of the master bedroom. I had been awakened by something, perhaps it was the brightness of the moon. I never bothered to put blinds up because I liked lying in bed looking at the night sky. I rolled over, away from the window. There on the bed, lying next to me, was Caleb, on his back, full lips slightly parted, relaxed in a restful sleep. I lay there watching him breathe, filled with unimaginable love for this man. At that moment, he turned to me in his sleep, as he so often did, gathering me close to him and rested his cheek in my hair. We clung to each other as if we were both unable to let go. I breathed the scent of him, a masculine, clean smell. He held me closer, murmuring 'I love you' and other soft comforts, as if I were a child afraid of the night.

"I know you aren't really here, but I just want to pretend for a little while longer," I whispered into his chest, tears wetting his skin.

"When I hold you and you quiver like that, I just want to give you my soul." Caleb breathed softly.

He rolled on top of me, I winced softly. He kissed me long and hard as he pressed his hips against mine. I relaxed and enjoyed the ripples of pleasure as they spread across my abdomen, taking over my entire body. Caleb was an exceptional lover. We shook in each other's arms as he followed my lead and let go. When it was over, he collapsed onto my chest.

Coming to my senses, I pushed him away, winded. He aggravated my breathlessness by kissing me deeply. I relented once again, accepting his deep kiss. Moving from his lips, I kissed his cheek, damp and salty. I could feel his heart pounding against my ribs and wanted nothing more than to stay there forever, not moving, making love and breathing the same air as him.

We held each other for a long time without speaking. Eventually, I murmured, "Why?"

"I didn't have a choice." Caleb finally choked the words out softly, putting his fingers tenderly over my lips to quiet me. Tears came silently as I dissolved into the warmth of his arms and drifted contently back to sleep.

* * *

Consciousness slowly fragmented into several small separate sensations. The softness of the pillow, the warmth of the sun spilling across my face, the smell of the ocean and pines, the fullness of my bladder. The feelings swirled and merged behind my closed eyelids into a glowing beam of daylight that roused me into a fully awakened state. I lay there resisting until I became aware of an odd feeling between my legs. The way I used to feel when I first realized my menstrual period had started during the night. I sat upright in a panic. What would be the psychological cost to me if I lost this baby? I knew in my heart that I was bleeding, and the baby was gone. All I had to look forward to in life was loss after loss. I was not yet ready to face it. I sat on the bed, shaking, tears coming uncontrollably.

'Okay Chloe, just go to the bathroom and check, it may be nothing.' I tried to give myself a pep talk. Of course, I knew what it was! It was always loss, always sadness, always bad news. Reluctantly, I finally rose out of bed, glancing back at the sheets. No blood. Some relief.

In the bathroom, I was comforted to find that I was not bleeding. However, I was confused to find what appeared to be remnants of intercourse. I sat in a state of shock thinking back on the dream during the night. Was this from me? An orgasm during the dream? The scent of Caleb and sex was all around me, engulfing me. I felt sick. I tore off my clothes and jumped into the shower. I wanted it gone—the smell, the fluids, the memories.

As the hot water washed over my body, flashes of the previous night played through my mind. Is this how a psychological fracture begins, I wondered? Things were getting strange. Last night was the second time I had experienced Caleb in a 'dream' that felt so very real, *it was real*—at least to me. Most of the time I dreamed about him, and it was just that, a dream. But not last night. Last night was incredibly realistic in every way. I was having a difficult time translating between what was factual and what was not. I had a bad feeling, a very bad feeling. Weeping softly, I scrubbed my skin until it was red and tender.

Later I had no memory of finding my way back to bed, but I must have done so, because I woke up there. I had slept for nearly two days, waking only to go to the bathroom or sip some water. When I finally looked in the mirror, I was alarmingly pale, and even the small effort of standing covered me with a cold sweat. I slept restlessly with dreams of purgatory, fire, demons, and padded insane asylums. I was in a state of torment with no apparent way out. Then at my darkest moment, Caleb returned to me. I awoke suddenly, heart pounding to find him sitting next to me on the bed.

"I'm concerned about you, Chloe, concerned for our child." His beautiful eyes were dark from worry. "I know this situation has caused you pain. You have to understand that this was never my intention." I stared up at him. I couldn't cry, I had no tears left. He took in a deep breath as he slowly removed my clothes. He then gently gathered me up from the bed and carried me into the bathroom. After lowering me into a tub full of warm water, he knelt beside me ringing out a washcloth and moving it tenderly over my body. "Chloe, we needed each other, and we found comfort in each other. Our love was real—it is real. It's just not conventional. But that doesn't lessen it. You must get better, Chloe. The baby needs you," he pleaded.

"Caleb, I am so confused. Am I crazy? Have I lost my mind?" I looked up at him, pleading for honesty. "Are you even real?"

"No, my love." He was softly kissing my forehead. "You are not crazy. Some things are just not meant to be understood. Some things are beyond the reasoning ability of your world."

"My world? Is it not your world too?" I inhaled, the hot steam opening my lungs.

"Think about it, Chloe. Aren't religious beliefs a mere leap into irrationality? Does religion not suggest the suspension of reason and acceptance of faith to believe that things can exist that are beyond comprehension?" Caleb's face took on a serious expression. I could tell he was hurting too, though the root of his pain I did not know. "What makes religion so 'natural', but anything else that is unexplainable is 'unnatural'? Please, Chloe, try and stay calm and keep an open mind. Will you do that for me?"

I nodded in agreement. I needed to play this out, even if it were only a figment of my imagination. I needed to know where the depths of my mind would take me. I was hoping for some level of understanding. Some measure of peace.

"Why do we accept that prayers will fulfill a person's wish to escape misfortune or mortality. Prayers. They are words spoken to a creator who lives discreetly in the sky, never seen, never heard from. He allows death, disaster, illness, and unimaginable travesties. Still, we speak words into the air in hopes that he will swoop down and save us from adversity. The saving never happens, not once, yet this behavior…these beliefs, are entirely sane?" Caleb paused to pour water over my hair, after which he squeezed out a dollop of shampoo and began massaging my head. I melted into his touch. "Chloe, you are not crazy."

"Who are you, Caleb?" I questioned weakly.

"I am exactly who I told you I was. Caleb Frasier. I have never lied to you, Chloe. Things are not always what they seem, but that does not make them a lie." He paused, trying to gather his thoughts before continuing. "Do you believe that most fairy tales of the supernatural and unexplained start with a bit of truth that becomes larger, embellished?"

"I guess so." I shrugged as Caleb rinsed the shampoo from my hair.

"Chloe, you are not yet ready for the entire story. You need to get yourself well first." Caleb had applied conditioner and was softly combing through my curls. "I just want you to know that I am here for you. I will always be here for you and our child. You are the most precious things in this world."

I stepped out of the tub and Caleb dried and dressed me. He again picked me up and carried me back to the room. Clean sheets were on the bed. I slid in between the covers and Caleb stripped down to his underwear and curled up next to me. It felt warm and wonderful. I fought the vortex of sleep, but was quickly sucked into the dark, quiet realm of a dreamless slumber.

CHAPTER NINE

Absolution

When I awoke, I felt better—no, I felt good, really good. I was famished and cooked myself a large breakfast. Afterward, I went for a walk along the cliffs. It was a gorgeous June afternoon. I arrived at my cliff and laid down on the sandstone looking up. The sky stood above me; a limitlessness one can only imagine. What lied beyond, with its whimsical clouds, and bright blue canvas, was anyone's guess. An immeasurable vastness so imposing that for me to even think of understanding it, I would have to step outside and view it from space, and then I would only find what I already knew, that it was too infinite to understand.

I thought back to my days as a high school senior. The yearbook team had polled all seniors with questions about careers, desires, all the normal stuff. I thought I had been so clever when I wrote under my own question: Greatest Desire: 'To witness a miracle.'

To try and comprehend what is not comprehensible, isn't that human nature? The need, the desire to understand. Don't we all struggle to orient our lives within these times of scientific revelation and mysteries that writhe about humankind like displeased serpents? Nevertheless, chase them we have, chase them we will, and chase them we must. For mystery is the great driving engine of the species. So why would I be so quick to write off that which I could not immediately understand?

Humans didn't understand the universe a hundred years ago, but now if we point our strongest telescopes at the furthest borders of our galaxy, we can see the distant past, right now. We have managed to fuse, bend, and distort time and space, creating a very strange relativistic elasticity. Isn't that a supernatural experience?

I would live only an instant measure of time, a cosmic blink of an eye. With all of this knowledge coming to light in the world, how could I question things I once considered out of the realm of possibility? Do gods exist? Do supernatural entities intervene in human affairs? Science wouldn't answer these questions for me. Matters that deal with supernatural explanations are, by definition, beyond the realm of nature, and hence beyond the realm of what can be studied by science.

That left me to question my personal faith and spirituality to find meaning in what was happening to me. Yes, acceptance was a choice—a hard one most definitely, but a choice, nonetheless. I needed to decide whether I would choose to believe in something my mind could not see as rational. Should faith or reason prevail when they are in such conflict?

I viewed religious enthusiasts as people who prioritize faith to the point that it became positively irrational. However, here I sat hypocritically contemplating, believing in ghost or spirits or whatever celestial being had been intervening in my life. What choice did I have? I saw two possible ways out: accept what was happening or fight against it. To fight meant to be miserable and defy the universe. Acceptance was like protecting myself with my own shield. Was unconditional approval of life and what it brings really such a bad thing? Life is unpredictable. Nothing is permanent, and everything changes. I had a choice to make about how these changes would impact and transform me. I would use care not to let this break me. I had too much riding on myself making it through. I had wasted enormous amounts of energy holding on to hate and betrayal and hostility. The only remedy I saw was to let go. Whatever happened with Caleb I would accept. Whatever happened was meant to be.

I headed home with absolution in my heart.

CHAPTER TEN

Things that go Bump in the Night

I felt my gown rise over my head, easing me awake. I opened my eyes to see Caleb looking down at me. "WOW," he whispered at last. "Chloe, you are the most beautiful woman I have ever seen."

A little reluctantly I took his hand into mine and drew him gently to me. He softly brushed my lips with his, then my neck, and slowly moved down to my breast. His breath was warm on my bare skin, and my body responded positively to his advances.

"Chloe, for the life of me I cannot look at you and keep my hands off you." His kisses moved down to the small of my belly. I was twenty weeks pregnant and had a tiny bulge to show for it. He laid his head lightly on the slight swell of my belly. "You know I love him already, Chloe."

"Him?" I questioned.

"I love him or her, but I have a feeling we have a son in there." He was still lying with his head against my baby bump.

"We will find out soon, I have a sonogram scheduled next week." I smiled at him, my heart swelling with love. "Are you as scared as I am, Caleb?" I ran my fingers through the dark mop of curly hair.

"I don't think I can be, babe. It's your body. I worry a great deal about you though." He was running his fingers lightly along my side as he lay there. It caused me to shiver. "You're cold?" He repositioned himself next to me and slid his arms around my waist. We were now face-to-face. I pressed closer to him, his bare skin against mine felt warm and comforting. I dissolved into him, and he responded by kissing me deeply. His hands exploring, touching and teasing. I was trembling, but this time it was from pleasure. I held him firmly, knowing neither of them could hold out much longer.

"Do you love me, babe?" Caleb groaned, as his lips broke loose of mine.

"Oh, Baby! YES, Caleb, I love you," I moaned.

He didn't answer, but moved abruptly, anxious to be closer. I was filled with yearning. I wanted him badly! My breasts ached; belly tightened. I wanted to be taken by him, wanted him to make me believe that he was real. I could feel his primal urge to let himself go completely, but I also felt the trepidation as he tried to be gentle.

I pulled him closer, digging my nails into his flesh. "Bad girl, Chloe." Caleb sighed, giving in to my desire to be his. His body heard my cries and responded, his grasp on my wrist tightened. He lightly nipped at my shoulder with his teeth between groans of primal pleasure. I could see the release on Caleb's face when he finally let go.

We lay pressed tightly together. He looked at me with unspeakable tenderness "I love you, Chloe." The moonlight spilled into the room, illuminating the wetness on his cheek—sweat or maybe tears. He held himself up, still as a stone statue staring down at me for a long moment. Then very gently, he rolled over and lowered himself to lie at my side.

We lay there looking into each other's eyes, Caleb's hand resting on the curve of my waist. "Will you stay with me tonight,

Caleb?" I asked.

"Of course, I will, babe." He kissed my forehead.

"No, I mean, can you be here when I wake up in the morning?" I pleaded. A shadow crossed his face.

"If that's what you want," he answered softly, hesitating just enough for me to barely catch it.

"I want you here all of the time, Caleb! I want it like it used to be, only more! I am so baffled by the things that are happening between us. Why can't you just tell me?" I implored. "I need to know why this is going on. Did you come back only because of the baby! How did you even know I was pregnant? I have so many questions, but I feel like if I'm not careful, you will just..." I paused, hesitant to continue. "You will just disappear forever." I finished in a choked whisper, tears flowing freely.

He closed his eyes and took a deep breath. "What do you want to know, Chloe?"

"Everything Caleb," I whispered. "All of it."

Caleb drew his finger over my collarbone. "The curve of a woman's neck and shoulders are the sexiest part of her body, the gatekeeper of all her mysteries. A bridge linking the vast wilderness of wonder between the mind and the body." He smiled, drying my tears. He continued tracing his hand down the side of my face and neck, over my breast, following the curve of my waist, ending the journey on my hip bone. "Are you sure you are ready? It is not an easy story to hear..." His voice faded to the point of being barely audible "...or tell."

I nodded, dreading what I might hear but desperately needing to know. "Caleb, no matter what you tell me I am prepared to hear it. I love you. I will continue to love you no matter your circumstances. I need a future with you, Caleb." I kissed him gently, placing his hand on the small swell of my belly, needing him to feel the love I had for him. "I've probably worked it up to be way worse in my head anyway." I gave him a crooked, sad smile.

"I doubt that," Caleb whispered, kissing me, then muttered, "That's why it had to be you, Chloe."

His last comment sent chills down my spine and caused a knot to tighten deep in my abdomen.

With pain in his eyes and apprehension in his voice, Caleb began to tell his story...

CHAPTER ELEVEN

Confinement and Other Entities

"This is very difficult, Chloe. You said you had ideas; I'd rather hear them first? What do you think is happening?" I could see the fear and pain in Caleb's face.

"Do you know that I went to the Frasier estate shortly after you disappeared?" I asked him.

"Yes, I knew you were there," he said, looking away as if ashamed. I wondered how he knew but I didn't want to change the subject. We were making progress and I needed to know the truth.

"Caleb, I saw the portrait, I saw the grave with your exact name and date of birth," I explained, and then asked, "How old are you?"

"Twenty-three." He answered promptly.

"Caleb! Was that your home that I was at?" I probed.

"Yes."

I thought for a moment, remembering the age on Caleb Frazier's tombstone at the Frazier estate was twenty-three. "How long have you been twenty-three?"

It was very quiet in the room. The silence seemed to go on forever before Caleb answered: "For some time now." He hesitated, looking down.

"Some time…" I contemplated his response and tried to piece together what he was saying. Not logically, just literally. "How are you still twenty-three?" I insisted.

"I don't age," he stated directly, honestly.

My breath seemed to catch in my chest, but I couldn't stop. "Are you immortal?" I quickly shot back, not truly even considering the question I was asking.

"Yes," he breathed, barely audible.

"Wh- How? What are you? Are you a vampire?" I was grasping, not sure if that was a serious question, but I just didn't know what to say. I knew I needed to press on before the opportunity slipped away.

"No." He chuckled briefly, nervously, but then his tone turned serious. "Does immortality frighten you, Chloe?"

"No," I answered honestly. If it were true, if he were immortal, it would be a relief. I had dealt with enough loss.

"Why not?" he shot back, apparently puzzled.

"I don't frighten easily," I kept my eyes on him.

"Chloe, there's a huge difference between courage and insanity. There are a lot of things at play here. Things that are difficult to understand. I would never harm you, but you are in grave danger because of me. I am not who you believe me to be. There is an entire world out there that you are not aware of—wars being raged, supernatural occurrences. Heaven," he paused, "and Hell."

I could tell he felt physically uncomfortable saying these things out loud but he pushed on. It was too late to stop. He had revealed too much already. "Do you know what purgatory is?" Caleb asked anxiously.

I nodded. "Yes. Well, in theory. My family wasn't Catholic, actually not religious at all, but I get the gist."

"Ok…" I could tell he was deep in thought. "Purgatory is a state where souls can remain after death, a limbo of sorts. It's different than what they teach in church. Not everyone goes there, only those in transition. I guess the best way to explain it is that I am in a state of purgatory." He kept a close eye on my face. I supposed he was looking for a reaction. I was determined to find the truth and was not going to do anything to make Caleb stop speaking.

"You died?" I whispered, reaching for his hand.

"Well, no," he assured me. "But I should have." Caleb shook his head and sat up, staring down at me. "So, I tell you that you're in grave danger and you are concerned that I may have died over 250 years ago!?"

"I'm glad I amuse you!" I glared at him, then caught myself and softly said, "I'm just trying to figure things out, Caleb! How did this happen to you?"

"My mom was a powerful healer. She was also a caster...um, a witch I mean." 'Witch' got caught in his throat. He hesitated a moment before he began again. "When I was twenty-three, I was in an accident." His fingers touched the scar on the left side of his back, "My mother knew I wouldn't survive it. She was grief-stricken, out of her mind. To save me she cast a spell. It created a doppelganger that took my place in death. I was thrust into this purgatory of immortality." He paused, watching me intensely. I knew he was waiting for me to say something.

"This is a lot to take in, Caleb. I'm trying to understand, to keep an open mind, but it's just a lot to process," I said reassuringly.

"There's a lot more to this, Chloe, but I think we had better go slow, give you some time. I'm not going anywhere." Caleb gave a brief smile, attempting a bit of witticism.

"So why did you have to leave me, Caleb?" I queried, trying to avoid being defensive.

"Well, that's a big part of the rest of the story. However, that should wait for another time. I know you are exhausted, and I don't want to lay too much on you at once. I mean, I already have, and you've only been well for a few weeks." I winced at the word 'well.' He was speaking of my mental breakdown. "We have to think of the baby. Make sure you stay healthy." He smiled sweetly at me and traced the outline of my cheek with his fingers.

"Do you still love me, Chloe?" Caleb asked.

"Oh, Caleb, how could I ever stop loving you? You saved me. You gave me hope. You gave me my life back! Yes, I love you." I thought about the dark weeks after he disappeared. I was lost, no one to talk to, no one to turn to. When he left, he took everything with him—hope, happiness, love. I felt the emptiness everywhere. The pain I felt was the only reminder that he was real. I squeezed his hand tightly. "Whatever the future holds, we will work through it together."

Caleb laid down next to me. I was lying on my back, accentuating the small rise in my stomach where our child rested. The moon had traveled out of our line of sight, leaving the room extraordinarily dark. I shivered, even though I wasn't cold.

"You're right, Chloe," He pulled me close, and I melted into his warmth. My body was relaxed, but my mind was churning through all the information Caleb had shared. It sounded like a fairy tale, or worse yet, a nightmare. All the same, Caleb was the father of my child, and I loved him. I loved him completely. I knew I would stand by him until the end. That's all that mattered. Nothing else.

Chapter Twelve

Heaven, Hell or Insanity

I awoke the next morning to Caleb by my side. I was so happy that he had kept his word and stayed. For some reason, his presence overshadowed all the ridiculously illogical things he had told me the night before. I loved Caleb completely, irrevocably, and nothing would change that.

I watched him as he slept, the sheet covered most of his pelvic area and right leg. Otherwise, he was naked. I thought he was gorgeous. The morning light fell brightly across the room, accentuating the tone of his muscles. Caleb suddenly opened one eye and squinted against the morning glare. His smile warmed my heart.

"Are you watching me sleep?" He laughed. He always woke in a good mood.

"Maybe." I shrugged, slightly ashamed.

"Stalker." He patted the bed next to him. "Come here, beautiful." I did as he asked. My body always responded favorably to Caleb, but during the pregnancy my desire for him had been so much more dominant. I wanted him constantly. Wanted him to devour me with his passion. I kissed Caleb's neck, chest, stomach. His fingers wrapped around my curls, unaware that he was guiding me to him. I loved that I could make him forget himself. He entered me with ease, and I moved my hips rhythmically.

"Stop, Chloe. Stop," he said suddenly. I didn't want to stop, but I did as he said.

"I need you." I moaned, very aroused, nearly on the verge of orgasm, and he had barely even touched me.

He kissed me deeply. "Be still, Chloe."

"No, Caleb, I can't!" I whined. My spasms pushed him over the edge, and he convulsed in answer to my orgasm. I loved Caleb for so many reasons, but sex had to be high on the list. I collapsed breathlessly on top of him.

"Are you going to leave me, Caleb?" I questioned, suddenly desperate to know.

"Never, Chloe. I will always be with you. You are my life now." He lifted my chin so that I was forced to look at him. He said it with so much sincerity that it touched me to my soul. "I see the pain I've caused you, the mental anguish. I never wanted that. Ever!"

"If this is the response, I'll get from you, you being here, loving me, talking to me, I'll break down more often." I smiled at him briefly, but then my mood turned serious again as I thought of him leaving.

"But you will leave. This morning, or tonight, or tomorrow—one day, you will leave me again," I said, defeated.

"Chloe, you don't understand—" I cut him off.

"So, make me understand!" I demanded.

"Chloe, I've been trying to understand this for more than 253 years, you're not going to come to terms with this overnight." He stopped and fell deep into thought. "My mother was always leery of using her magic. She always told me that no magic is without consequence. I guess she thought the price was worth it, and this life would be better for me than death. But because of her decision I've been wandering around this earth with no purpose or human connection for hundreds of years. How can that be better than death?" He shook his head, pain etched into his expression. "She was right about one thing though; magic does come at a cost. To complete the spell, a doppelganger had to be buried in my place. Doppelgangers are created by pulling the souls of fallen angels into the dead person's body. When I woke up in this state of purgatory, I was still the same, but somehow I was different."

Caleb looked down, his brow tense in thought, then he looked up at me and continued. "I had to go into hiding. I didn't age, so I couldn't stay in any one place very long. I didn't get sick. I would never die, yet everyone in my home thought I was dead, so I could never see my family again." I could physically see how much remembering this hurt him, yet I had a nagging feeling there was more to the story, much more.

"At first I was very confused. I didn't understand how to handle what had happened to me. After several years away, I decided to risk seeing my mother. My mistake cost her everything including her life. People saw me, and it came out that my mother was a witch. My father was outraged at what she had done to me. He said she had cursed my soul to Hell's damnation. It was a different time back then Chloe, people handled things differently. Often the mob got the best of the situation. My mother ended up dead because of me, because I didn't listen to her. She told me never to come back." His voice cracked, and he paused briefly to recover. "My mother just wanted a normal life for me. I was too young to die. I was her only child, and she did what she thought was best, and here I am, an abomination." He rubbed his eyes with the palm of his hand then looked at me with so much love that I thought my heart would break.

"Chloe, until I met you, I was destined to walk the world alone. I tried..." he insisted. "I tried to leave you alone, but I just couldn't. You have such a beautiful soul it makes my heart ache. Sometimes there are consequences for the choices we make, even when we make those choices with no intention of doing harm to anyone."

"So, it sounds like we both saved each other," I said softly.

"Apparently we did." He flashed a heartwarming smile my way.

"So why am I in danger if you stay here with me?" I questioned, pressing him to continue.

"So that's the thing. It turns out fallen angels aren't keen on being transformed into doppelgangers. Then there's the matter of the Divinity. Let me give you a little inside information about the Deity, otherwise known as God. He's a control freak. He cast his angels out, but then he takes offense when someone interferes with them. Hence my mother facilitating the making of a Doppelganger and robbing him of a soul, mine. Yea, the almighty is a real ass about those things. Luckily the realm that I exist in, this purgatory, is a kind of magic free zone. Well, that's a bad example, but the point is I'm difficult to find as long as I stay on the move." Caleb was watching me carefully. I was having a hard time digesting this but was trying hard to keep a neutral expression. "I'm like the supernatural public enemy number one, babe." He shot me a quick smile then looked down, embarrassed.

"So, you're telling me that not only is some demon angel out to get you...but God, the human God, himself, has you on his hit list?" I asked hesitantly.

"Well, God having a hit list may be a little extreme, but these guys don't play nice. What surprises you most? That there is a God or that he doesn't like me very much?"

"Both I guess!" I sat up, pulling the sheet around my chest. "Are you saying that I'm in danger from God?" I asked, startled.

"Anytime that I have intertwined myself in the human world for any amount of time, terrible things have happened, which makes me believe that my involvement with people put me, and them, on their radar." Caleb wrapped his arms around me. "Look, there are all kinds of reasons that I am not right for you or good for you, yet here we are. I think the baby bonds us so tightly that we are now forced to ride this out, regardless of the danger. Do you agree?" he asked, his voice full of hope.

Our lives had merged into a single strand. Cut one lifeline, and both fell. If he were not there, I would not be able to live through that. What I had learned over the past few years was that I did a good job of blocking painful things from my memory. That was a skill I was going to need going forward.

"Caleb, I don't know how else to convince you of this, but I love you. I love you unconditionally. No strings attached."

He leaned over and kissed me hard. "Once upon a time an angel fell in love with a demon."

"You are not a demon!" I disputed.

"Chloe, no one has to convince me of anything. I know what I am," Caleb said very solemnly.

Lucid dreams

The greatest trick the devil ever played was convincing us all he doesn't exist. The greatest trick the devil ever played was convincing us all he doesn't exist. The greatest trick the devil ever played was convincing us all HE DOESN'T EXIST. The greatest trick the devil ever played was CONVINCING US ALL HE DOESN'T EXIST. The greatest trick the devil ever played was convincing <u>YOU</u> he doesn't exist......

I sat up in bed drenched in sweat. What the heck! Another nightmare. I got up to pee and washed my face. Wondering if lucid dreaming was a part of pregnancy. I always had dreams, but nothing like this. Recently the dreams were so realistic that it was hard to tell whether I was awake or asleep.

When Caleb was with me, I rarely dreamed, but he was apprehensive about spending too much time together. He had shared his story—at least most of it—and I was grateful for that, but I also wasn't sure how to process the information Caleb had shared. What I knew was that he believed it.

All of my life I had struggled with the belief of God, Heaven, and Hell. It all seemed odd that there could be a God living somewhere in the sky fighting for mortal souls, all the while knowing about every single experience that is occurring on Earth. It was even more difficult for me to comprehend why a loving deity would allow the greatest of human injustices to happen. I couldn't wrap my head around it. Not the small personal things that were devastating to one person, like my family dying. It was the large-scale insults on humanity, like the Holocaust, that I couldn't fathom. These were massive tragedies. One crazy man orchestrated the murder of six million Jewish people in an effort to kill every single human being of Jewish descent in the world. If there was a God, why wouldn't he just take that one person out? Instead, he's chasing Caleb around. It just seemed far-fetched. The only problem was that Caleb seemed perfectly reasonable and sane as long as we weren't talking about this particular subject.

I always had a theory that people's actual religious concepts often diverge from what they believed they believe. What people tell them—family, friends, school, church. No one has proof that any of this exist, yet the majority of people believe in something. Why shouldn't I believe in Caleb? I had seen the portrait. I had seen the gravestone. Ernie, the groundskeeper, supported these facts, at least somewhat. Faith and reason were both sources of authority upon which beliefs can rest. The problem was that I lacked faith, and none of it was reasonable to me.

My mom often quoted her grandmother. "To one who has faith, no explanation is necessary. To one without faith, no explanation is possible." Maybe without proof, none of this would ever be real to me. I wondered if one day this would end up coming between me and Caleb.

For now, things were great. I had my second sonogram earlier in the month, and the baby was a normal, healthy boy. We were thrilled. I didn't care much about the gender, but a son seemed to make Caleb happy, so that was good. The healthy part was most important to me.

I could hear Caleb downstairs. I was always relieved when he showed up. I felt as if his presence was so fragile, if I spoke about my fear of losing him any louder than a whisper he might vanish forever. We had planned on going for a walk along the cliffs. I was a little more than twenty-three weeks pregnant and had a small, growing bulge to show for it. Caleb had asked me not to hike by myself anymore. I resisted briefly, but then decided it was an easy excuse to require Caleb's company more often, so I agreed.

When Caleb left my place, he stayed at his family estate since it was nearby. He explained that the reason the trust had been inconspicuously set up and maintenance paid through the Portland attorney's office was because he discreetly frequented the family home. It sounded legitimate. It was more reasonable than a bunch of attorneys' holding a property in trust while they looked for descendants for over a decade. All the while paying the maintenance and even remodeling. Some things were still vague, but I was trying to give him space and not pressure too hard.

Maine's climate was very different from Texas. It was late August, and the weather was gorgeous, blue sky, ocean breeze, temperatures in the low 80's. I could fry an egg on the sidewalk on an August afternoon in Texas. As kids, Mia and I once did cook an egg on the pavement. It took hours, but it worked. Sunny side up. Before the experiment was complete, a neighborhood dog came by and ate the test subject.

Caleb held my hand as we strolled along the edge of the cliff.

"Caleb, when you stay at the estate how does Ernie not see you?" I asked.

"Is this all we are going to talk about from now on?" He smirked.

"Well, not all... But I am curious," I stated.

"I know you are trying hard to believe me, Chloe. I get it. This isn't the usual baggage you get with a new boyfriend. I am just worried that the more questions you ask, the stranger the answers will be and the harder this is going to be for you to understand."

"It's ok Caleb. I'm hooked, I'm not leaving no matter how crazy I think you are." I smiled and jabbed him softly in the ribs with my elbow.

"Isn't that sweet." He winked at me then paused. "I think?" He took a deep, exasperated breath. "Okay, I'll try to explain it."

"I'll try to keep up." I laughed.

"I can control who sees me. I can enter in and out of a parallel dimension, a plane that humans cannot see and are not aware of. I guess I could best explain it as moving back and forth through a tear in the fabric of this dimension. Except I can see everything, even interact, but no one on this side can see or communicate with me." There was an awkward moment as he looked directly at me. "Well, usually that's how it works, but I was coming to the house to check on you every night while you were searching for me. The only problem is you did see me. You have this peculiar ability to see through the veil. It seemed to happen mostly when you were sleeping. You thought you were dreaming. It was odd. I don't know, it's never happened before."

"You are crossing over to another dimension, and I'm the odd one?" I flashed him a crooked grin. "Anyway, how do you know? Do you regularly go sneaking into women's bedrooms at night?" I asked with a tinge of jealousy and actual seriousness. He had never spoken of previous relationships, and now my interest was piqued.

"No, not regularly." Caleb was amused by my jealousy. I stopped walking and looked skeptically at him. "Okay, not ever, babe. I told you, you are special. I couldn't resist you. A long time ago when I figured out I could do this, I mean there wasn't like an instruction book or anything that came with this lifestyle. I was thrust into this. I practiced. When I figured out I had this ability, that's when I started returning home. I had a lot of guilt to deal with, and it was killing me. I needed some closure."

"Did it help to be able to visit your mother's grave and see your father?" I questioned.

"Nope. But several years later I figured out the thing about guilt. Guilt is like carrying a bag of rocks around. All you've got to do is set it down. I mean how long could I beat myself up over what happened. I didn't ask for this, and I didn't mean for anything bad to happen to my mother. Anyway, my father died shortly after I discovered this gift, and then there was no one left. Plus, I had bigger things to worry about." He shrugged as he said this.

"Yeah, like what?" I asked.

"Like not being discovered. It was a lot different back in my day. There were fewer people, it was easier to be recognized. There was always a chance that I could run into someone I had previously met, no matter how much I moved around or how careful I was. I tried to be tactful, but mostly I lied a lot. It was tough to keep everything straight," he answered thoughtfully.

We had arrived at the cliff and decided to sit there for a while so I could rest.

"There was also the matter of avoiding..." Caleb said pointing a thumb up to the sky. "He's such a hypocrite. Think about it. He authors this book that contradicts itself at every turn. He tells us to follow the rules or you don't get into Heaven. Not only that, but he will cast you into Hell to be tortured for infinity if you don't follow the rules—then he makes rules which no one could possibly understand. It's like he put us here for his amusement. While we're jumping through his hoops, what is he doing? He's watching us like some sick puppet master, laughing his demented ass off at us! It's ridiculous. Luckily, he's built up to be quite a bit more than he really is. The church is full of propaganda bullshit. He's not the invincible God humans tend to think he is."

"How do you know this stuff, Caleb? I mean it's not like you've met him... the Deity, right?" I queried. I wasn't insulted by his comments because I was very neutral in my beliefs but nonetheless it sounded crazy, him speaking of God in terms as if he were a mere acquaintance.

"Yes, I've met him. Chloe, he wants to kill me. Of course, we've met," Caleb scoffed sarcastically. Then he turned to me. "Babe, I've been around for a long, long time. I've seen things, done things, been a part of stuff that would be very difficult for you to understand. I know I sound mad to you, but trust me, I'm not crazy. I cannot tell you everything but believe me when I say it is for the best that you don't know everything."

"So, when you met this deity, what did he say to you?" I prodded cynically.

"Well, let's just say we didn't see eye to eye on some very fundamental issues, and sometimes there just isn't any way to come to a compromise." He took a deep breath. "Chloe, he's an angel of sorts. He's been exaggerated and immortalized by the church. There are many, many angels. He just calls himself the king. If I call myself Zeus that doesn't make me Zeus now does it? The almighty is jealous and vindictive. It's not exclusive to my world, he feels the same about you guys too." Caleb looked at me intently and stopped. "OK, less heavy subject. Did I ever tell you that your property used to be part of the Frasier estate?"

"No way. WOW, your family owned a lot of land, huh?"

"Yeah, we were kind of a big deal, I guess." He shrugged. "Not that it matters, material things can be gone in the blink of an eye. What matters is this," he said reaching out to place a palm on her swollen belly. "Do you know how happy you've made me, Chloe? This is the best moment of my very long existence. I never thought I could have this. You and our son. Chloe, I know he is the key to a new future. He's going to change the world. He's a special kid." Caleb spoke with such pride it made my heart swell.

"Wow that's a lot of pressure, let's get him out of the birth canal first before we start laying world ruler on his plate." I laughed.

Caleb leaned in and kissed me. I hugged him tightly, thinking about their earlier conversation. Chills ran down my spine, causing small waves of muscle spasms to spread across my body involuntarily.

"Are you chilly, babe? Maybe we should head back to the house."

I looked up, smiled and nodded, and we started on the path back home.

Chapter Fourteen

Danger in Plain Sight

It was suffocating. The dark clouds rolled in as if to crush me. The storm made its presence known with a sudden flash of lightning, thunder rumbling like an angry monster a split second later. It was September, and I had a bad feeling in the pit of my stomach. Change was coming. Summer to fall. Good to Bad. Caleb. The Baby. I didn't know for sure, but I felt it, something was very wrong.

It probably didn't help that my twenty-five-week obstetrical appointment had not ended on a positive note.

Betty had recommended an amniocentesis. Once the doctor had reviewed the ultrasound, he was concerned about the volume of amniotic fluid present, and Dr. Price was recommending additional testing. Betty had explained the procedure briefly. A needle would be inserted through my abdomen and a small amount of amniotic fluid would be withdrawn and tested. Supposedly, amniocentesis was 99% effective at discovering issues with a fetus. The scary part was that it could lead to miscarriage in one in every two-hundred women.

Caleb was waiting for me when I arrived at the house. I was visibly upset, and he knew something was wrong the second he laid eyes on me.

I explained everything to Caleb, then ended with, "It's probably nothing, but, Caleb, if it weren't for bad luck, I'd have no luck at all." I started to cry. I was distressed, on emotional overload. Caleb wrapped me up in his arms, comforting me, protecting me. Not rushing or trying to make things better, just giving me time to grieve.

"Chloe, you don't have to do the test if you don't want to. You're healthy, the baby's healthy. I mean, finding out ahead of time isn't going to change anything, is it?" He asked after I had begun to recover.

"I don't know Caleb, they told me that sometimes treatments could be done before birth, depending on what they find. I guess I should do it. They made the appointment for Friday." I was on the verge of more tears.

Caleb looked deep in thought. He didn't seem overly concerned but appeared to be more confused. "OK, well..." Caleb paused. "I'm going with you then," he offered suddenly. "I'm not going to let you go through this alone."

I smiled. "You would do that?"

"Chloe, I would be there for every appointment if it wouldn't put you at risk. I love you. You and this baby are the most important people in my life." He took me into his arms and held me so tightly that all of my grief melted away.

* * *

Thursday, Caleb spent the night with me, and Friday, as promised, he accompanied me to the amniocentesis. Caleb was a man of his word, he always stuck by what he said. We checked in at the receptionist desk then took seats in the waiting area. Finally, I was called into the office. I was directed to change into a paper gown. Caleb and I waited for Betty and the Doctor to return. Caleb immediately began teasing me about how sexy I looked in medical attire. Obviously, a distraction technique.

A few minutes later, Betty came to obtain consent for the procedure. She seemed different, not as upbeat as usual. I introduced her to Caleb.

"This is a friend of mine, Caleb." Chloe could see Caleb wince as she said friend, but she wasn't sure how to go about the introductions. "Caleb, this is my Nurse Midwife, Betty."

"Caleb?" Betty repeated coldly, eyes narrowing as she sized Caleb up. Then she swiftly added, "You're the baby's father." It was more like a statement than a question.

Shocked by Betty's egregious question, I sat silent, unsure of what to say to get Caleb out of the spotlight.

"Yes, I am," Caleb answered sternly, glaring back at Betty. Betty turned her entire body quickly in Caleb's direction, eyes now widened. Her knuckles turned white as she clutched the clipboard tightly—so tightly I heard it crack under the pressure.

I couldn't understand what I was missing. Did they know each other? If they did, it certainly was not on friendly terms. I felt vulnerable lying semi naked on the exam table, but the tension between Betty and Caleb made it a million times more uncomfortable. Betty completely stopped the explanation of the procedure and unsteadily laid the consent aside. A look of panic, no terror, fell over her face.

"Ok, Chloe," Betty said, patting my arm. Betty hurried to remove herself from the room. "Dr. Price will be right in." She said as she rushed out, consent completely disregarded.

I looked at Caleb confused. "What the hell was that all about?"

Caleb tossed my pile of clothes to me. "Come on Chloe, get dressed. We're getting out of here."

"What?" I demanded, startled. "What do you mean getting out of here? What's going on, Caleb?"

Caleb had walked over to inspect the amniocentesis supplies that had been laid out on the metal mayo stand. His eyes scanned the instruments, syringes, and tubes that sat on top of several blue towels.

"Chloe, these people aren't who they say they are. Please trust me. Just get dressed!" Caleb had turned back toward me and gathered up the rest of my belongings. I was shaking, I didn't know what to think, what to do. Obviously, Caleb and Betty knew each other, but I couldn't understand why Caleb was rushing me out of the office as if our lives depended on it. Nevertheless, I did as Caleb instructed, sliding into my yoga pants and t-shirt, then moving over to the chair to put my tennis shoes on. Before I could finish, Dr. Price entered the room.

"Hi, Chloe," he said as he walked into the room reading the information within the manila envelope. When he did finally glance up, he noticed that I was fully dressed. "What's going on, Chloe? Betty should have gotten you into a gown by now." Dr. Price looked confused as he turned around to see Caleb standing by the sterile procedure stand, eyes piercing, arms folded across his chest and head cocked slightly to the side.

"Who is…." Then the doctor stopped in his tracks, as if in sudden recognition of a long-lost acquaintance. "Who are …." His sentence broke again before he gained his composure. He stood straight, defiantly. "You? What are you doing here?" Dr. Price demanded, but unable to hide the fact that he had been caught off guard by Caleb's presence, and again clearly aware of who Caleb was. I was perplexed.

"Well, I guess I should be asking that same question," Caleb snarled in a low, throaty voice that shocked and frightened me. "So, Dr. Price, I presume," Caleb said ominously, emphasizing the words 'Dr. Price.' "What exactly did you have planned here?"

"Um." The Doctor stumbled. "Well, I was scheduled to do—"

Dr. Price attempted to pull himself together. "Just a routine amniocentesis," he answered with false innocence. He seemed unsure if he should continue the charade. The gig was up no matter what action he took.

"Why are these syringes full then?" Caleb looked down at the surgical setup. "Shouldn't you be removing fluid during an amniocentesis?" Caleb interrogated, as serious as I had ever seen him.

"Well, yes." Dr. Price choked on his words, trying to stammer out an answer, but speech ultimately failed him. Suddenly he said in an overly animated, ah-ha moment, "Anesthesia. That's what the syringes are full of."

"OK then, that's a relief." Caleb nodded cynically. "You should be fine picking up the syringe and injecting yourself with…the anesthesia."

Dr. Price was at his breaking point, sweat dotting his brow. You could see the facade dissipating by the second.

"Come on," Caleb ordered calmly.

The doctor was scared now. "Don't do this! I was only following orders!" Dr. Price held his palms up defensively in front of his chest and rapidly shook his head as he pleaded.

I knew they had known each other!

"PICK. UP. THE. SYRINGE!" Caleb said forcefully through clenched teeth, punctuating each word as he said it.

It was as if an invisible force was guiding Dr. Price's arm. He was resisting, but apparently wasn't as strong as the energy he was wrestling against. He picked up the syringe and jabbed it into his own neck, pushing the plunger with his thumb, releasing the fluid into his bloodstream.

"Now the other one!" Caleb continued in mercenary style.

"Caleb!" I cried, shaking, not knowing what to do. It was as if Caleb was in a trance and couldn't hear me.

"How could you do this, it's a child!" Caleb said disgustedly.

"IT'S *YOUR* CHILD!" Dr. Price yelled through clenched teeth, face flushed a dark shade of red. His breath was becoming labored, shallow, and his hand shook as he was forced to jab the second needle into his neck and push the plunger of medication until it was empty.

"No. It's *HER* child!" Caleb said calmly, shaking his head as Dr. Price fell to the floor. "A human child! They are supposed to be under the realm of your protection!"

"It's the beginning of..." Dr. Prices' voice cracked as he dropped to his knees, face turning purple, "...the end," he whispered with his last breath and fell to the floor.

I sat hard into the chair, shock taking over. Caleb looked up at the sky and yelled through clenched teeth, "LEAVE HER ALONE!" I swore I felt the walls shake.

Betty came running into the room, scalpel in hand, straight towards me. Caleb turned toward the disturbance and put his palm up in the direction of Betty. Betty froze in place as if a force field had been put up between her and me.

"Caleb, you know this doesn't end here. She won't be safe as long as you are with her and that wretched thing is inside of her!" Betty screamed.

Caleb smiled smugly and tilted his head, eyes narrowing intensely as if reading Betty's thoughts. Fear took over every muscle in Betty's face. She gasped and pulled the scalpel across her throat, blood pouring down the front of her uniform and squirting out in pulsing red tides that turned the walls crimson. Betty crumpled like a rag doll onto the ground.

"What the hell, Caleb!!!" I cried.

Caleb grabbed my hand, and we stepped over Betty's body and pushed out the door, bloody red shoe prints marking our path to the exit. I glanced back just in time to see Dr. Price's body burst into flames.

"Come on Chloe, we've got to get you out of here!" He pulled me by the hand, and we walked hurriedly down the hallway and through the waiting area. Two women were sitting in chairs, flipping through magazines.

The receptionist called out, "Do you need to make your next appointment, dear?"

We ignored her and continued briskly walking toward the car. Caleb thrust me into the passenger side, taking the time to attempt at putting the seatbelt around me.

"I've got it!" I yelled frantically, trembling.

"Let's get out of here!" I pushed him away.

Caleb slid behind the wheel, and we sped off. Behind us in the distance, there was a loud explosion. I watched black smoke fill the sky through the rear-view mirror.

I was quivering uncontrollably, tears streaming down my face.

"Caleb, stop the car," I said softly, trying to gain composure. Caleb continued driving. "Caleb," I repeated louder. I felt sick. A burning sour taste was quickly rising into my throat. "CALEB! STOP THE CAR!" I screamed. Caleb slammed on the brakes. I jumped out and immediately vomited. When it had passed, I leaned against the car and sobbed. Caleb had come around and put his hand on my shoulder. "I'm sorry Caleb," I whispered softly. "I'm sorry I didn't believe you."

"Love, means never having to say you are sorry, and I know you love me." He smiled tenderly.

"What was that?" I looked Caleb directly in his chocolate-brown eyes and whispered, still terrified.

"That was your so-called God!" Caleb explained visibly agitated. "To God, humans are all expendable. I mean, he has the recipe, he can make more, why should he care? Humans are the only ones who value human lives. To think that God values human life is an elaborate human delusion. To him, humans are nothing. Nothing unless they become a threat, and then they are the source of his vengeance and the object of his wrath."

"Why would God want to harm me...our baby?" I cried.

"Chloe, I should have never gotten you mixed up in this. This is my battle, not yours." Caleb looked defeated. "Baby, I have to get you out of here, and then I have to leave. I have to go far away from you and never come back." A tear rolled silently down his cheek, the pain on his face so visible it hurt me to bear witness to it.

"Caleb, I'm all right, the baby is fine, it was nothing!" I comforted him.

"Nothing... Yeah, you're right. Nothing compared to what it could've been. I promise I will never put you through anything like this ever again. I'm going to get you some place safe, and then I'll leave, and that will be the last time I will ever put you in danger. Then you will be safe. You and our son will be safe."

For me this was the day that civilization swiftly crumbled into a primal landscape of predators and prey, as two people fled in search of sanctuary.

Pain

Caleb kept driving until we hit the interstate, he continued for several hours after that. We both sat in silence. I was in shock. Then without warning, Caleb pulled into the parking lot of a hotel. "We need to get you some food," Caleb said, barely above a whisper.

"I'm not hungry," I said flatly.

"I'm getting you food," he insisted. I shook my head no.

"You're not stubborn at all, are you Chloe?" He looked at me with eyebrows raised, then added with a flash of sarcasm, "Said no one ever." He leaned over and quickly kissed me before jumping out of the car. He returned shortly with keys to a motel room and an armful of snacks and drinks from the vending machine. "We can order pizza or Chinese when we get to the room." He parked the car and we got out. Walking in silence down the corridor to the elevator, I quietly followed him.

Inside the room, I fell onto the bed, exhausted. "How can I hide from God, Caleb?" I challenged him quietly.

I could tell this agitated Caleb. "Trust me, he's not the God you think you know. Look at me. He's been chasing after me for over two-hundred-fifty years, and I'm still here. He can't be that all knowing." Caleb punched the nightstand, breaking off a small piece of wood. "Listen, babe, don't worry, we've got people on our side too. This is all new to you, but it's a battle I've been fighting for a very long time."

"Who's on our side?" I questioned.

"Angels," he answered flatly.

"Were *they* angels? Betty and the doctor," I pushed.

"Yes. They were just on the wrong side," Caleb answered with a dangerous tone.

"Wrong side of what?" I continued, not deterred, eyeing him suspiciously.

"Me!" His eyes flashed a wicked darkness that resonated inside my soul. He turned away and quickly disappeared into the washroom.

The hotel was nice, nicer than any hotel I had ever stayed at. I laid back on the bed and stared at the ceiling. Caleb returned a few minutes later, scooping me up and carrying me into the bathroom. He had prepared a bath. There was a very large two-person jacuzzi, full of warm water, jets whirling. "Get in." He pointed to the tub. I obeyed.

It felt wonderful. Caleb slid in behind me, his arms encircling my waist, hands resting on my swollen stomach.

"Thank you, Caleb," I mumbled, not really sure what else to say.

"For what?" he asked, taken aback.

"For saving me," I breathed out as a tear silently ran down my cheek.

"Chloe, you were only in that situation because of me," his voice dripping with anguish.

"Caleb, how did you do those things, back at the doctor's office?"

"When angels cross over it releases energy, and that allows me to harness certain powers. It only works in the presence of angels.

When I'm around humans, and there are no angels, I'm pretty basic," he explained.

"Caleb, I don't think anyone could ever describe you as basic."

We sat quietly, water swirling around us.

Caleb gently kissed my neck, I cried silently. I felt comforted, safe in Caleb's embrace, never wanting the moment to end. However, it did end. We climbed out of the tub and dried off, donning robes from the closet. I glanced in the mirror; my brown eyes red-rimmed from tears.

Caleb stepped up behind me, taking me into his arms, and holding me tightly. My nose brushed Caleb's hair. It smelled clean and fresh. All I could think was kiss me, dammit. I mentally implored him to kiss me, but I was frozen, body and voice. My heart was pounding as I took a deep breath.

"Caleb, let's just forget this supernatural stuff for one minute. Right now, I'm just a girl, vulnerably standing in front of a guy, asking him not to leave her. I need you Caleb. If you leave, how am I going to stop myself from sliding back into some dark place like before?" I was openly crying again.

"This is not a choice, Chloe! It is not what I want! Nevertheless, you must steer clear of me. I'm not good for you. Look what happened today. I don't even want to think about what could have happened to you." I heard the sharp intake of his breath.

I stood up straight, pulling him closer. I kissed his lips, his cheek, along his jaw. He moaned softly. My kisses slowed as his breathing became heavier, his eyes were closed, a look of relaxed pleasure on his face. Suddenly he grabbed my wrist.

"Stop, Chloe. It's not your job to make me feel better. This is all my fault!" He picked me up and carried me to the bed. "I want, no I *need* you, but let's do it right."

He laid down next to me. I felt ravenous, aggressive. I was invincible, elastic around him. His hand on the side of my neck, gently grasping my throat, chocolate eyes peering into mine. He watched me intensely, taking in every detail of every expression, as if his survival depended on it. He made love to me with the single-minded devotion of a dying man trying to hang on to life for another brief moment. During our love making, my eyes fluttered open to see a dark desire on Caleb's face. It frightened and aroused me at the same time. I felt insatiable.

When it was over, he softly whispered, "I love you Chloe." He took me into his arms without a word and held me tightly, leaning in and placing one more sweet kiss onto my forehead. Within moments he was sound asleep.

It was later when I was lying in bed trying to sleep that I allowed my thoughts to drift through the events of the strange day. I kept coming back to the moment when Betty and Doctor Price killed themselves. Or had Caleb killed them? It was confusing, and it made me angry. Angry at them, angry at Caleb, just angry. They meant to kill our baby, kill me. The film reel repeatedly played non-stop until I fell into a restless sleep.

I woke up just before daybreak, Caleb was still asleep. I pulled on a robe and ventured out onto the balcony to get some fresh air. I had a difficult time sleeping and felt hungover. As I stepped out of the dark room and onto the terrace, swiftly, without warning, a cloud moved over the morning sun and the sky became dark. I looked up into the sky to see a man. He was levitating. He seemed at least seven feet tall and perfect, beautiful. He sported huge wings. I could not take my eyes off of him, but I wasn't afraid, I was calm, at peace.

"Genesis 6, Genesis 6, Genesis 6, Genesis 6, Genesis 6, Genesis 6, Genesis 6, Genesis 6." The phrase was repeated quietly, almost like white noise in the background, as he hovered there.

Then he spoke. His voice now boomed with the power of a raging ocean wave crashing against the shore during a squall. "The second set of gods who came to Earth and interacted with humanity were the evil angels who took human wives and had offspring..." The angel's voice broke off, and I was overtaken by a white light.

"Chloe." The scene was interrupted by Caleb's voice. A hand on my shoulder, my eyes softly fluttered and opened. Caleb was sitting over me, fully dressed.

Holy shit, it was a dream. Damn dreams! "What time is it?" I asked Caleb, slowly coming around.

"It's eight am." Caleb gave me a minute to get my bearings. "I'm leaving Chloe. I needed to say goodbye." He choked the words out, eyes shining with tears.

"*What!* Leaving? But I thought—" I frowned, shaking my head. Tears filled my eyes, and my head was spinning with rejection. "Wait a minute," I said, standing up, pulling my robe on. I took a deep breath trying to find my voice.

"Chloe, this is hard enough, please don't make it any more difficult." He put his hands onto my shoulder, holding me at arm's length, carefully watching me. The only thing running through my mind was how much I wanted him, needed him. Finally, he pulled me close and kissed me deeply. I could feel the tears mingling on our cheeks. Then he pushed me away. Devastation set in. He didn't want me! He really didn't want me! The thought kept repeating over and over in my head.

"Goodbye love," he said with one last gentle forehead kiss. He looked desolate as he walked away.

I slumped to the floor crying uncontrollably.

CHAPTER SIXTEEN

Goodbye My Lover

With a wave of nausea, I realized I had not misunderstood. Caleb had left me. I was numb. This didn't make any sense. Cognizance of what just happened was beginning to creep through me. I sat down because I was shaking uncontrollably. I could hear the blood pounding in my ears. I tried to slow my breathing, so not to hyperventilate. I needed to focus, find a way out of this nightmare.

I laid there for hours, days, weeks. I didn't know for sure, because at this point time made no sense to me. I rolled onto my side so that I could breathe and curled up into a fetal position. Drifting in and out of sleep, I woke at some point and noticed that the room had grown dark again. I didn't care. I dozed back off. When I awoke again, the sky was no longer dark. It seemed as if the sun was beginning to rise. My stomach growled, but I couldn't bring myself to get up. I thought about my last night with Caleb, and agony ripped through me with the memory of his face. I lay there motionless until I fell back to sleep.

At some point, the door swung open and a woman came into the room. I was still lying on the floor.

"Are you okay?" she asked, leaning over my pregnant unmoving body. She had a thick Spanish accent and was obviously startled. I could barely understand her—not for any reason other than I didn't care to. What did it matter? I knew she was speaking, but it was like she was under water. I stared up at the dark-haired middle-aged woman, bewildered. The lady was nervous. I could tell by the way she was looking at me.

Caleb must have paid for the hotel room for more than just one night, because no one had called or come by until that day. I finally pulled myself together and stood up, leaving the frantic woman standing apprehensive but relieved. I went to the bathroom, washed my face and put on clothes. Stepping out of the washroom, I began looking around the room for the car keys, finding them on the desk. They were lying on top of a piece of hotel stationery.

Chloe, please take care of yourself. Anything I have done or will do is out of love for you and our child. The address below is a safe place where you can go to be alone. No one will bother you there. I will have your things sent. Love always and forever, Caleb

I didn't even go through the trouble of reading the address. I wadded the note into a tight ball and tossed it into the wastebasket, taking the keys and leaving with no more than the clothes on my back. My purse was in the jeep; I was thankful for that. I had it with me at the doctor's office but couldn't remember if I had grabbed it in all the chaos that ensued.

I drove directly to the nearest fast food drive through, ordered greedily, then pulled out, merging onto the highway, headed west.

I would start over because I had to. I didn't feel like I had it in me, but I thought of the baby I carried, and knew life would go on. It had to. I was not the first person to go through a breakup. I had gotten through worse—well, kind of, and with the assistance of drugs and a good deal of professional help. Then a voice in my head laughed, reminding me, the thing about being psychoanalyzed was it didn't work unless the person being analyzed could be reasonably truthful. Sure, I could tell the truth—if I wanted to spend the rest of my life in an insane asylum. I would have to work this one out on my own.

I continued to drive for eighteen hours straight before stopping again. I woke the next morning and started driving again, going as far as I could each day. Until one day, I finally ran out of road to drive on. I was at the Pacific Ocean. I didn't know where, but it really didn't matter. This is where I would stay.

I went through the motions of renting a furnished bungalow on the beach. The next week I found a doctor as I began trying to acclimate to a somewhat normal life again. Like life had ever been normal since my parents died.

I slept, I ate, I walked on the beach, and wrote a little. Life was mechanical. I had been in my new home for almost two months.

The muted light of yet another overcast day eventually woke me. I lay with my arm across my eyes, groggy and dazed. Something was nagging at me, a dream trying to be remembered, I struggled to break into my consciousness. I groaned and rolled onto my side, hoping more sleep would come. And then the previous months flooded back into my awareness.

I sat up so fast it made me dizzy. I was confused, as I often was, since leaving Maine. I still wasn't used to the new house. My thoughts were hazy, still twisted up into dreams and nightmares. It took me longer than it should have to realize where I was. The room was too generic to belong anywhere except a hotel, yet it wasn't a hotel, it was my home. I laid back down and rolled over noticing that the oversized flat screen was still on, volume low, with a movie playing out. I must have fallen asleep while watching television. It often happened these days.

Now at nearly thirty-five weeks, my stomach had grown to the point of enormity. I could barely move. Therefore, I didn't. I lay quietly, listening to the wind whip at the windows, until I heard a rapid succession of knocks on the door. Maybe that was what woke me a few seconds earlier—someone was knocking on the door. Probably, Damien, a friend I had met shortly after I arrived in Oregon. Sometimes I felt like his pet project, but he was sweet, and he kept me from being in a perpetual state of loneliness. I slowly opened the apartment door, firm in my assumption that it was Damien. A cold breeze blew in, sweeping under my gown and robe, chilling me to the bone.

Despite the freezing temperatures, I stepped outside to greet my guest with a quick hug. The sky was cold and damp, filling the horizon with a gray blankness that blended into the gray mist of the ocean, perfectly complimenting the grimy cover of last week's snow. I shivered, stepping back inside and closing the door behind us.

"Morning, sunshine." Damien smiled. He was a handsome man, nearing thirty, tan skin and striking hazel eyes. Damien was an entrepreneur of sorts. He started when he was young buying up oceanfront properties and building vacation villas. He was also a kindred spirit who loved hiking and had suffered a great deal of loss in his young life. We had become fast friends. "I brought you a chai tea latte and that Mediterranean bagel that you like so much. Extra balsamic." He walked by, giving me a friendly kiss on the cheek as he passed.

"Thanks, Damien, but you don't have to do this," I said.

"Yeah, but I want to. Plus, it gives me a reason to stop by and visit." He was already laying out the spread on the table. "Come sit down."

"You can just stop by; you don't have to bring me anything." I smiled, being careful not to give the wrong impression and encourage him.

I excused myself to the bathroom. I didn't know myself, inside or out. The face in the mirror was basically that of a stranger, eyes dull and red, feverish spots of crimson across my cheekbones. After I brushed my teeth, I worked to straighten out the tangled chaos that was my hair. I splashed my face with cold water, trying to wake up and appear 'normal', with no noticeable success. I went back to the breakfast nook to meet Damien.

Damien was a friend, and I needed a friend right now. I got the feeling he may have wanted more than that someday, which was surprising. I was hugely pregnant. He knew that I was fresh from a bad relationship. I left out all the supernatural details. Damien knew about me being in love past the boundaries of sanity. What he did not know was that the object of my affection was immortal, but Damien got the gist of my emotional state. He was given the information that he needed to know—I was hurting over the breakup; no other details were necessary. Still, he always looked so damn excited to see me, like I had made his day better by just allowing him to buy me a bagel. I supposed that the attention made me happy too.

Caleb didn't know where I was, we hadn't had any contact. It had been months since my last night with him. I had resigned to never seeing Caleb again.

I didn't feel like eating, but I did sip the chai latte—it was warm and delicious. I could feel Damián's eyes on me as I peppered the bagel and grabbed a fork. I looked down at my food on the table, and then paused. I hadn't been feeling well lately, and this morning was no exception. One of the many reasons Damian had been bringing breakfast nearly every morning. The doctor had been concerned about my blood pressure at the last appointment and had rescheduled me to come back weekly to be evaluated. I was still leery of doctors. I was wary of everyone really, but what choice did I have? I couldn't deliver this baby on my own.

"Can I get you anything?" I asked, not wanting to be rude.

Damian rolled his eyes. "Just eat dear."

I sat at the table, watching him as I took a bite. He was gazing at me, studying my every movement. It made me self-conscious. I cleared my mouth to speak, to distract him.

"What's on the agenda for today?" I asked making small talk.

"I've got a couple of meetings this morning, but I am free for dinner if you'd like." He answered.

"I don't know Damian; I really haven't been feeling well. Just tired carrying around this extra weight." I answered back.

"Well, that's ok. I'll call you this afternoon and if you like I can bring you something for dinner. Save you having to cook for yourself." He offered.

"Damian I really don't want to put you out like that, plus I'll probably just turn in early anyway." My accompanying grimace was limp and unimpressive, then I quickly added, "I'm sorry, I really appreciate the offer though."

My apology sounded a little flat, even to me. I'd thought I'd been doing him a favor. Keeping him from suffering right along with me. The truth was that I had no interest in being around people. I only wanted Caleb, and no one would ever compare to him. I felt my face crumple. It was so unfair. Sometimes as I laid awake at night, shunning sleep, I questioned why I had thrown the paper away with the safe house address that Caleb had given me. If I still had it, at least I would have had some reference point to try and find him, a connection. It was too late for that now. We were over, it was a clean break. Well, as clean as it could be with a baby between us.

Damian's palm came down on the table, causing me to jump. "We both know what's really going on here, Chloe, and it's not good for you." He took a deep breath. "It's been months. No calls, no letters, no contact. You can't keep waiting for him."

I glowered at him. The heat almost, but not quite, reached my face. It had been a long time since I'd flushed with any emotion.

This whole subject was utterly forbidden, as he was well aware.

"I'm not waiting for anything. I don't expect anything," I said in a low monotone.

Damian smiled at me with tentative friendliness before he excused himself and left. My answering smile was just a little late, but I thought that he saw it.

The rest of the day passed slowly, my thoughts focused on past traumas, as always. The thick haze that blurred my days now was sometimes confusing. I was always surprised when I found myself in my room each night, not clearly remembering the day's events. But that didn't matter. Losing track of time was a relief from life.

I didn't fight the haze as I turned to my bed for much needed rest. I scanned through the television stations until I found a program that was harmless. I awoke later that night to a rerun of walking dead. The movie was comprised of macabre zombie attacks and endless screaming from the handful of people left alive, their numbers diminishing quickly. I would have thought there was nothing in that to disturb me. But I felt uneasy, and I wasn't sure why at first.

It wasn't until almost the very end, as I watched a gaunt zombie shuffling after the last screeching survivor, that I realized what the problem was. The scene kept cutting between the terrified face of the leading lady, and the dead, unemotional face of her pursuer, back and forth as it closed the distance. Then I realized which one resembled me the most.

Something strange pulsed through my veins. Adrenaline, I realized, long absent from my system, hammering my pulse faster and fighting against the lack of sensation. It was strange why the adrenaline when there was no fear? It was almost as if it were an echo of the last time I'd seen Caleb. That night in the hotel a lifetime ago. I saw no reason for fear. I couldn't imagine anything in the world that there was left to be afraid of, not physically at least.

One of the few advantages of losing everything. I sat up and got up out of bed. It was three AM.

I put on a coat and went out onto the balcony, sitting down on the chair outside I tried very hard not to think of the irony. But it was ironic, all things considered, that, in the end, I would wind up as a zombie. I hadn't seen that coming. Not that I hadn't dreamed of becoming a fabled being once, just never a grotesque, animated corpse. I shook my head to dislodge that train of thought, feeling panicky. I couldn't afford to think about what I'd once dreamed of. It was depressing to realize that I wasn't the heroine of my story anymore. My story was over.

I could see my breath as I tried to slow my respiratory rate. I took in the beach neighborhood. A tourist spot in warmer weather. The little shops lining the street were all locked up for the night, windows black. Half a block ahead, the streetlights started up again, and I could see, farther down, the bright golden arches of the McDonald's.

Across the street from the restaurant there was one open business. The windows were covered from inside and there were neon signs, advertisements for different brands of beer, glowing in front of them. The biggest sign, in brilliant green, was the name of the bar Peg Leg Joe's. I laughed, wondering if there was some pirate theme not visible from outside. The metal door was suddenly propped open; letting out a burst of music from the club. It was dimly lit inside. The cold night air carried the low murmur of voices and the sound of ice clinking in glasses floated across the street. Lounging against the wall beside the door were two men and one woman. I watched the scenario for several minutes concerned with the woman's safety. However, it soon became too cold outside and my interest was lost as I headed back to bed.

I didn't want to go back to the empty house. Tonight, had been particularly brutal, and I had no desire to revisit the scene of the suffering. Even after the pain had subsided enough for me to sleep, it wasn't over. There was never any doubt that I would have nightmares. I always had nightmares now, every night. Not nightmares really, not in the plural, because it was always the same nightmare. You'd think I'd get bored after so many months, grow immune to it. But the dream never failed to horrify me, and only ended when I woke myself with screaming. There was no one to check on me. No one came in to see what was wrong, to make sure there was no intruder strangling me or something like that.

My nightmare probably wouldn't even frighten someone else. Nothing jumped out and screamed at me. There were no creatures, no ghosts, no psychopaths. There was nothing, really. *Only emptiness.* An endless maze of trails, so quiet that the silence was an unnerving pressure against my eardrums. It was always dusk on a cloudy day, with only enough light to see a few feet in front of me. I hurried through the fog without direction, always searching, searching, searching, getting more frantic as time stretched on, trying to move faster just made me clumsy. There would always come a point in my dream, when I couldn't remember what it was that I was searching for. Then came the point where I realized that there was nothing to search for, and nothing to find. That there never had been anything more than just the empty, dreary forest, and there never would be anything more for me, nothing but emptiness.

I curled into a ball, pressing my face into my pillow and trying to breathe. I wondered how long this could last. Maybe someday, years from now, the pain would just decrease to the point where I could bear it, I would be able to look back on our few short months together and enjoy the memories of those times. Those times that would always be the best of my life. And, if it were possible that the pain would ever soften enough to allow me to do that, I was sure that I would feel grateful for the time he'd given me. More than I'd asked for or dreamed of. Maybe someday I'd be able to see it that way.

But what if this hole never got any better? If the fresh edges never healed? If the damage was permanent and irreversible?

I held myself loosely together, for the baby. 'This would make it better,' he said. He could take away my security, my home, reclaim his gifts, but that didn't put things back the way they'd been before I'd met him. The physical evidence, the child, was the most insignificant part of the equation. I was changed, my insides altered past the point of identification. My appearance looked different; my face ashen, white except for the purple circles the nightmares had left under my eyes. 'I'd be safe,' he said. That was insanity. It was a promise that he could never keep, a promise that was broken as soon as he'd made it. I was on a slow course with death every single day.

I screamed into the pillow, trying to distract myself from the sharper pain in my heart.

Later that week, two days before my next doctor's appointment, I was sitting on the couch when I felt a wetness between my legs. I stood up to see bright red blood spilling out onto the pale tan fabric of the sofa.

CHAPTER SEVENTEEN

The Darkest Hour

In a panic, I bent over to pick up the phone. I could barely see it beneath my huge stomach. "Just hold on little fella," I said, and patted my stomach trying to stay calm. Then the pain shot through me with a sudden, stabbing burst, as I was preparing to call my doctor. "It's not too early, you'll be fine son," I was talking to myself to try and maintain my composure.

The pain was incomprehensible. Exactly that - I was confused. I couldn't understand, couldn't make sense of what was happening. My body tried to deny the pain, as I was sucked more and more into a blackness that cut out whole seconds or maybe even minutes of the agony, making it that much harder to keep up with reality.

I tried to separate them.

Non-reality was black, and it didn't hurt so much. Reality was red, and it felt like I was being sliced in half, trampled, torn and quartered, all at the same time. Reality was feeling my body twist and flip when I couldn't possibly move because of the pain. Reality was knowing there was something so much more important than all this torture, and not being able to remember what it was. Reality had come on so fast.

One moment, everything was as it should have been.

The next moment, I was gripped with excruciating pain followed by a muffled ripping sound from within my abdomen. And then one tiny, trivial thing had gone wrong. Inside me, something had yanked the opposite direction.

Ripping. Breaking. Anguish.

"Oh!" I gasped out in agony. The pain caused a blackness to quickly overtake me, and I dropped the phone and slumped to the floor.

"Chloe?" I could hear Caleb's voice. I tried desperately, but I couldn't open my eyes. He was clearly in a state of alarm. A horrendous pain tore through my side, and I managed a scream—at least I thought I did. I could feel my eyes involuntarily roll back in my head, and then I was retching. Drowning. I could taste the metallic tang of blood.

My heart was pounding so fast it was practically a flutter. I was scared, but Caleb's voice comforted me. I knew it was impossible, a manifestation of my fear, a trick my mind was playing to protect me, provide me comfort. I could hear him talking, but the words were quickly fading away into a distant mumble. My entire body was vibrating, and then everything went black and quiet. I was still mindful of my internal workings, but everything outside was evaporating from my awareness. I could hear the beating of my heart, fast at first, but beat by beat it was slowing down. I was cold, the coldest I had ever been. Had someone left the door open?

The pain faded away again, though I clung to it now. My baby, my baby, we were dying.

How long had passed? Seconds or minutes? The pain was gone. Numb. I couldn't feel anything. I still couldn't see, either, but I could hear. There was air in my lungs again, scraping in rough bubbles up and down my throat, like sandpaper. The weakness was too much. My arms felt like empty rubber hoses, and then they felt like nothing at all. I couldn't feel anything. I couldn't feel me.

The blackness rushed over my eyes more solidly than before. Like a thick blindfold, firm and fast. Covering not just my eyes but also my body with a crushing weight. It was grueling to push against it. I knew it would be so much easier to give in. To let the blackness push me down, down, down to a place where there was no pain and no weariness and no worry and no fear.

If it had only been for myself, I wouldn't have been able to struggle very long. I was only human, with no more than human strength. I'd been trying to keep up with the paranormal for too long. But this wasn't just about me. If I did the easy thing now, let the black nothingness erase me, it would hurt more than just me. I held the blackness of nonexistence at bay by inches. It wasn't enough though - my determination.

I couldn't focus on anything except the slow beating of my heart. No two, there were two beating hearts. One very rapid and the other sluggish. That gave me a huge sense of relief. I latched onto that sound, my one link to life. The fear began to slip away. It was dark and cool and peaceful. I felt like I was floating on the ocean. I could hear sirens closing in, but before they arrived the beating of my heart slowed to the point it faltered then went silent. I tried to feel my heart, to find it, but I was so lost inside my own body. I couldn't feel the things I should, and nothing felt right.

All awareness left me. I was no more.

CHAPTER EIGHTEEN

Parting is Such Sweet Sorrow

Caleb knew Chloe was in trouble the minute she stood up. He had rushed to her, but he was too late. She was hemorrhaging profusely, vomiting blood. He held Chloe's body, bleeding, twitching in his arms as if electrical shocks were traveling through her nervous system. Her beautiful face was pale and blank, for a moment they locked eyes before she became unresponsive. Her eyes were red, bloodshot. Blood covered her face, shirt and pants. He held her head up, desperately trying to clear her mouth so that she could breathe again. She had gone from pale to blue, her eyes wide and staring but not seeing anything.

He could hear the ambulance in the distance. Why the hell wasn't it here yet!

'CPR? Yes! I should do CPR.' Caleb's mind was frantic.

Caleb laid Chloe flat and began pushing on her chest with a single-minded ferocity. He didn't count he just kept pressing until he remembered, "Get her breathing! You've got to get her breathing!"

Another shattering crack inside her body, the loudest yet, so loud that he momentarily froze in shock waiting for her answering shriek. Nothing. Her legs, which had been twisted up in agony, now went limp, sprawling out in an unnatural way.

Caleb gasped in horror. And then he bent over her head. Her mouth looked clear, so he pressed his lips to hers and blew a lungful of air into it. He felt her twitching body expand, so there was nothing blocking her throat. Her lips tasted like blood. He shuddered as he blew more air into her.

He could hear her heart, thumping slowly, unevenly. Keep it going, he thought fiercely at her, blowing another gust of air into her lungs. Keep your heart beating. With a last dull lub-dub, her heart faded and went silent. He blew more air into her mouth, but there was nothing there. Just the lifeless rise of her chest in response.

At last, there was a thump at the door, the EMT's had arrived.

"She's pregnant! She started to bleed and passed out!" Caleb tried to stay calm and move out of the way, but the words came out as a yell. He paced back and forth as they worked frantically on her. Finally, they scooped her up and loaded her into the ambulance. The lights inside were brilliant white. Chloe was on a stretcher, her body exposed, cold and still. The paramedics hooked her up to monitors and machines as they injected syringes of medications through her veins. A loud screech continuously blared from the equipment. A flat line rolled across the screen where Chloe's heartbeat should have been.

"You stay with me Chloe!" Caleb yelled at her. "Do you hear me? Stay! You're not leaving me. Keep your heart beating!"

"Asystole," the paramedic yelled as he began doing chest compressions. Another paramedic removed the bag that had been forcing air into her lungs and slid a tube down her throat. He then connected the tube back to the bag, which he squeezed several times, causing Chloe's chest to rise and fall. As the bulb collapsed and expanded, Caleb watched Chloe's chest move mechanically with the force of air. A few more breaths and the bag was removed and connected to a small square ventilator that took over her breathing. The second paramedic continued with chest compressions.

The ambulance driver sped toward the hospital. It seemed like forever before they arrived. Chloe was turning a sickly shade of blue, despite the paramedic's efforts. Her eyes wide, staring, empty.

At the hospital, the medical team stood by the door ready to jump into action as they brought Chloe into the emergency room. They rolled past the trauma room directly into an operating suite. Caleb was stopped at the door and sent back into the waiting room. He had never had such a human experience in all his existence. He had never hurt this badly.

Frustrated, Caleb crossed into the alternate realm and followed Chloe into the cold, sterile operating room. Yes, the Deity could easily locate him in this parallel dimension, but he had to be there for Chloe. He had to know.

In the operating room, CPR continued. Caleb heard another sickening crack from inside Chloe's body, a rib breaking. He felt ill. How many times had he fantasized about his beautiful Chloe? He couldn't even look at her now, shattered and dying.

Like a television in the distance, Caleb heard the doctor say, "We've got to get the baby out, we are barely picking up fetal heart tones during CPR!"

In the bright light of the operating suite, Chloe's skin took on a blotchy scarlet hue. The huge bulge of her stomach was exposed, mottled. A nurse painted Chloe's abdomen with an orange-tinged liquid, an antiseptic odor filled the air. There was a squelching sound as the doctor slid the scalpel across her skin.

Caleb promised to keep Chloe safe and look after her. As hard as he tried, he could not block out the soft, wet sound of the blade ripping across her stomach. Blood and fluid gushed onto the floor. How she had any blood left, he didn't know. The nurses were pumping bag after bag of fluid and blood into her, but she had to be losing it faster than they could replace it.

Caleb moved to be by Chloe's side and began whispering into her ear. "You stay with me, Chloe!" he demanded. "Do you hear me?" Tears ran uncontrollably down his cheeks. "Stay! You are not leaving me!" Caleb was openly weeping. "I've been dying over the past few months watching you from a distance." He desperately wanted his voice to be the hope she clung to if hope was at all possible. He needed her to hear him. "Do you want me to tell you something funny?" Caleb forced a laughed through his tears and kissed her cheek. "I was ten shades of jealous over that Damien fellow." Chloe's eyes were open, looking at him, but seeing nothing. Caleb's cheeks were wet, tears stinging like ice in the frigid operating room as they soaked his face. The room was so cold, so sterile. "Chloe, I fucking love you! I need you! Please stay with me. Please," Caleb begged in desperation. "I'm sorry for everything. *I AM SO SORRY FOR LEAVING YOU!*" His voice broke and came out in a whisper. "I thought I was doing what was best."

The medical team continued to give CPR as the doctors performed the emergency cesarean section. Then it was done. A soggy, squirting noise followed by the sound of more fluid sloshing onto the floor and the baby was out. Tiny, limp, blue, and silent. Everyone paused briefly at that moment to look at the motionless, tiny child. Then in an instant, they sprang back into action, splitting into two teams. They were back at work trying to save the child and its mother.

A smaller medical team took the little cyanotic baby and placed a mask over the infant's nose and mouth, each squeeze bringing a rise to his tiny little ribcage. The other group remained at Chloe's bedside, working intensely on her. Caleb could tell the team with Chloe was grasping in desperation at a life that most likely could not be saved. Her blood was beginning to congeal, it was still dripping off the table, but was thicker, moving slowly and clumping. The CPR continued, pushing the now-viscous blood through Chloe's veins. Caleb stood to the side, helplessly watching.

He focused on the man's large hand as it squeezed the blue bag that pumped Chloe's lung's full of air. There was nothing there, just the lifeless rise of her pale chest in response. The nurse doing CPR continued pushing on Chloe's sternum, counting aloud, while the rest of the team worked frantically over her. Hanging fluids and administering drugs, pumping in blood, bag after bag. There were fluids, trash, and medical supplies strewn everywhere.

Caleb fell to the floor as the realization sunk in. They were working on a corpse. There was nothing left of the girl Caleb loved, only this shattered, exsanguinated, mangled shell. He knew she was gone. From this nightmare, there was no coming back. Not without a miracle.

In desperation, Caleb crawled onto his knees, exposing himself to all celestial beings, and screamed to the human God. "Okay my brother, I surrender! I give up! Take me! Just leave Chloe!" Caleb cried up to him, fists curled in balls at his side, fingernails cutting into his palm. "This is your chance you SICK FUCK! You can snatch me out of existence right now, without a fight! Save all of humanity the pain, the suffering. This war could end now, here, be over in an instance."

However, this was his day. This battle was his. Caleb knew his brother was too self-righteous to take him now, during this moment of weakness. The deity would not let him surrender. He didn't care about bloodshed or war. He didn't care about the further loss—loss of angels or humans. He needed Caleb. He needed someone to blame for all that was wrong in the world. He needed Caleb if only to keep his own image pure and clean, untarnished. Selfish bastard!

The deity was called the king of man because, only he, had the power to intervene and save a human life while it was in its earthly form. No other angel had that power, the power to reverse death. Caleb knew Chloe's soul would be his, but Caleb was selfish, he wanted her in the flesh. He wanted her now! He didn't know how much longer he would be stuck here in perpetual immortality fighting this prophetic battle of wits. All the while Chloe would be out of his reach. Oh, yes, God was a vengeful deity. Caleb sat, vulnerable, quietly giving the deity the opportunity to consider the offer, on his knees, hands up in submission, begging for intervention. Nothing.

The deity would pay for this injustice, even if it meant the war of all wars. Here it begins...tonight. Oh, he would pay alright.

Caleb didn't feel any reason to be beside Chloe any longer. She wasn't there anymore. What was the purpose of all his power if he couldn't save the one person he truly cared about?

Caleb wanted to run away, get out of there, never come back. Yet, he stood watching, entranced as they pushed Chloe's dead heart faster and harder until he just couldn't take it any longer and he finally turned away. Caleb would leave them with the dead. In his defeat, he slowly walked over to the baby.

To Caleb's surprise, the infant suddenly began to cry. Caleb thought he was surely dead, and all was lost. Tears filled the new father's eyes and again spilled over. The child lived! Its heart was beating. Hers wasn't. At least Chloe's death wasn't completely in vain. She'd freely sacrificed herself to bare Caleb's beautiful sweet demon child. Therefore, her fight was over, but Caleb and the baby's was just beginning.

Caleb trembled, trying to block out the sound that was coming from behind him—the sound of a dead heart being forced to beat.

CHAPTER NINETEEN

Gone

Caleb went back out to the waiting room and took his place as the anxious grieving father and boyfriend he was supposed to be. When the doctor came out to tell him, of course, Caleb already knew, but his emotions were still fresh, raw, so he played the role well. No acting required.

His son was in the neonatal intensive care unit with a fair chance of survival. He would soon be transported to a higher-level of care facility in Seattle. Chloe was dead. Sudden placental abruption is what they said, but Caleb knew better. He sat in the waiting room single-mindedly plotting his revenge. Yes, he may die in the process, but so would the deity. Caleb didn't much care either way. The other angels would avenge Caleb if he fell, but none of that mattered. All that Caleb cared about was his own justice. His vengeance.

Somehow, the deity had found Chloe, gotten to her and facilitated her death. If Chloe had survived, she would have wanted Caleb to focus on the baby. However, the baby would be okay. He was the most important person in the world right now and would continue to be for many years to come—if he survived his human birth, that is.

Caleb would burn the deity's entire kingdom to the ground.

His murderous ideas had distracted him from the pain. The visions of revenge repeatedly played in his head until a hand on Caleb's shoulder interrupted his thoughts.

"Sir," I'm Kelsea from the NICU, would you like to come see your baby before he's transferred?" she asked compassionately. Caleb had been too far gone in his insane rhetoric to even think about seeing the infant. He thought to himself, what kind of shitty father am I going to be?

"Um, yes," Caleb managed to choke out. "Of course." He followed the thin nurse with olive skin and loose curls. The entire way she talked about incubators, tubes, and monitors until Caleb eventually just blocked her out. Everything she said was just white noise. Kelsea stopped him before entering the NICU. "Sir, would you like me to call the chaplain for you?"

Caleb stared at her blankly while he processed what she was asking. He questioned the nurse's intentions quietly inside his head. *Like to pray for me!* Ha, what a joke. The deity had these humans eating out of the palm of his hand.

Caleb couldn't help but let out an angry "humph" of a laugh. "No, ma'am, we'll be fine. Thank you," he managed to choke out, as kindly as possible. He was fairly sure it didn't come off as very genuine, or kind for that matter, but he didn't care.

The nurse had Caleb wash his hands and put on a plastic gown before leading him into the intensive care unit. The child was so tiny, lying there. He was a pinkish-purple, no longer the sickly blue he had been right after birth. The doctors had put a tube down his throat to give him extra oxygen since he wasn't breathing when he was born. The nurse assured Caleb that he was taking spontaneous breaths now and the tube was only temporary. Caleb laid his hand on his son's chest. He could feel the tiny thrumming of his heart. It made Caleb think of his last moments with Chloe and the sound of her dead heart being compelled to beat.

Then unexpectedly from behind the tangles of wires and tubes, the baby's eyes suddenly opened and stared up at Caleb, more focused than any newborn should have been. Bright blue eyes, the color of a summer sky. Caleb's heart melted. He was perfect!

As Caleb gazed upon the tiny, fragile child, everything inside of him suddenly came undone. Everything that he ever thought was important, every stressor in life, every flaw, every plot of revenge just snapped, like a tremendous tension had been released. Everything that made Caleb who he was, his love for the dead girl, his love for power and immortality, his loyalty to the angels, and hatred for his enemies, floated free like a boat breaking away from its moor, drifting out into the vast ocean. Caleb was not sailing alone; he was securely anchored. A heavy, steel, indestructible anchor. He knew immediately that this child would be everything to him from this point on. Caleb's knees involuntarily buckled. He fell backward, sitting down hard on the rocking chair positioned beside the baby's warmer. Caleb would give his very existence for this child. Moreover, he knew he might have to.

The nurse eventually made Caleb leave when the transport team arrived to take the child to the larger, better-equipped hospital in Seattle. It was just after daybreak when Caleb arrived at Chloe's house. The pain that had faded away was back again, though Caleb clung to it now. *My baby, my baby, my son.* He tried to keep his mind focused on the child. Why did I come back here? Caleb thought as he sat in Chloe's Living room looking at the blood-stained furniture and floor. So much blood. He could hear the ticking of a clock. Or was it the beating of his heart? He wanted to be close to her, he just didn't know how. Chloe's house seemed like the best plan at the time. Eventually, Caleb noticed that it was again dark outside. How much time had passed? Seconds, minutes, hours, days? The pain was gone. Caleb was numb. He couldn't feel anything. There was air in his lungs, and his heart was beating, but he felt nothing else.

Why did Chloe have such a profound effect on him? What was it about her? He instinctively walked through her house, ending up in her bed, her scent surrounding him. His head hurt, his heart ached, and there was a hollow pit in his stomach. Caleb's arms and legs felt like empty rubber hoses. He couldn't feel them. He couldn't feel himself. He welcomed sleep, or death, but neither came.

It was the pattern of his life. Caleb had always been strong enough to deal with anything he came across. Yes, humanity was always outside of Caleb's control, but humans were weak, fragile beings, and he had never vested any deep interest in them—until now. Chloe was the typical human, frail. The only thing he had ever been able to do was to keep her going, help her endure, help her survive. Caleb felt as if he had failed her miserably.

For him, the pain would be eternal...for he was eternal. For humans, pain was easier. Time passed and healed all wounds for them. It felt like something was stuck in his throat. He swallowed against the thickening of it. Caleb would not forget this pain. He had felt guilt and a semblance of pain for some of the things he had done. However, immortals, like Caleb, we're very easily distracted. Grief and guilt never stuck around long. Now Caleb had upped the stakes and fully vested himself in this little human love triangle. There was no getting out of it—not easily anyway, or without intense, lasting pain. Sleep finally did come, and Caleb embraced it wholeheartedly.

CHAPTER TWENTY

Hindsight is 20/20 Even for a God

Therefore, time passed. Months of it, even when it seemed impossible. It passed even when each tick of the clock ached like a hammer coming down on a fresh wound. It moved unevenly, in sprints and drags, but pass it did. Caleb buried Chloe, and his grieving continued. The only reprieves were the daily visits to his son in the neonatal intensive care unit. As the child improved, Caleb was able to stay with him for longer periods. The infant's smile warmed Caleb's heart, and the baby's eyes glowed with the wisdom of an elder. Caleb loved the child with every diminutive molecule of his being.

Each morning, Caleb opened his eyes and realized he had survived another night. It wasn't a surprise to him since he was immortal, but more of an unwelcome ending to the comfort of sleep. Caleb had a lot of time to think about his immortality and put things into perspective during the weeks after Chloe's death.

In the dregs of despair, Caleb had almost forgotten who he was. He knew Chloe was okay. She couldn't see him, and as Caleb, he couldn't see her, but the angels in his realm would know what to do. Chloe would be the queen of his kingdom. That's the thing about angels, they knew their rank and place. Yes, Caleb had been gone a long time in human years, but for immortals it had been just the blink of an eye. There had been angels who crossed over and given him updates about the other realms. Eternity was a long time of running when you pissed off a stronger entity—none of his angels would risk that. He didn't think the archangels would take that chance either, except on the deity's orders. There was no one more powerful than Caleb, especially when he was in his own realm.

Caleb wondered what a human soul's experience was in the process of death and transition. He had never been human, so he didn't completely understand their shift between realms. He had also never taken the time to ask a human on the other side. He never cared until now. He was well aware of what happened after the death and evolution when crossover was complete, that's all that had mattered to him.

His body was a charade. It was not his first, but it would likely be his last. When the witch cast the spell that opened Caleb's body up, allowing a dark angel's soul to enter, he decided it was time. Two hundred and fifty years ago things were different. Men were shorter, bad teeth, gnarled-up young from illness and injury. The wealthy young man's body was a real prize in its time. It suited Caleb. It was much easier to get what you needed when you looked like Caleb Frasier. Looks were especially important when he had to spend most of his time acting mortal. Other than being veiled in the parallel dimension, using his supernatural abilities put him on the radar. Really, unless the angels were nearby his powers were minimal in this realm anyway.

A confrontation with the deity would force the last war that the deity wanted so badly. It could wait in his opinion. Caleb had spent thousands of years in war, and what did his leagues get out of it? Loss of legions is what they got. They flexed for each other, flaunting their 'unique gifts.' It frustrated Caleb how duped humans were by the bible. Historically he had won battles, the deity had won battles, and neither the deity nor he were greater than the other. When they were at their greatest is when they fought as a team. They were invincible then. The one thing they both are is eternal. Both direct descendants of the spirit, the first creator. Over the centuries his brother branded him with many names. Brethren, Beelzebub, father of lies, deceiver, god of this world. The spirit called him Lucifer, the Shining One. While in this realm he would be called Caleb.

After Caleb had acquired his current body, he spent a long phase of time relishing in the experience. He also spent a lot of time remaining veiled, so the king of man wouldn't be able to locate him and start the last war. Time just escaped Caleb. Two hundred and fifty plus years of it. Until Chloe, that is, that's when Caleb began to slip and let his guard down. That's when they found him, and ultimately found Chloe. What a stupid damn mistake. It forced Caleb's hand, and now the prophecy is compelled to be played out. Chloe provided Caleb with a son. A boy who, as a man, would change the world, the realms, the kingdoms. Their son would right the wrongs that the human god put into place thousands of years ago. Their son would take his place as king of all kings. His power would one day rival both the deity and Caleb's.

The deity who calls himself the human god orchestrated that joke of a book to scare humans into submission. Blaming Caleb for all things wrong and taking credit for all things good, when in fact the deity is the king of man. He should have just stepped up and admitted that he never gave a damn about humans. Therefore, bad stuff happens, because he lets it. The deity has the ability to right wrongs, just like Caleb does, but you don't see the deity running around saving human lives. He also has more power over man than any other celestial being, including Caleb. The god of man has the power over humankind's life and death. All angels can change things for humans, to a point, but they cannot raise them from death, or even intervene with the process of death for that matter. If Caleb had that power, Chloe would be alive now. The truth was angels rarely interfered with humans. To celestial beings, it would be like a human intervening in an ant's life—what's the point? Angels all have unique powers; some are stronger than others. The deity and Caleb being the oldest and most powerful of all the celestial beings other than the spirit creator.

Those fanatical witches were always opening the deity's little loophole by creating doppelgangers, which allowed fallen angels to cross over into the human realm. The witches believed angels resided in the corpse. However, they were mistaken. Were they kidding? The angels would take over the living body, the human just died, as it was intended. Again, only God has the ability to intervene with saving a human life from imminent death. Especially on Earth, in this realm, Angels are weaker when in human form.

The deity has always had control over mankind's mortality, which is his special power. Most angels could care less about that particular power. What did it matter if he has power over the weakest, frailest creatures in the universe? Big deal. That's definitely not the best party trick Caleb had seen. Furthermore, the book and the stories the deity had disseminated for centuries about Caleb along with that God of all Gods bullshit, it never bothered Caleb—until now, until Chloe. Caleb also could have cared less about that prophecy nonsense he wrote. The deity orchestrated that book to blow smoke up his own skirt. This power over humans went to his head. Now he had forced Caleb's hand, and the real prophecy was being fulfilled. Caleb would have his revenge, in this existence or the next. His son would rule over everything. He would be the downfall of the so-called king of king's reign over humankind. Likewise, one day Caleb would return to his kingdom to rule side by side with Chloe, and the human god will take the role of fallen angel.

But Caleb was digressing. He needed to stay focused.

There were two items on Caleb's agenda right now. Find out more about this Damien fellow who had been hanging around Chloe before she fell ill, and to prepare a home for his son at the safe house in Seattle.

Damien had disappeared immediately after Chloe's death, a big red flag. Caleb knew he was involved. He had Kira trying to find out who Damian was and where he was. It was likely that Damien was an opposing angel, he just didn't know which one, but he would soon. Kira would make sure of that.

The loophole angels had safe houses around the world. Most angels were here because of the witches, but some angels possessed the ability to temporarily travel between realms in their party trick repertoire. The deity's angels had free reign among man's realm as long as they didn't get too involved with the humans. For instance, fornicating—and especially procreating—was definitely an eternal death by fire no–no. Caleb found this fairly hypocritical seeing as how the deity himself had been known to go off on a tangent with a human or two, even resulting in an offspring of his own. Everyone knows how that turned out. The god of man didn't even care enough about his own half human son to intervene in his torture and murder. Why would any person think that this same god would care about them?

Sebastian was preparing for the infant's homecoming. The baby was scheduled to be released from the hospital soon. Caleb called him Azaiah. Azaiah, being half human, had struggled at birth but had survived and was now thriving. Azaiah had leagues of angels protecting him. His birth had been long awaited among the celestial kind.

First order of business for Caleb, Azaiah was going to need a mother, a human mother. The Angels couldn't care for him having to remain in this realm all of the time. If the angels stayed for extended periods, the deity would be able to locate and destroy the child easily.

Caleb's heart wasn't ready for wooing another female right now. He sincerely, irrevocably, loved Chloe, and her absence still weighed heavily on his heart, but the child was a priority now. So, it was now Caleb's duty as a father to locate a female who was worthy of raising the next king of kings. This parenting gig was a stressful job.

CHAPTER TWENTY-ONE

Pretender

"How's the search for Mrs. Right?" Kira smiled sarcastically.

"It's a hard job, but somebody has to do it. Maybe I'll start going to church and see what I come up with." Caleb smiled back mockingly.

"I bet there are a lot of heartbroken ladies out there." Kira laughed. "Well, at least you can have fun while you are searching."

"Kira, if you only knew," Caleb shot back seriously. What he wanted to say was this quest was breaking his heart more than she could ever understand. He knew that they felt differently about the human girl than he did. It was understandable. However, his love for Chloe was not something he could easily explain to them. It transcended time, space, Heaven, and Hell. Before Chloe, he would not have understood it either. If one of the angels had come to him speaking of a human the way he talked about Chloe, he would have thought them insane.

Either way, Caleb's search might be over. He had found a suitable candidate. She certainly wasn't Chloe, but she was a good person, smart, and she would make a great mother. Luckily, she was also easy on the eyes. Caleb had tried to take the relationship to the next level, but she was holding out. Therefore, she had some principles about her. She was young but had just finished college. An elementary school teacher, same goal as Chloe. Chloe never actually was a teacher, but it was her intended pathway before fate intervened.

They had met at a night club. Caleb with his easy charm, introduced himself, she saw in him exactly what she needed: someone with confidence about the future and a sense of humor that drove all her fears away. He was handsome, intelligent and driven, a successful businessman, several years older than she, and he pursued his job with passion. She understood his vigorous pursuit of success, for her father and most of the men she met in her social circle were the same way. Like them, he'd been raised that way, and, in the class system of the South, where she was from, family name and accomplishments were often the most important consideration in marriage. In some cases, they were the only consideration.

Though she had quietly rebelled against this idea since childhood and had dated a few men best described as reckless, she found herself drawn to Caleb's easy ways and had gradually come to love him. Despite the long hours he worked, he was good to her. He was a gentleman, mature and responsible. When she needed someone to hold her, he never once turned her away. She felt secure with him and knew he loved her as well and that was why she had accepted decided to date him.

Caleb would have to be careful to be as humanly normal as possible, but he just wanted to get on with it. Get on with the sex, the marriage, and then her stepping into the role of wife and mother. She was a sweet girl, but there would be no great passion on his side. She would never know how he felt though. He was a master at deception, probably the best. But then, he had to be good at it. It's not a survival skill that most people need. Most people were not Caleb.

He picked Hayden up at eight pm, went for dinner, then he brought her back to the house on the pretense that he wanted to get home to Azaiah. Caleb wanted Hayden to become attached to Azaiah, and he needed to see the attachment to make sure she would work out. She had been around him many times over the past months, and they got on very well. Besides, maybe tonight would be the night that the deviant wildcat sex goddess would emerge. Well, a man can dream, can't he? Damn physical desires got Caleb every time. He did love human sex.

Hayden was a beautiful woman with pale olive skin and brown curls. She was tall with a curvy, athletic build. She had a great sense of humor, and conversation was easy with her. Caleb almost felt sorry for pulling her into this, but there was a higher calling at stake. Her sacrifice would serve humanity. He did feel fond of Hayden, don't get it wrong, he would provide her a good life. She would feel loved. However, children were out of the question. Additionally, there was always the possibility of her ending up as collateral damage. Look what happened to Chloe. They would cross those bridges when they came to them. Tonight, was all about romancing Hayden.

Azaiah was three now, and very intelligent. He had the sweetest temperament, which was very useful. The angels watched with careful eyes as his powers grew. He seemed to be strong without having to siphon power from the presence of other angels. He, himself, was a great source of power. They all worked with him, teaching him control and containment. His guardians tried hard to balance the emphasis of hiding who he was, without making it seem shameful.

One morning, Caleb entered Azaiah's room to find him sitting upright in his bed, eye's open, staring forward. Caleb could not get him to awaken. He picked him up and sat holding the child closely, looking for signs of trauma or illness. There were none.

However, as Caleb held him a warmth radiated from his body. Not heat, but light and peace. Caleb recognized it. It was home, his realm. He immediately felt comforted. He also felt the presence of Chloe.

Caleb hadn't been home for hundreds of years; it was the most peaceful feeling. The tighter he held Azaiah, the more peace he felt. He had the sensation of Chloe stroking his hair, saying that she loved him, thanking him for taking such good care of their child. He even felt the soft warmth of her lips on his. He could sense her love radiating through Azaiah into him. It was spectacular. Then suddenly it was gone. It was like abruptly awakening from a dream. Fragmented memories and sensations lingered as he sat dazed, sorting through what had just occurred.

Azaiah looked up at Caleb with his beautiful blue eyes and chubby round face and smiled. "Mama," he said.

Then the child's eyes closed, and his head fell back limp. Caleb examined the boy carefully. Azaiah's body temperature was cooling down, normalizing. His chest rose and fell with a regular pattern of breathing. Whatever had happened exhausted the child. Did his son have the ability to travel across realms? He laid him softly on the bed and curled up next to his sweet child and cried once again for the loss of Chloe. She would have been such a wonderful mother to the child. That relationship had been stolen from them.

"Yes, baby, that was Mama," Caleb whispered to his son as he swallowed against the lump in his throat, tears running freely down his cheeks. "Your mama is very special; Daddy loves her and misses her too." Caleb kissed the top of Azaiah's head, tears still quietly flowing. Caleb missed Chloe so much, his heart was breaking being so close yet so far away from her.

Azaiah stirred, and his eyes fluttered open. A tiny hand touched Caleb's face.

"Is Daddy sad?" Azaiah put his little chunky hands on each side of his daddy's cheeks.

"Daddy is just sad that Mommy can't be here with us, that's all. But it's ok, because if Daddy is patient, we will all be together again one day." Caleb smiled at his sweet toddler, hugging him tightly.

* * *

Caleb spared no expense when it came to Azaiah. He had the best nanny, the top private preschool tutors, the finest toys and clothes. Between the angels and humans, this kid had a great life. He rarely got angry or threw tantrums. He was generally mild natured. The few times he had become angry it was very good that angels were around to intervene. Sebastian could control human memories, what they thought they had seen, what they remembered seeing.

Angels could not outright control humans, that would have made things so much easier, but free will was a bitch. For instance, Caleb possessed the ability to force humans to act physically, like stab themselves with a pencil. What he could not do is force them to change mentally or think differently. He couldn't force Hayden to fall in love with him just by telling her to. What a time saver that would be. No, that was all his natural charm and good looks.

Several weeks into the relationship Hayden was becoming very close with Azaiah. Most evenings she insisted on putting him to bed and participating in the bedtime routine. She would usually stay for a while afterwards, spending time with Caleb. Tonight, they sat in front of the fire, drinking wine and talking. Caleb knew all the things to say and do to win this girl over. He almost felt guilty. Like a spider and its prey. It was getting late, and he wanted to either bed this girl or go to bed. It had been long enough, there was a breaking point for everyone. With the flash of a smile, Caleb leaned in and kissed her softly. She kissed him back.

"Hayden, do you want to stay over?" he asked hopefully.

She hesitated. If it wouldn't have been rude, Caleb would have rolled his eyes, but he restrained from any negative connotation. "It's okay, baby, if you aren't ready. I understand. I can give you a ride home."

"It's just that…" She stopped. Caleb thought she would never continue. He took her hand gently into his. "It's just that I've only ever been with one man, and I thought we would marry, and he would be the only one for life. Obviously, that wasn't how it worked out." She observed Caleb closely, monitoring his expression. Shit, how did I keep finding these girls. I guess standards and good breeding was synonymous with you are going to wait forever to have sex.

But he said, "Hayden, its fine. I love you. Yes, I want you, but I can wait until you are ready." He offered as comfort to her, "I've got loads of time. I'm not going to give up on us." He smiled warmly at her. She hugged him tightly. He had to keep things in perspective. This wasn't about him; it was for the child.

"This may sound old fashioned, but I just always imagined being unspoiled until my wedding, but it seems to get to the wedding you have to taint yourself these days," she huffed nervously.

'Great!' Caleb thought. 'How long do I have to wait to propose?'

"Hayden, I swear it's fine. That's a decision I can respect." He kissed her deeply. "It'll give me something to look forward to." He helped her up off the couch. "Let me get you home now."

She seemed happy with how Caleb had handled things. He was fine with waiting. A sacrifice he was willing to make for an acceptable mother candidate for Azaiah. A means to an end.

He drove her home. She did look gorgeous in the moonlight. She had a great body too. It really was something to look forward to. He walked her to the door and kissed her goodnight. Maybe if things progressed, he could propose to her on Christmas? Perhaps her birthday in February? He would speak to Kira about that, see if she thought it would be too soon. Kira could pick out the ring and engagement venue if she decided it would be appropriate to proceed.

February came, marking four months of regularly, tediously dating of Hayden. Many times, they were intimate to the point of sex, but never including the actual act of intercourse. Caleb was romantic and charming and everything a girl could not resist. It was no surprise when Hayden accepted his proposal of marriage. She rarely spoke about her family, so after the proposal he asked if he would be meeting them, if they would be involved in the wedding.

Hayden firmly stated, "No." She didn't offer up an explanation other than, "The only thing worse than not having a father was having mine."

Caleb smiled and took her hand. "I can relate, believe me, I have family issues myself. Don't worry, you plan the wedding I'll pay for everything." He took her into his arms. "You've made me a very happy man, Hayden. I want you to have your dream wedding." And she had indeed made him a happy man.

After the proposal, Hayden became a daily fixture in Caleb's life. It was helping him and Azaiah get used to her. He couldn't stop thinking about how truly happy he would have been to do this exercise with Chloe. That's how he got through each tuxedo fitting, cake tasting moment, by picturing Chloe. If there had really been a score to keep for the number of sins committed, Caleb would have quickly been racking up his tally. The tedium was not something he ever grew used to. Every day with Hayden seemed more impossibly monotonous than the last. He was very good at hiding it, she never expected anything.

They were married the August before Azaiah turned four. It was a beautiful ceremony. Hayden was a lovely bride. They were both happy for different reasons. Her because she was starting a new chapter in her life, marrying the man of her dreams. Caleb because this deplorable cat and mouse game had finally come to an end. The child had a mother. He could up his "job responsibilities," travel more and be away from them as much as possible, lessening the risk of the deity locating Azaiah, something Caleb always worried about. Everything had worked out and he congratulated himself on a game well played.

That night Hayden no longer had to worry about being an untarnished bride. Caleb had been having sex all along, just not with her. However, she was sure the suspense had been killing him. She was beautiful to look at, and the idea of her excited him. She was restrained in her love making. Lack of exposure possibly. He was gentle and thoughtful and everything she had dreamed of for their first time. Caleb, of course, thought about Chloe the entire night.

CHAPTER TWENTY-TWO

I love you. I hate you.

Hayden acclimated to the role of Azaiah's mother very well. Caleb was away as much as he could manage. He made sure she felt spoiled and loved whenever he was there, even though the only thing he really wanted to do was spend time with his son. Everything was going great until their three-year anniversary. Azaiah was seven, and he had started school full time. Hayden developed a strong maternal yearning to have a child of her own. At first, Caleb played along. After a year of infertility, she wanted to go for tests and doctors' visits to find out why she hadn't conceived. He dragged his feet, making excuse after excuse. For the next two years, he began to slowly pull away. He explained that work was stressful, and they had a lifestyle to maintain, assuring her that they could focus on children in a few years. However, she wasn't happy with that. She was ready now.

One beautiful crisp autumn day they were strolling through the park with Azaiah. He was nine. Caleb remembered thinking that the sky was so blue you could literally drown in it. It remind- ed him of sitting with Chloe by the ocean in Maine. Hayden and Caleb were walking, hands linked, when she stopped mid stride and turned to him. There was a faint crease between her eyebrows.

"Caleb, are you seeing someone else?" she blurted out. The

bluntness of the question took him off guard.

"Why would you ask that, babe?" He responded, shocked. Of course, he was seeing other women. Many, many women over the years, but never anyone on a regular basis. That was about as much faithfulness as he could muster. Very few repeat customers. He could tell this conversation was going to be unbelievably frustrating.

"I knew it. I can tell when we are making love, or when I'm playing with Azaiah. I can tell when we are walking through the park, like now. When we are talking, and you look right through me. You are thinking about someone else. Women know these things, Caleb." She was crying, and he could clearly see the pain on her face.

Oh hell! Damnit Chloe! He always thought about Chloe when he was with Hayden. Always. He couldn't help it, thinking of her. It's what got him through the dullness of each day. Caleb had to be there, he needed Hayden, but he apparently could not mask his unresolved feelings for his lost love. He was eternal, therefore his love for Chloe was eternal. No human could understand that. The thing was Chloe and Caleb would be together again one day. Pain fades for humans in death because deep in their hearts they doubt they will ever be with their loved ones again. They lack true faith, they lack dedication, loyalty. They honestly don't believe that they will be reunited after death. No matter what they say. If they actually did have faith and truly thought they would be reunited, then it's likely they would wait it out. Nope, eventually they move on. Always! It's different for immortals like Caleb. They rarely fall, but when they do, they fall hard. How could he explain this to Hayden in a sensitive way that she could understand?

"Let's sit down love." He pointed to the park bench. "Hayden, you know I lost Azaiah's mother suddenly. I do think about her at times. I can't help it. I see her in you and you in her. It makes me happy that you love Azaiah so much, and I think about how happy Chloe would be about that. There is no one else. Only you, babe." Caleb put his palm against the curve of her cheek and leaned in for a kiss.

All the time he was thinking, 'I am on a roll, I might as well get the whole traumatized by pregnancy thing out of the way while I'm at it.'

"That's why I am so reluctant to push this pregnancy issues. It scares me. I couldn't risk losing you...like I lost her." Caleb felt like he deserved a Golden Globe for that performance. Unfortunately, Hayden wasn't so impressed.

"Caleb, I'm not her. I could never be her, and I can't live with her ghost any longer." Tears were spilling over onto her cheeks. He was becoming more and more irritated with this conversation. WOW, this was going to be harder than he thought.

"What can I do, Hayden? I can't change history. I can't just forget because you want me too." He asked her with total seriousness now.

"Caleb it's been nine years!" Her voice trembled. "I wish I could give you what you're looking for, but I don't know what it is. There's a part of you that you keep closed off from everyone, including me. It's as if your' mind is on someone else. It's like you keep waiting for her to pop out of thin air to take you away from all this..." Her breath caught in her throat and the tears were flooding her face.

"Are you okay baby?" he asked, a thousand other questions on his face. "I'm sorry, Hayden. It kills me to see you cry. I will try harder, but I'm not sure what else you want. Our past is our past. It's always there. It's not like it can be erased to make someone else happy." Caleb pleaded with her. He really didn't want to lose Hayden. Azaiah was used to her, and he needed her. Nevertheless, he was becoming increasingly annoyed, and he wasn't sure how much more he could endure.

"If you loved me enough it could!" Hayden was openly weeping. A lump had risen in her throat, and she was now speechless.

She stepped back, trying to compose herself, wiping away the last of her tears. She tore herself from Caleb's grasp and hurried across the park toward the car.

Thank goodness, Caleb thought. He knew that he was obligated to follow her and try to win her back, but at least he could have a few minutes reprieve to gather his thoughts.

Hayden shut Caleb out after that. It was the beginning of the end of their marriage.

A few months later Caleb came home after a 'business trip.' Hayden had been drinking, taking a mixture of antidepressants and anti-anxiety pills and who knows what else. She was a mess. She had been seeing a psychiatrist regularly since that day at the park, but Caleb didn't think it was helping. When Kira saw what was happening with Hayden, she popped in to look after things. They still had the nanny, although at nine Azaiah really had no need for one. She was kept on because she minded her business, Azaiah liked her, and Hayden was slightly unstable at this point.

Caleb set his suitcase on the floor and asked Kira, "What's going on?"

"Your wife is having a meltdown," she said dryly, twisting her face at him and pointing to the master bedroom. "Drinking herself into a stupor and mumbling about a ghost and you not loving her...blah, blah, blah. I don't know, she's half-baked."

"Oh, great!" Caleb said, pressing his palm against his forehead, hoping it would help relieve some of the tension he felt coming on. "She's jealous, say's I still love Chloe." He couldn't contain his aggravation.

"She's right. It's very apparent, Caleb," Kira said, pouring herself a glass of chardonnay from the open wine bottle. Caleb raised his eyebrows and bit his lower lip. "What?" She shrugged, looking at her glass of wine. "It's a good year. You leave it uncorked like that it will go to waste." She winked and smiled.

"I should have fallen for you, Kira. Life would be a whole lot easier right now." Caleb shot her a smile, and she rolled her eyes at him.

"You wish." She took a sip of her wine. "Anyway, I have principles. I'm not playing second fiddle to no dead girl! You can bet on that." Then her tone became a bit less playful. "That dead human girl is going to be your downfall, Caleb."

"For fuck's sake, you're telling me." He nodded his head in acceptance, acutely aware that she was giving him sisterly advice masquerading as a sarcastic remark.

"I am immortal, I have conquered legions, I control realms, I have brought the human deity himself to his knees, but I just can't get that girl out of my head." Caleb looked at Kira solemnly. She shrugged, shooting him a mocking half smile and continued drinking her wine.

Towards the end of their relationship Hayden began to travel back home to the south frequently. A month later she visited Caleb and told him she'd met someone else. He understood. They parted as friends, and the following year he received a postcard from her saying she was married. He hadn't heard from her since.

CHAPTER TWENTY-THREE

Foul Play

Caleb shook his head, agitated with himself. Chloe ruined me. At the very least set the bar high for the next woman. He was sure Chloe would have wanted it that way. Many times, over the years Caleb would find a wife prospect, a woman he thought might fit the bill. Then she wanted to have sex immediately, like the first date immediately. Okay, he went along with it most of the time. Well, to be honest, he fucked all of them, but who wants to wife-up that kind of girl? He didn't think it would be good for the kid. She had to have values.

Caleb wasn't judgmental. He was totally in favor of a good time. It's not like celestial beings see morality the same way humans do. Caleb and his kind knew that idiotic book was a crock, nothing more than a bunch of ramblings written by hallucinating lunatics. Celestials would never let themselves be defined by a book written by humans, most of whom were clinically insane. Besides, they knew the deity firsthand, knew that he was a hypocrite. He absolutely did not know every hair on a human's head or watch every move they made. Come on, people, does that even seem logical? Oh yeah, faith. Caleb always forgot about that. That was a smart move by his brother, Caleb gave him that. He convinced humankind that believing in illogical, unreasonable, ludicrous things was…logical. Smart move, but just about as ridiculous as a child's prayer saving him from the monsters under his bed in the dark of night.

Humans knew deep down that this stuff didn't make sense. They all prayed, but only for things for which no proof of results could ever be verified. They prayed for a cure for the cancer of a loved one while the medical team worked diligently with science to actually answer those prayers. Have you ever met a human who prayed for something tangible? For instance, prayed that an amputated leg would grow back? No, because all faith and fairy tales have limits. People could give God credit if the doctors save their loved one from cancer but are they going to blame God if a leg doesn't grow back? No, because no one truly expects it too. Because God doesn't answer prayers in the first place. All prayers accomplished was feeding the deities ego.

So many times Caleb had heard that god has a plan for everything, but then humans are told to pray – for their loved ones to get better when they fall ill, for safety in the storm, for the home team to win the big game. Do humans think that means god will change his plan if they pray hard enough, or the right way, or get enough other people to pray for the same thing? This seems to suggest that god doesn't have much of a plan at all, since he's apparently willing to simply do whatever gets the most prayers or favors those who ingratiate themselves the most or who have prayed the best – not to mention that it's a rather arbitrary, even capricious, approach to human suffering.

Christians are always going on about how Jesus died for human sins, but if he came back after three days then he didn't really die at all; more like being in a brief coma, which is a drag, but not exactly the ultimate sacrifice that the crucifixion is cracked up to be. If you go dig up a three-day old grave, regardless of what you think may have happened to that person's immortal soul, odds are there's still going to be a body in it. Jesus' tomb, on the other hand, was empty, meaning that following his resurrection he was either a zombie or he was fully alive, neither of which is dead.

Jesus was willing to call out hypocrisy, and he did care somewhat about social justice – at least with regard to poverty and leprosy – but otherwise he was still the enforcer of some rather distasteful rules. And don't even get Caleb started on the biblical tale about Jesus being his own father – a concept that, in addition to being patently bizarre on its face, makes Jesus himself the very same god of the Old Testament that Christians like to dismiss as no longer relevant, except, of course, when it comes to hating gays.

Caleb knew why the bible was full of rape, murder, genocide, slavery, and every manner of atrocity – and not in a, 'This is what our enemies do so don't be like them' way, but in a 'As long as you are one of mine, have at it' way. The deity is a rather narcissistic and not particularly family-centric god. The mighty deity had been trying to find Caleb and Azaiah, and they were still here, in the same location for over a decade. Therefore, did people really think the deity was following them around with a notepad keeping track of every lie they told? Caleb knew he wasn't going to change a thousand lifetimes of bad information getting crammed down humankind's throat, but he couldn't help but wonder why humans had a brain but refused to use it for common sense.

Historically, Caleb saw the point of this ridiculous doctrine. Back in the day, it was a lawless time. Everyone would have killed each other if the deity hadn't scared them into submission. It would have been mayhem, only the strong would have survived. The Bible served its purpose in that respect. However, those times were long over.

Anyway, the bible never set the moral bar very high. Let's face it: Don't rape people, don't own people, don't hate people, and don't hurt children are kind of no-brainers when it comes to morality. Jesus and his old man not only failed to make these things clear, but in many instances, they encouraged, condoned, or commanded them. Sure, Jesus said a few things about loving your neighbor and being kind to strangers, but he also said that not believing in him was the worst offense a person could commit and that anyone who didn't believe would burn in Hell for all eternity. And seriously, the Ten Commandments as a basis for all morality? Checking out your neighbor's wife is worse than raping your daughter? Taking the lord's name in vain is worse than owning slaves? Nice priorities. Add to this the fact that god himself does not follow his own rules, to which Christians usually respond that mere mortals cannot understand or judge the morality of god. But if the bible defines morality, and god has a different set of rules for himself than for humans, and we are not allowed to know or understand his rules except that we are expected to do as he says but not as he does, then how exactly does that provide any kind of moral baseline whatsoever? It was mind boggling to Caleb for a group that loves to point fingers at 'sinners' for supposed moral relativism, what could be more relative than that?

It's all just way too convenient. Got what you prayed for? He answered your prayers. Praise Jesus! Didn't get it? He has another plan. Praise Jesus! Don't have the answers? You're not meant to. Praise Jesus! Figured out the answer? He chose you. Praise Jesus! Sad about the deaths of your loved ones? They're in a better place. Praise Jesus! Sad about how much your life sucks? You'll be happy once you're dead. Praise Jesus! Honestly, when the answer to every question is exactly the thing that should make you feel the need to use your own human intellect. It should send up a huge red flag that maybe you're not being completely objective.

Humankinds buy in to the bible, faith, the organization of religion would always be something Caleb didn't understand, especially in such an educated century as the current one. It was easy for him because he knew the story, firsthand. He had been there, had lived it. But one day humans would see what kind of god they had been worshiping and Caleb would be there to witness the truth unveiled. At that time, he and his son would bask in their glory.

As far as the female mom candidates, it was about standards and good breeding, not morals. Caleb would have loved to find the perfect mom who became a kinky ball-licking wildcat at night. However, at this point it was about the kid. He needed to fit in with society while flying under the radar. He really needed to get his game on track.

Kira strolled into the room. Her presence never went unnoticed.

"Zi's down for his nap," she announced. Caleb gave her a nod of thanks. Kira was one of the original fallen angels. Standing at six feet tall, nothing but firm muscle, her dark skin was smooth, shiny, and perfect. She wore her hair in a tight afro. Her neck was lean and long, her facial structure and high cheekbones making her a beautiful creature in any realm. Moreover, she was strong and stealth and a great warrior. Kira and Caleb had battled side by side for eras', and he was thrilled to have her on his side and lucky to call her his oldest ally. There were no secrets within the friendship, so Caleb quickly noticed when she cut her eyes at Sebastian, also an original.

"OK, what's going on?" Caleb's eyes darted back and forth between the faces of both of them. He could tell this was serious. Sebastian raised his eyebrows but made no other move.

"Why haven't you told him?" Kira quickly called Sebastian out. They faced each other in silence for a long moment. Caleb had reasonable intuition that this was something he was not going to be happy about. Otherwise, why be so reluctant to share the information.

"Caleb, Chloe has disappeared from the other side," Sebastian conveyed as calmly as he possibly could.

He immediately felt the heat rise in his neck as he tried very hard to stay calm. *Damn, I am having a very bad week!*

Caleb knew that essentially nothing had changed. So, the deity had not given up, but had he believed for one moment that he had? This only confirmed what he had already known, that there was no fair playing field with him. There was also no reason for fresh panic. Chloe was Caleb's soul, she belonged in his realm, he must have seized her as a pawn in his last war chess game. The deity was just begging for a fight, so a fight he would get.

Caleb was in fact the only danger to the deity, and vice versa. No other angel had the power to kill either one of them. In the past, neither of them would have actually killed the other either. War was just a game between bored gods. They were brothers, always would be brothers. They especially would not have sought the eternal death of a brother over a human, but Chloe was different. Caleb wasn't sure the deity realized that. Maybe he didn't care and was committed on provoking him into the final battle. *Goddamnit!*

"Sebastian, bring me one of the archangels. DON'T harm them, I just need some information. Someone new to this world," Caleb said sternly. Sebastian nodded and left without hesitation. Archangels didn't need a loophole, though sometimes it was referred to as a loophole for uniformity. He needed someone who had recently crossed over so he could acquire fresh intelligence.

* * *

Caleb already had a lot on his plate with Azaiah and now this. Fucking Chloe! He had loved that girl before he even knew her. Her heart called out to him long before they met. She was weak and helpless and in need of rescue. And so eternally beautiful. He shook his head at the memory.

God of humans. Ha! Caleb was more of a god to humans, always had been, minus that one special power over life. Why not? He was here on the ground, playing the part, watching it all since the whole thing began. He had cultivated and perfected every sensation man had ever had. He cared about what humans wanted and never judged them. Never rejected him. Despite all the imperfections and weaknesses, Caleb had been a fan of the human race! Did anyone ever, in a million years, think the god of humans would lower himself to come down to earth and live as man among men? Hell no. He was a megalomaniac. A tyrant. Humans had no idea what kind of monster they were worshiping.

Well, no going back now. He couldn't stand the thought of Chloe's soul in any realm other than his. She was and always would be *HIS*! He owed nothing to humans, but he owed everything to her. So, if the deity wanted this war that badly, then war he would get.

Before the days end Sebastian had arrived with an archangel in tow. A low-ranking member, unimportant, but still one of the deity's throngs, nonetheless. He nodded at Sebastian in thanks. He was a close ally, and Caleb considered him a dear friend. Caleb could not die easily, but he could be sequestered, and if that ever happened, Sebastian and Kira would be charged with raising Caleb's son. A great honor bestowed onto them. Sebastian had a daughter of his own, he understood the responsibility of that charge. Kira would give her life for Azaiah.

"What's your name, son?" Caleb asked the unidentified angel. Even if he knew him, he rarely could recognize an angel in their human form, at least not immediately. He always felt the presence of another angel. As for the deity and himself, they would recognize each other anywhere, in any form. His senses were much weaker when in human form, but still present. The deity and Caleb had a type of telekinesis, ever present, except when they were veiled or in certain opposing realms.

"I am not your son!" The angel spat vehemently.

"OK, that's fair." Caleb smiled at him, then repeated sternly, "So what's your name?"

"James," he stammered.

"James," He confirmed. "Whose legion do you belong to?"

"I am son of Ezekiel," he stated proudly.

"OK, James, son of Ezekiel," Caleb answered respectfully. "What's going on in your realm?"

"I don't know what you're talking about." He stood proud and sounded convincing, but Caleb sensed a twinge of nervous energy, so he pressed on.

"Has the deity hijacked one of my souls?" he asked, remaining very amicable.

"Is this a test?" James laughed sarcastically.

"Isn't everything?" Caleb looked at him, eyebrows raised, palms held out as if the answer were plainly there.

"The souls of man are his. He is the king of humankind. So, when you ask me if he abducted one of your souls, the answer is no, he has not," James said, looking smug and pleased with his answer.

Heat again rose in the back of his neck. "Listen, son." Caleb grabbed his shoulder firmly, causing James to wince. "I am trying not to lose my patience with you, but don't push me." He had intended to let this lowly angel go free initially, but he was now skating on thin ice by pushing his buttons. His tolerance was wearing thin, and as forbearing as he was, his tolerance ended with Chloe's involvement.

"That the sons of God saw the daughters of men, that they were fair, and they took them as wives, of all which they chose.

When the sons of God came in unto the daughters of men, and they bared children to them, the same became mighty men of renown." James began to regurgitate verses from that deplorable doctrine.

Caleb pressed his fingers into his forehead. But James was not deterred.

Caleb joined in with James as if in a perfect chorus. "And God saw that the wickedness of man was great in the earth, and that every imagination of the thoughts of his heart was only evil continually." James stopped and watched Caleb, wide eyed.

"James, I know you don't fully appreciate the predicament you are in. Therefore, I'm trying to give you a pass, but you are making this hella□ difficult. I suggest you stop rambling. I have been force-fed that shit for over four millennia." Caleb was becoming angry. "You want to quote the doctrine to me?! Okay, here's some doctrine for you." Caleb was within inches of his face as he began to forcefully speak the scripture. "The purpose of these relations was to corrupt the human gene pool and prevent the birth of the eventual Messiah, who God prophesied would be born of a woman and eventually destroy Satan." He stopped and composed himself. "Tell me, James, how did that work out for him?" He grabbed James by the throat. James coughed and stiffened up. "Now James, *the girl*. Does he have her?" he asked calmly.

"You won't kill me," James insisted.

"Won't I?" Caleb stared at him blankly.

"It would cause a war between legions," he said, confidence clearly wavering.

"James, I have news for you, war is no longer imminent... *WAR IS HERE!*" Caleb dropped him to the ground, letting go of his neck.

"I'm not asking you to betray anyone. I just want to know about the girl. That's all, then you go on your way," Caleb said, walking away in a gesture of peace.

"You must have forgotten, in the Bible you lose," James said, composing himself. "You are destined to lose."

Caleb laughed, walking back slowly toward him. "Well, consider the source, James. This is my time. The twentieth and twenty-first century have been and will be entirely mine. Son, this is not a theological debate. This is your last chance to answer before I take you out of existence. *WHERE IS THE GIRL!*"

"Yea, he's got her, but that's all I know. It's not like I am high ranking, so you're talking to the wrong guy here."

He was right, but he had confirmed the only information that he really needed to know. Chloe was with the deity. Caleb placed his hand on the archangel's shoulder and squeezed slightly.

"Thank you, James. See that was easy enough." Caleb smiled and then immediately gave James eternal death, his human form catching fire and turning to ash.

Sebastian sucked in his breath at the unexpected maneuver.

"What, Sebastian!?" Caleb looked at him wide-eyed, taunting him to say a word. He knew what he had done. Caleb and the deity felt it when any of their legions were ripped out of existence. The deity could feel the loss of this lowly angel. Caleb didn't care. This was a battle that the deity began, but Caleb would end.

"I sent a message," he said, calming down.

"Sir—" Sebastian started, correcting himself, "Caleb." He was always leery when any of the angels started a sentence with "Sir." "I don't mean to be disrespectful—"

Caleb cut him off abruptly. "Well then don't."

"Okay, but is this human girl really worth starting the war of all wars over?" He was definitely unsettled asking this question, but he felt the need for it to be asked, and that took courage. Caleb took a deep breath, choosing his words carefully.

"Well what do you think, Sebastian? She is the mother of the goddamn king of all kings. Do you think she is worth saving?" Caleb paused, cocking his head slightly to one side and holding full eye contact. "Plus, how do you think Azaiah would feel about us leaving his mother at the mercy of his mortal enemy?"

"Do you really think he would harm her?" Sebastian asked.

"What part of mortal enemies is too complicated for you to understand, Sebastian?" Caleb answered. Sebastian responded with a nod.

" I have some place to be." Caleb put his hand on Sebastian's shoulder and looked him in his eyes. "Thank you for being such a loyal friend." He walked out, leaving Sabastian with a sigh of relief.

CHAPTER TWENTY-FOUR

The Beginning of the End

Sebastian had received intel regarding the realm where Chloe's soul was being held. He took no time getting his legions together for battle. They stood waiting in the combat realm.

"Be calm, Brother. We have time to sort this out. No need to rush." Sebastian took Caleb's arm in a firm Roman handshake.

Caleb had seen red when he learned that Ezekiel's legions were holding Chloe.

Now he stood firmly in the consequences of his decision as the opposing army advanced. There was a great production about their entry. They came in a rigid, ceremonial formation, moving together, perfectly synchronized, as if choreographed. Ezekiel was always one to put on a show. From where they stood, the outer perimeter was an undefined blur that darkened with each line of soldiers as they fell into procession. They flowed into infinity, every beautiful face glaring Caleb's way, but they were too disciplined to show any more emotion than that. The faint brushing sound of wings was regular, hypnotic, a melody, a complex rhythm that never faltered. The pattern folded outward, appearing ominous. Their advancement was measured and thoughtful, with no urgency, no pressure, no concern. It was the stride of the invincible.

Caleb watched the lower ranking angels take their place on the frontline with the older, higher ranking seraphs spread out among the flanks. Ezekiel took his position precisely in the center of the frontline. Each movement of the group was closely controlled and thought out.

The opposing army showed no surprise or dismay at the collection of Caleb's legions that would stand against them, a presentation that rivaled their own. They revealed no astonishment at the legions that stood in their midst. Caleb possessed one-hundred-twenty-two legions. There were one-hundred-twenty of them on the battlefield this day. The other two legions were to watch over Azaiah if Caleb were sequestered, or in the less likely scenario that he be destroyed. This could happen only if the deity decided to show up himself and fight. The deity's presence was highly unlikely.

Angels were a stunning sight. Naturally, they were beautiful, strong, athletic, and cunning. This would make for a stellar battle, Caleb thought. He didn't like killing angels, but it was repetitively a necessary task because of his brother's wrath, so he had become accustomed to it.

"What a display of grandeur. Did you bring all of your legions, Ezekiel?" Caleb asked mockingly. "For such an insignificant battle against me? I'm flattered."

Then, as if their numbers were not enough, while Ezekiel slowly and majestically advanced toward Caleb, more angels began entering the clearing behind them. Caleb and his generals watched everything as it unfolded, paying attention to every detail. He made mental notes as the procession on the battlefield continued. He watched Maliki, Ezekiel's lieutenant, take his position. Caleb especially watched Ezekiel, every muscle contraction, every eye movement, right down to the position of his head, in anticipation of his next move.

"Are you planning to take me down personally, Ezekiel?" Caleb stood perfectly still as Ezekiel took his place of defiance in front of him.

"We both know that's not possible, Caleb," he mocked. "I hear that's the name you are using these days." Caleb shrugged and nodded with a grin.

"Yes, we do know that is not possible. You also know that I can take out half of your legions single handedly before this battle even gets started. So why are you here? Why give so many of our beloved eternal death for the cost of one human soul?" Caleb questioned with absolute seriousness.

"I could ask you the same Caleb, "Ezekiel answered simply. "So, it is written. So, it will be." He smiled broadly with confidence exuding from every particle of his being.

Caleb laughed and scanned the seemingly endless influx of faces. Did they really think the intimidation would work on his legions; Caleb wondered as more unexpected forces moved in? As for Caleb, he expected nothing less than this show of power. They were secure in their overwhelming numbers. Caleb was secure in his legions being unstoppable warriors who were battle ready.

Caleb stood in front of this angry mob as they salivated for righteousness. He had never fully realized the tenacity that the archangels felt for playing out the doctrine's prophecy. It was always a big laughable joke to him. Caleb need not question their intentions toward his half-immortal child who would one day rule them all. It was clear that this mob would pounce on the child if Caleb were ever sequestered.

The deity would then spread the word that the evil brother was eradicated, the king of man of course having acted with nothing less than justice and impartiality. That would never happen. Caleb had too much to lose. This was nothing more than a game to the god of humans.

Most of the angels had the stern look of battle about them. As if they hoped for more than just an opportunity to observe, they wanted to help destroy the destroyer. They didn't have a prayer. Even if they could somehow neutralize Caleb, his legions were strong, old, and well trained by epochs of constant battle.

The two commanding angels advanced from each of their opposing forces. Caleb immediately recognized Chloe in the distance as she struggled in between her two abductors, her expression clearly that of fear and shock. Chloe scanned the faces of all the soldiers that stood across from her until her horrified gaze eventually locked onto Caleb. She promptly realized that he was there to rescue her. She then relaxed and smiled with relief. Anger rose in the pit of Caleb's stomach. For the first time on a battlefield, he felt fear. He felt the potential for loss, for death.

Sebastian snarled a very low but fervent sound. Kira grabbed Caleb's arm and held it tightly. "Have mercy, Brother, for they know not what they do," she whispered.

"They will soon. I can promise you that," Caleb answered back furiously.

Chloe was a diversion, meant to throw them off. He knew the game. Ezekiel walked just a few paces more. Cocking his head to one side, he looked at Caleb intensely with profound curiosity at the apparent reaction he saw when Chloe was brought forth.

"HA! It's true!" Ezekiel screeched enthusiastically, as if he had discovered the secret to Caleb's defeat. He was showing more excitement than a commanding general, leading his legions onto the battlefield, should have.

"We have found your weakness, Caleb. The chink in your amour." He laughed a bizarre high-pitched laugh that echoed throughout the battlefield.

Caleb continued to fight off the anger that rose inside of him. He would not show weakness again, as it would be exploited at all cost. He knew that all too well. He gathered his composure.

"I see you have done the right thing and brought Chloe back to us. We both know that her soul belongs to me," He stated calmly.

He could feel the doubt traveling through the legions. It infuriated him. The uncertainty and hesitation crept about him like a malicious rumor. Caleb's legions doubted him because of Chloe. Despair hung heavy in the air, pushing him down with more pressure than he had ever felt before this moment. He would deal with his legions later. After this battle, they would never doubt him again, ever, despite the human girl.

"I see where you could be confused about that. The wretched sinful human souls are yours, but the deity has accepted her as one of his children. She has been forgiven. She was not wicked, or evil, only a non-believer who fell prey to your games," Ezekiel stated accusingly. "Therefore, she is his."

"Fair argument, Ezekiel," Caleb calculated with the utmost composure. "However, she is the mother of the devil's own spawn." Then he added in a thunderous voice. *"SHE IS MINE!"* Caleb quickly regained his self-control. "Let's handle this peacefully, Ezekiel. We have no animosity towards each other. In another time, long ago, we stood as brothers. Fought side by side on the battlefield. You pledged your fealty to me as your general."

"True. Yet, that was long ago." Ezekiel nodded in thought, as if retrieving those memories. "And, those words seem out of place considering the ensemble you've pulled together and brought here to stand against me." Ezekiel turned with his arm extended, motioning toward the legions that stood behind Caleb.

Caleb shook his head and stretched his right hand forward in a gesture of peace, there were still almost fifty yards between them. "You know that was never my intent. I am weary of battle."

"I know nothing of the sort," Ezekiel challenged. "Did you not give eternal death to one of my angels?"

Chloe stared at Caleb blankly, her face like that of someone who had not yet fully roused from a terrible nightmare. Irritated, Ezekiel snapped his fingers. One of the captors moved to Chloe's side and shoved her roughly, propelling her forward. She blinked and then walked slowly toward Ezekiel in a stupor. Chloe was forced to stop several yards short, her eyes still wide, but focused on Caleb. Ezekiel closed the distance between himself and Caleb by half. He was now within striking range. There was something terribly humiliating about the way Chloe was being held by her captors. Probably more for Caleb than for her. It was like standing by while someone abused a small defenseless animal. Chloe noticed that Caleb was watching her. She adjusted her posture, straight and rigid, her eyes focused on him in defiance of her captures.

"So many pointless rules, so many unnecessary decrees you hold yourselves to, Ezekiel. How is it possible for you to defend those laws when they are ever changing?" Caleb paused not wanting to directly challenge Ezekiel any further. "They are *your* laws; they do not govern me. The deity can have his kingdom of men. I just want one soul...*her soul.*" He pointed in Chloe's direction.

"Do not treat us as fools." Ezekiel's voice rumbled through the masses. "If I were to give you this soul, nothing would change. You would still position your demon child in an attempt to overthrow the only real king."

"Ezekiel. Brother. I've been here for thousands of years. You know me, I'm not an instigator. Your deity is the adversary. I admire the humans. I do not wish to rule them. I live among them, as an equal, does that seem like someone who wants to rule all the realms? We can all live in peace," Caleb disputed.

"Yes. We can all live in peace, if you will present me with your son. The half mortal, half immortal child that is prophesized to cause the Last War." Ezekiel requested Azaiah to be handed over as if he were asking Caleb to borrow a quarter. He continued to speak, turning toward the two angels holding Chloe in place. "Conceived and carried by this soul while she was still in human form. I am suggesting a deal. A contract that will ensure peace among our kind, and among humankind. Your son in trade for this human soul." He pointed at Chloe.

Caleb could not stomach looking at Chloe as he negotiated her life, for the life of their child. Ezekiel was a monster under the guise of an archangel. Caleb did look at her. She was adamantly shaking her head and mouthing the word "no." He didn't need her confirmation, but he wanted it. Beneath the charades, the opposing needs tore at him. Heaviness pushed down on him, crushing him so firmly it felt like his bones might shatter from the pressure of it. Chloe or Azaiah.

"Yea, that's not going to happen Ezekiel," Caleb answered with disappointment.

"The deity would never harm a child...*your child*. He is your brother." Ezekiel tried to convince Caleb, placing an emphasis on brother.

"Yes, Ezekiel, how did things work out for his son?" Caleb asked, his voice dripping with contention.

"That was you're doing!" Ezekiel shouted back.

"My doing? Is that the story he tells?" Caleb asked pointedly. "I tried to save the boy. I told him what would happen. I offered him a place with me, offered my protection. He trusted my brother and look what happened to him! That will not be the fate of my son!" He shouted, causing reverberations through the crowds. "He sacrificed his son...and for what? For a ridiculous story in a book that doesn't even make sense. I mean sin is rampant here—war, greed. What exactly did Jesus' death accomplish?" Caleb calmed himself and continued to speak in a level, composed tone. "What did it accomplish?" No, his son would not be handed over to that monster. He looked at Chloe, even though he told himself he would not. She was beautiful, and he wanted her badly, but not at a price that neither of them was willing nor able to pay.

Ezekiel raised his right hand high into the air and Caleb watched as Chloe was escorted to the midpoint between the legions and Ezekiel. He kept her slightly closer to him than she was to the mob behind her. Ezekiel's smug smile peaked Caleb's rage. He wanted Caleb to break, he wanted him to make the first move. Then the beginning of the end could be placed on Caleb's hands. Games, always games. It had to be exhausting, the incessant scheming.

"So, what is your next move, Ezekiel?" Caleb was tiring of the mockery and wanted to get Chloe out of their clutches. He needed to move things along. "We've got masses at our disposal. We fight, or we shake hands and go home to live another day." Caleb was furious but trying to maintain a tranquil facade. "This war doesn't have to happen now...this war doesn't have to happen ever. *I DON'T WANT THE HUMANS!* My son can live a full life of glory. I have many realms at his disposal. He can still be a great ruler." Caleb paused, beseeching reason with Ezekiel. "Do not force my hand, Ezekiel. Do not do it! Do not do this, Brother!" Caleb yelled as the signal was given. "This is your last chance to make the right choice," Caleb spoke in a whispered threat as he leaned closer, speaking more to Maliki than to Ezekiel, noting how unrelenting Ezekiel had been. Maliki's face was desperate as he looked to Ezekiel for answers. Caleb realized at that moment they had not come here to battle, they came here to present a ransom, thinking Caleb would hand over his child. *Fools!* "He is the liar Maliki," Caleb roared. "We are brothers. I have fought by your side. You know what I am capable of," he said as he positioned himself for battle.

Caleb made another attempt to thwart this fight. He knew the signal for execution. He did not wish for this battle, but he would not stand by and allow them to take Chloe out of existence in front of him without a fight.

Caleb moved again, a few inches toward Ezekiel, a few inches away from Kira. She was watching closely. Sebastian's gaze zeroed in on the gap between the commanding angels. Ezekiel was unaware of the slight tactical movements that were going on. Caleb's army's trained eyes would not have missed them.

It would take the angels less than a second to kill Chloe, they only needed the tiniest margin of opportunity. Even more slowly this time, Caleb repositioned his shield.

Ezekiel again held up a hand to his legions and gave the sign of advancement. Therefore, it began.

As they clung to Chloe and she struggled, Caleb's anger exploded, greater even than the raging hatred he had felt the moment the negotiations began. He could taste the fury on his tongue, felt it flow through him like a tsunami of unadulterated power. His muscles constricted, and he reacted out of habit and battlefield experience.

This was all occurring within milliseconds. Caleb slid his feet forward and to the side. He was ready. Ezekiel circled too far around when giving the execution signal, overcompensating. He leaned forward onto the balls of his feet and thrust.

Caleb threw his shield with all the force in his body. Flinging it across the impossible span of the field, it flew like a discus. The breath rushed out of him with the exertion. The shield released from his grasp with the power of sheer energy, a streak of liquid steel. He could feel it from the apex of his soul. It sliced through Ezekiel's neck like a hot knife through soft butter. His head rolled across the ground and lay at Maliki's feet. Before the legions could react, Caleb was at Chloe's side, his sword impaling both of her captors before they even understood what had happened. Then he was able to breathe again. Chloe was in his arms.

Simultaneous to Caleb's actions, Kira and Sebastian followed his lead, calling the legions into battle. *"It's starting!"*

In an instant of raw force, he saw the backlash of what he had done. Caleb had started the war. Before his legions could get to the frontline, Caleb held up a hand and threw a field of fire toward the opposing frontline troops. They all felt instant eternal death. Caleb pulled back and remembered that he had Chloe, there was no reason to battle to the death. He concentrated and set his forcefield free, stopping all troops in their tracks. The forcefield burst out of Caleb, covering at least five hundred yards in front of him. This was done effortlessly, taking only slight concentration on his part. It flexed like any other muscle, obedient to his will. He pushed it along, shaping it to cover over half the legions—the front half, the only half that mattered at this point. He thrust the force field further, covering the length of the clearing, then he exhaled in relief. Caleb's eyes were riveted on Maliki, who was now in command.

"Maliki!" Caleb called out as he held the opposing army at bay. "What is your decision?"

Caleb watched the muscles in Maliki's back tighten. Caleb had a captive audience for a few more seconds. He was going to use the time to try and prevent any further bloodshed.

"Did that battle play out as it was written?" Caleb yelled, spitting on the ashes left where Ezekiel once stood. "Do you all still believe that travesty of a doctrine?" He had let go of Chloe to make his stand against Maliki, but she remained close by his side. This will lead you to death and despair, and for what? For the glory of a madman who sends us all to our doom for his entertainment?" He looked squarely at Maliki. "I will wipe you out of existence if you choose to go forward with this fight. In the blink of an eye I brought eternal death to the multitudes. There is no glory in this battle. Your deaths will be pointless. The deity will lose masses that he will not be able to rebuild, giving me the opportunity to rise and conquer during his moment of weakness." Caleb was speaking loud and forcefully. "Think, brothers!" He pointed to his head with the hand that grasped the sword. The other he wrapped around Chloe's waist pulling her close to him. "*Think!* As this is not a wise decision. This will be the beginning of the fall of the king of kings." Caleb tried to reason with Maliki.

Maliki was an experienced soldier, but he was not an original, and he was out of his league without Ezekiel. Maliki knew that, and Caleb was exploiting it.

"You don't have to die today," Caleb said calmly. "Vengeance won't benefit anyone if carried out in haste without forethought, Maliki. Think about what you're doing. If you attack, you will all die. The demise of thousands of souls will be on your conscience. But you have a choice. You can walk away right now."

Maliki's shoulders hunched with defeat as he lifted his arm and gave the signal for retreat. Caleb took a deep breath of relief. They had seen Caleb's power. They knew there was absolutely no hope for them if they continued what Ezekiel had started.

Maliki gave the legions their instructions to retreat. There was no fear in his voice, only resolve and acceptance. If the deity's troops were lost here, it was true, Caleb could have risen against the deity, and likely won. Maliki's decision was the right one.

Sebastian snarled out a dark laugh. "It would have been a regrettable waste to our kind to have lost any more of you. Brother go back with your head held high. Know that we would be glad to welcome any of you into our ranks. You don't have to die for his lies."

Maliki stared at him sullenly.

The opposing troops had retreated. The battlefield was quiet. Kira and Sebastian released Caleb's legions.

Then Caleb remembered Chloe. He dropped his sword and wrapped her up in his arms.

Chapter Twenty-Five

Blink of an Eye

Caleb held Chloe tight. He felt if he let her go, she would again be gone forever. His heart pounded against her chest.

"Take me to see our son," she said suddenly.

"Chloe, we have some time together, but not much," Caleb replied.

"What do you mean?" she asked, sounding startled.

"We cannot remain here. This is a temporary realm created for battles. A neutral zone of sorts." He struggled to explain in terms she would understand.

"Can't I go back with you?" she pleaded, tears welling up in her eyes.

Caleb shook his head, his heart breaking. "No, babe, you are a celestial being now. Your human body died." Chloe held up her hand, looking at it intensely.

"In this realm we are a reflection of how we believe things to be. Have you ever heard consciousness creates reality? Perception is fundamental, and matter is derived from consciousness so everything that we regard as existing, postulates consciousness." His point was that in this realm the souls, as individuals or on a collective level, shaped and created whatever reality they preferred for themselves. The entire realm was a manifestation based on what the beings that entered it believed it to be. It did exist in a physical way, but that was at a level of understanding that no human could grasp.

Chloe nodded. "So, get me a body Caleb!" she demanded wearily. "I need you. I need to see our son!"

"Chloe, if I could do that, I would, but only angels can take possession of a human body." He was hurting, arguably more than she was, but he was trying to keep up pretenses so not to frighten her.

"But aren't you... I mean, you are a god!" she said, grasping. "Look at what you did here!"

"There are limitations to all of our powers. I am much more powerful when I am in my own realm. I am weakest in the human realm, we all are. I could give up my human body and return with you, but Azaiah would be on his own, and we cannot do that to him. He is too important, and too many people want him eliminated." He winced at his own words.

"You called him Azaiah." She looked up at him and smiled, "I like that. He is a beautiful child. I know you have raised him well." She paused and whispered, "No, of course you cannot leave him." She sounded resigned. "So, what happens to me now?"

She had been through an ordeal already, and he knew she was fearful of her fate. Caleb wanted to comfort her. Needed to comfort her. "You take your place as queen of my realm and wait for my time here to be complete." He pushed a stray curl off her forehead. "You will find that time for you will pass much faster than it did for you as a human. A hundred years will be gone in the blink of an eye." He offered a comforting smile.

"So, you can come see me?" She was nearly begging.

"Chloe, I cannot. I cannot cross realms like that. If I left this body, it would immediately begin to desecrate. If I were to leave it for any amount of time, it would degrade, and it would no longer be habitable."

"So, get a new body!" she offered.

"Again, it's not that easy. Witches play a part in that. And even if I could get a witch coven in league with me, there are a lot of variables at play." Caleb paused, wanting to explain but not to overwhelm her. "Each pass through a realm takes a toll on us, weakening us. I would slowly but eventually recover, but it could take years, decades. Angels know when you pass through a realm. They will know when Azaiah lacks my protection. He needs me strong." Caleb kissed her softly on the forehead. "I know this is a lot to take in, and, Chloe, our time together here is limited. I can promise you this. You will be cared for and treated as I would be treated. You will be a monarch until my return, at which time we will rule together. You are very important now. To every angel and human, you will be known as queen." He cupped her face with his hands and kissed her soft, full lips. "Chloe, I have missed you terribly. I was a lost, ruined, soul in your absence. You have affected me like no other."

"I love you." She smiled.

"Yes, I know that too. But when I left you, I left you unprotected, vulnerable. And then you were attacked, and I lost you." Caleb shook his head, shamefully looking at the ground. "I just need you to know that I am sorry for that. It was a serious lapse in judgment."

"You were doing what you thought was best. You were protecting me, protecting Azaiah." She shrugged it off.

"I knew I would gain your forgiveness, but that doesn't let me escape the consequences. *You died, Chloe!* Azaiah needed you, and I let you die." Caleb could feel tears burning behind his eyes.

"I should have known you'd find some way to blame yourself. Please stop. I can't stand it," Chloe demanded, her arms pulling him close. "Just say, 'I'm sorry. I shouldn't have left you because I love you more than my existence' and be done with it already." She looked up at him with a soft melancholy grin.

"At least let me suffer a little. I deserve it," Caleb demanded.

"No." She shook her head, looking at him with so much love.

Caleb nodded slowly. "You're right. Keep being understanding, that's probably worse."

"I love you so much," she said, changing the subject suddenly. "How much time do we have?"

"Not enough," he answered. "Until the new day comes."

Caleb kissed her deeply, relishing in her warmth. His heart pounded loudly against his ribs, and his breath seemed to get stuck in his throat. He felt Chloe's eyes on his face, but he refused to meet her gaze.

The sun had gone down and the moon was bright. Just a few yards away there was a large body of water with glistening ripples. Chloe's fingers caressed the back of his neck, wiping away several drops of sweat. Were two souls ever meant to be together more than Chloe's and Caleb's? He knew the answer to that. No, there were not.

"It's beautiful," she said, looking at the moonlight moving across the water.

"I didn't even notice." Caleb flashed a smile.

"No?" She sounded surprised.

"Chloe, it pales in comparison to the beauty standing before me," he whispered genuinely.

She shot him a look of annoyance and took him into her arms. Her lips brushed against his throat, sending chills down his spine. She moved her lips down his neck to his shoulders. Caleb scooped her up into his arms and he headed for the water. She was unfastening his shirt with lightning speed, and once undone he shrugged it off, dropping it on the ground. Caleb stood her up in front of him at the water's edge, slipping her shirt off over her head. The muggy, humid air was all around them.

They fell onto the soft grass, a tangled ball of arms and legs. Caleb reminded himself to breathe. How did she do that? Have this effect on him. Finally, they lay naked in each other's arms. Warm sweat soaking their bodies, sliding against each other as they kissed, long and deep.

Caleb wanted her, desired her badly. As if she read his mind, she released him and said, "I need you, Caleb."

Stopping for a brief moment to take in the sight of her. She lay naked in the dark, perfect skin desaturated of all color by the moonlight. She was a goddess. Deserving of a god. Deserving of more than Caleb was, or could ever be.

A rush of heat flashed across his skin as she moved her hips towards him in anticipation. He was basking in the pleasure. He could barely wait, yet he wanted to surround himself in her beauty, her perfectness for just another moment before it was over. But desire won out. She shuddered. He felt every spasm, every tiny movement she made. He was torn between needing her and wanting to extend and lavish in their moments together.

"Don't be afraid," he whispered. "We belong together. Here or there, we will be together. My love for you transcends time and space." Caleb was abruptly overcome by the reality of the words he said. This moment was so perfect, so right. There was no way to doubt he was correct.

Her arms wrapped tightly around him, holding him against her, it felt like every nerve in his body was on fire.

"Forever," she agreed. "Oh, Caleb," Chloe moaned loudly, taking away any reasoning skills he had left, forcing him to give in to animalistic instincts and desires. He took her. He took every ounce of her—her body, her heart, her soul, her love. She was his eternally, and he was hers.

This would be goodbye, but not forever. Eternity was a very long time, and they still had a great story ahead of them. However, they would have to wait. Wait a decade, a century, a millennium, or the blink of an eye.

END PART ONE

The Book of Azaiah

Prologue (Azaiah POV)

I can remember the day I was born. I know it sounds bizarre, but it's true. I can remember that day, and every day since.

Birth

A pair of gloved hands slid me from the safety of my dying mother's womb. I came into the world just as I would likely leave it, surrounded by death and destruction. I was not more than a few minutes old and my mother was already dead. Her forehead slick with sweat, her skin cool with the pastiness of refrigerated butter. I was still connected to my mother by a terrible appendage. A grossly twisted, shiny, blue cord. The pulsating life force that once flowed through it had ceased.

I could no longer breathe. The beat of my heart resounded in my head, very fast but it was beginning to decelerate. The electrical impulses originating from the sinoatrial node triggered my heart to contract. These impulses were occurring at intervals further and further apart, until the node finally failed completely, causing my heart to beat erratically. As the normal pathway was disrupted the backup atrioventricular node took over which led to ventricular tachycardia, until it too failed and asystole commenced. The lack of a heartbeat caused the blood in my veins to become sluggish and ultimately stop flowing altogether.

As everything ceased, I could feel a sudden renewed flow of the stagnant blood with each involuntary beat of my pulse coming in heavy waves, as if compelled by an outside force. I was growing colder. The coldness stung my eyes and pierced my skin, but I knew my priority was oxygen. I vividly remember what my mother looked like lying in the distance, battered and bloody, the medical team working frantically trying to save her life. I was no longer connected to her and that gave me a sense of isolation.

My mouth was open, my throat completely contracted. My body limp, my mind was going blank, I gave up on all effort. I just let go, like a balloon snapping free from the string that tethered it. My flaccid body feeling as if it was floating. My lungs had given out. There was no pain, just comfort, even though I was suffocating. Darkness was closing in and I too was no longer of this world.

I was sinking into a dark, deep pool of icy black water, plummeting slowly beneath the surface into the world of unknown. The sounds and voices in the room drifted farther and farther away. Just before everything went black, my sense of hearing seemed to intensify. I heard echoes of prayers from heaven and echoes of screams from hell.

The blood in my body was stagnant, too viscous to flow, my lungs full of blood and fluid instead of air. My pain had been replaced with peace. There was no excitement, no struggle, and no tangible awareness as I faded. Everything became insubstantial, like it was there but it was not. Something wasn't right, but whatever it was, was no longer important.

Quick blows continued to be delivered to my chest, forceful, each compression causing a swooshing in my ears. I knew they were continuing the resuscitation efforts because I saw it happening before the darkness moved in. It was like watching it happening to someone else, yet, somehow, I knew it was me.

For some seemingly inexplicable reason I unexpectedly had a huge burst of energy and the will to get out of this predicament re-emerged. I could feel myself rising, moving toward the surface, faster and with more force. I had the sense of suffocating, drowning in a body of water, but I was rising to the surface, I could see the darkness fading as light moved in, I was almost there. Maybe I could make it. Perhaps I would make it. I broke through, gulping in the cold air. I had made it. I began to understand what was happening. This sudden surge of liveliness occurred just after something slid down my throat. There was a hiss of suction, my airway was cleared, and finally I took a breath. My oxygen-deprived mind was playing out a scenario in which I was coming around of my own accord, gasping for air as I successfully emerged from a body of water.

After taking in the much-needed lungful of air, a bout of coughing ensued. The drumming of my heart grew louder, stronger. Blood flowed smoothly in my veins as precious oxygen flooded my lungs. My chest expanded, and everything slowly came back. Bright lights besieged me. Unexpectedly, I lived.

The weeks after that were a bit of a blur. A lot of white noise and medical sounds. Considering babies possess a limited pool of experiences along with their brains' immaturity, I now know that the fantasy worlds I visited and dreams I had during this time were exactly that, but at the time they seemed so real that the actual and imaginary worlds simply blended together.

Nothing appears more peaceful from the outside looking in than a sleeping baby. But behind my serene little expression fantastic dramas were unfolding, like theater performances behind closed stage curtains. Newborns spend half their sleep time in eyeball jerking, body twitching, rapid eye movement or REM sleep. Dreaming for the equivalent of a full eight-hour workday. That's a lot of mileage to get out of the few images I had collected as a newborn.

The images I had were not the typical crib mobile, stuffed animals and parents cooing faces. No, the images I had were the stuff nightmares were made of. Constant beeping, mechanical noises, different masked faces showing up to poke, stick, and painfully prod my tiny body. The visions from my birth were burned into my memory. I was unquestionably aware of things going on around me, but in the absence of knowledge as to my whereabouts, situation, and circumstances, I was unable to rationalize or relate them with any reference points to the real world. This is why I made stuff up in a parallel fantasy world. I didn't know the rules, so I made the rules up as well, no matter how foolish or ridiculous the outcomes were. I had no context to compare. I had no real-world experiences.

Dreaming is a cognitive process that supposedly arises in early childhood, once children have acquired the capacity to imagine things visually and spatially. I can attest that this is not the case. My dreams were typically static and plain. My lack of self-knowledge strongly correlated with the vibrancy and amount of plot structure in my dreams, so my dream characters lacked significant movement or action. They were more like individual 3D film clips, repetitive flashes of the short life of horrors I had endured. On good days the sound effects were the beeps, whooshes, muffled chatter and alarms of the intensive care unit. On bad days the theme music consisted of the screaming tortured souls in hell, or even worse, the haunting melancholy never-ending chanting of prayers from heaven. These dreams evoked deep emotions and memories. They lacked structured narratives, because as a baby I lacked a clear understanding of language.

Babies naturally lack self-awareness which is necessary for the insertion of the self into dreams. I however did not lack self-awareness, so I was present, a part of these dreams. However, I had never actually seen myself, so the dreams occurred through my eyes. I was a bystander watching a horrific accident unfold, helpless to change the outcome.

Luckily during a large part of every neonate's day, the brain is occupied with a completely different function, building neuropathways, becoming integrated with the rest of the body, and grasping an understanding of language. While all that grunt work was going on, my brain lacked the capacity to dream and I was given peaceful reprieve.

My first weeks on earth were comparable to Dante's journey, a perplexing expedition through the nine circles of Hell, Purgatory and Heaven.

I truly believe that birth was my last chance to die as a good person.

Chapter One

Current Era I

"I wish you'd quit reading those kinds of books," Kira said pointing to my advanced historical theology textbook. "They're bad for your mind."

"It's necessary for my theology class, Kira, a requirement for graduation." I laughed. She "hmphed" back at me with a breath of annoyance.

Seattle had always been my home, so I was thrilled when I received the letter of acceptance to The University of Washington. It was extremely competitive. I fully expected to be accepted but was still thrilled. My father, Caleb, wasn't home so I handed the letter to Kira, smiling smugly. She was like a second mom to me. I had several 'mom' types over the years, but my father couldn't keep his head straight when it came to relationships, so the women never hung around for long.

Watching these women spend time, energy and emotion on a man who would never be a part of their future gave me a firm understanding of the female psyche. All too often these women would tell themselves, Well, he wouldn't commit in the past, but I'm different. I have more patience than the other women he dated, and I am more understanding than most women. I can help him. That's what they all thought.

I would watch from first date until relationship after relationship painfully began to unravel. At this point delusion usually took over. They became increasingly intimate, and the female would tell herself, I know he really likes me. I give him unlimited space, wonderful sex, and we laugh a lot. This will work. What was really happening was the women were invested in the relationship and Caleb was just there for the sex.

That was even an understatement. Caleb had officially flown that extra bat-shit mile since my mother, Chloe, had died. No woman would ever match up to her. Eventually my father's girlfriend's self-esteem would take a hit. They would continue to invest themselves in Mr. Non-Commitment, and he would never return the affection they needed. In little ways they began to feel unworthy. They trudged forward, openly willing to risk the heartbreak from a man who could not commit. He never mistreated them, but he never gave himself to them either. It always ended in a one-sided tear fest. When the day came for them to admit that the relationship was a wishful-thinking-fantasy, somehow Caleb had the magical touch of making the women feel grateful for the time they shared with him. He always got out before it came to the point of anger and hatred.

He was a great father and protector, but husband material he was not. Caleb, being who he was, the theoretical king of deception and all, one would think he would be a bit better at inciting these women, but that wasn't the case. He was, and always would be captivated by his lost love. Everything changed for him when he met her. The thing that Chloe had loved most was his humanity. The funny thing was humanity was something that Caleb completely lacked before he met my mother. Azaiah knew their love was epic. The kind of love that only comes around once in a lifetime.

Fate had brought them together. Whether it was serendipitous, destiny, or just crazy coincidence, there are people that just seem destined to touch each other's lives, people meant to meet, and there are those magical moments where the universe seems to do everything it can to make that happen. Whether it was for love, friendship, or just a much-needed conversation with a nameless stranger, chance encounters happened every day.

I recalled several stories my father had shared over the years. "We hit it off straight away and spent hours just chatting. I can't recall precisely what we talked about, but I left very impressed by the fact she didn't watch television and was 'mostly' a vegetarian. She was very beautiful, and her warm nature just shone through. I was nervous to approach her at first. I walked slowly behind her for the entire morning, hoping I would become better looking really quickly. Practicing my powers of charm and wit until I finally decided I wasn't going to get any prettier or funnier and finally just went up to her. If there was ever such a thing as love at first sight, this had to be it."

Caleb admitted to a bit of manipulation in getting Chloe to Maine and making sure she got the house she did. The rest was fate. Caleb insisted that one day I would bring them back together and all things would be as they always should have. That's what he wholeheartedly believed.

The other moms were only needed for my protection. The more humans that cared for me the less often the supernatural's had to be around. That kept me off the archangel's radar. I had a human nanny until I was sixteen. Yes, sixteen! She was about a hundred years old at the time she retired from being my nanny. It was around that time that my dad also gave up on trying to keep a wife around. I was even happier about that than getting rid of the nanny.

No other woman would ever have made Caleb happy. When he was especially melancholy, he would sit on the back patio and reminisce with me.

"When I think of Chloe, what I miss the most about her is the way she used to lie her head on my chest at night. Sometimes I couldn't move, I even held my breath, but I know she felt safe... complete. Every time we would go out, she would worry about me catching a cold. I've never been sick in my existence. I don't even think it is possible." Caleb chuckled. "*Well it's cold today, wear a scarf,*" she would demand. A shadow drew over Caleb's face. "But lately I've been forgetting little things. She is fading and I'm starting to forget her, and it's like losing her all over again. Sometimes I walk through every detail of her face, focus on the exact color of her eyes, lips, teeth, the texture of her skin and hair. Sometimes, not always, but sometimes, I can actually see her. It is as if a cloud moves away and there she is. I could almost touch her, but then the real-world rushes in and she vanishes again." He paused for a moment but then continued. "For a while I did this every morning, but it was too painful for her to appear and disappear like a sunrise or sunset. Everything about her was always so ephemeral. Just like every other human life, they appear and they disappear, so important to some, but no matter how important, they are just passing through."

"Cheers to passing through." I smiled at my father.

I had a mom. A real mom. She was not of my world, but she was ever present in my life. I also had a gift that allowed me to see into other realms and communicate with souls, angels, or whatever existed in those realms—this included my mother. I entered these realms through portals, inter-dimensional openings, that transported entities from one realm to another. Reality is nothing more than an electromagnetic network which contains many other realities. When one moves through portals, either with the body or the mind, one moves from realm to realm. These portals link to ever present energies of time and space. These corkscrew energies allow our consciousness to move from one grid reality to another.

As I learned about my powers, I found that gateways exist everywhere that open and close from one dimension to another. In space, these portals have been identified as wormholes. Portals contain universal networks where information and entities flow seamlessly back and forth. For thousands of years humans have believed in these dimensions, in the forms of Heaven and Hell. To believe in Heaven and Hell humankind surely has to believe that there is movement between these realms.

To me these portals are places of initiation. They awaken the information I could never access in my physical body. My gift was that I could existed interdimensionally. Other realms are similar to a dream state. If you want to know what the afterlife is like, pay close attention to your dreams. There is a connection. The dream realm and the afterlife realms are both realms of the mind, soul, and spirit. In the realms of the mind, all thoughts and things are possible. Death is merely a process of freeing your true essence from all physical limitations of having a body. It's a realm of thought and spirit. In the afterlife realms, what one thinks is what matters most, because thoughts are deeds in those realms.

There is no hiding from who we really are. The human belief that the soul only exists as a speck in a seemingly endless universe is only an illusion. After death, the soul expands and transcends the physical universe. After death, the soul travels through the various dimensions of the realms. All of us are aware of the conscious mind and, to a lesser extent, the subconscious mind in sleep and dreams. When the soul enters the spirit realms it is as pure super consciousness, the human's highest spiritual potential.

To travel to the highest realm, completely outside of our universe, put me into a seizure-type state. My body temperature soared. For hours afterward I would be in a postictal state—febrile, dehydrated, weak, exhausted. The human body is fragile, and it was not meant to endure frequent travel through the other realms. Crossing over wasn't an easy act, but when I needed to, it was within my power to do so.

It was as a toddler that I began seeing these other realms. I also began communicating with my mother. The universe is indescribably vast and magnificent. There's so much that humans still don't know about. Our five physical senses perceive much less than 1% of the physical world, so we must realize there is much that we cannot perceive or even imagine. Just as we perceive with our sight, hearing, taste, touch, and smell, so the spirit world can be perceived by a set of spiritual senses—which are not limited by the physical laws of nature. Because most of us are not attuned to our spiritual senses, we become aware of the spirit world only when we pass into it at the end of our physical lives.

It is correct to say that we are fundamentally spiritual beings who possess physical bodies. When we die, we take off our physical bodies as one might take off a coat. The essential person remains.

One day I was extremely upset. I remember crying, and then my mother was there, comforting me. She was patient and kind and loved me and my father so much I could feel it to my very soul. What I quickly realized was that she had not come to me, I had gone to her. My physical body remained in the human realm while my soul traveled through the portal. As I traveled, I was in a structure nearly identical to my physical body, but lighter, subtler, and more vibrant. The other realms seemed wispy and ethereal to me, but not to their residents, like my mother. Their world seems as solid and real to them as ours seems to us.

My mother had been released from her humanly body when I was born, but she was not prepared to progress. She was hurting but she tried to hide it from me. She missed my father. She suffered daily because she was not there to raise me. She felt like she had let me down. Her sorrow was so deep rooted there was no way for her to hide it, no matter how hard she tried. My mother's love provided me a piece of mortality that nothing else could have. She was my moral compass. She was my humanity. She was pain, love, and heartbreak coiled up so tightly into a ball they could never be separated. I loved her with every ounce of my being, and she loved me even more. The rare times I saw her it was a gift, and I always learned so much from her love. I badly needed her morality, because crossing realms was not my only gift.

My powers were apparent from the time that I was just a few months old. I could hear most human thoughts, but not every human, and none of the angels. At first it was difficult to tune out the babble of voices that gushed like steam from a volcano inside of my head. When it came to the human mind, I'd heard it all and then some. There was no protecting me from it. Luckily, before I learned to control it, I wasn't around humans very often. My nanny was elderly, and her thoughts were very tame.

As I got older, I could block out almost anyone—and I did, out of courtesy and revulsion. I tried not to listen if I could help it. Try as I may, still...I knew things about people that I didn't want to know. And I felt guilty reading others' minds because I knew there were things there that they wouldn't want me to know. If anyone thought about me, it was almost the same as having my name called aloud. I was glad that my given name was unique. It would have been annoying to be named John—anytime anyone thought of any John my head would turn automatically.

I acted as a lookout, for lack of a better word, for my family. To protect us. If anyone ever grew suspicious, I could give us early warning. That never happened.

I could also move things without touching them. One evening when I was three, I was extremely irritated with one of the angels who was enforcing my bedtime. The anger built up inside of me until there was a bright flash overhead, followed by a gun like pop as a lightbulb sizzled and went out. My nanny cried out with surprise, and it occurred to her that this kind of thing always seemed to happen around me when I was upset. The thought was gone almost as quickly as it had come, until the next time.

At times my mind seemed to stretch, a curious mental bending, almost like the flexing of a muscle. One summer afternoon when I was no more than five, I became so angry it knotted up in my stomach and my throat grew tight. Things started to crash, shake, and break around me. Bottles, glasses, I don't know what all. And then the side window broke open and the kitchen table flew halfway through. It was a big mahogany thing; it took the screen with it. It must have weighed three hundred pounds.

'*How could a child throw that?*' The nanny immediately wondered how she was going to explain this to Mr. Frasier. She stopped and turned from the window to look at me, her face haggard from trying to recall all that had happened. One hand played nervously with her casually styled silver bob haircut. After telling the story my father asked her if she was implying something.

"I'm only telling you," she insisted, suddenly distraught. "I'm not asking you to believe-." Her head began to feel tired and fuzzy, throbbing with the beginning of a headache. Her eyes were hot, as if she had just sat down and read the Book of Revelations straight through. Powers like that just evolved. As a toddler my powers grew and expanded, they continue to increase and intensify to this day.

When I was younger, I was aware of my powers, and I knew what I was doing when I used them. However, at the time I didn't always understand the consequences. There were a few times when people got hurt, angels even died.

Light brown curls framed a cherubic face with round cheeks

and full lips. An adorable three-year-old with dimples and powers that could wipe out Seattle during a single temper tantrum. I didn't mean for it to happen, and I remember those times vividly, even though I was small.

I can remember standing around hills, but not hills of earth and rock, hills of bodies, battered and lifeless. Too late not to see the faces. I knew them all. Blank eyes staring, burning into my soul before bursting into flames.

Nobody wanted to believe I was capable of that, not even now. We never spoke of it. All my family, my protectors, denied it, as if that could make it go away. But then there's this, *it really happened*. There were lots of angels who saw it happen, and it was just as real as the nose on their face, but denial was a real mental power. No one could laugh this off. Too many people were dead. My protectors were frightened of me. I felt it.

I quickly learned to control my powers afterward, but still those times, the things I did, the people I hurt, are the driving forces behind my nightmares to this day.

My father, Kira, and the other angels started my battle training very young. I needed self-control first and foremost. Tolerance was next, along with tactical intelligence, and lastly, I needed to be a great warrior. Because of my powers and training in the art of battle I was unquestionably a tough sparring opponent. My schooling was also a high priority. I was educated privately in several countries. I spoke seven languages fluently, but I could understand human's thoughts in any language.

I achieved a perfect score on my SAT's. I had my pick of any college. My father was hoping I would reconsider and go with MIT, but I had been away from home enough and I wanted to study law at the University of Washington.

My life did come with a price though. Supposedly I was the prophesized Antichrist. My father was present as the Bible was penned. According to him, the book was a farce written by men who were either crazy or influenced by the deity to support his cause. These writings were passed down and embellished over the years. Then the Catholics got a hold of them and hand selected the parts that they thought pertinent to their cause, making the content even more confusing and diluted. Viola, you have the Bible.

The book eventually became a hotchpotch of examples of man's battle with his own perceived demons, projected as sin onto humankind. My family was not a fan of the Bible. Knowing how my father was misrepresented in the doctrine, I had no reason to place any faith into its accuracy either. My father had always been a friend to humanity, and he certainly wasn't looking for any war. Unfortunately, he did believe this holy war would eventually come to pass because of what his creator passed on to him. My father's maker was the original spirit, and he foretold that one of his two sons would sire the king of all kings with a human. The outcome of that is still yet to be determined, but so far, it's seemed to fit the description of me.

I wouldn't say I'd had a normal teenage life, but it's been okay. We found out around age fourteen that I had always been veiled from the deity and his angels, so I was off the radar on my own accord. The angels could be around me without disclosing my presence to the deity. I guess that's another one of my superpowers. Life got a lot less hectic after we figured that out.

My best friend, Taybor, had grown up with me. Her father, Sebastian, was one of my father's oldest friends and commander of his legions. Taybor was clever and a great warrior. We had studied together, fought together, and been friends for as long as I could remember. She had really helped me through some tough times. Especially figuring out my powers and just generally sorting out who I was in the whole scheme of things. It's a lot to be laid on a kid, to know that you may be the cause of the war of all wars, the fall of humankind as we know it.

I used to be plagued with nightmares. Every night for years I had them. Sometimes I was not sure exactly where a memory ended and a dream began. I had intense flashbacks. Everything was gray, barren, and the air was thick with the scent of fire. I seemed to be invisible to everyone around me. Invisible to everyone except him. He was always lurking, shrouded in an ashy cloak. I knew if I saw the person's face it would be the end. The end of what I didn't know, but the end regardless.

There was one very tough period in my life, night after night same nightmare, repeatedly played out like a horror movie. It wasn't even that particularly scary. No demons or angels or deity, but it scared the heck out of me each time. That was the worst month ever.

In the nightmare I was lost in a never-ending maze, a hazy fog stung my eyes, and the silence was deafening. I hurried through the tunnels, disoriented but always searching—searching for what I didn't know, but searching, nonetheless. No matter which direction I took, I always ended up in the same exact place, surrounded by annihilation. Then there was finally a point in my dream, like a buildup of pressure in my chest, panic maybe, where I would burst through the end of the last tunnel to find nothing, just more destruction leading to more fog and more tunnels. It was horrible. I would take the nightmares of war any day over that one.

My dad was caring and loving and a great father, but you just don't go to the god of fallen angels to complain about bad dreams. What would I say? "I'm having nightmares, Dad."

When I was younger I went to him about a bad dream and he told me, "Son, that's a human trait. Your mother had nightmares like that. You, child, are the entity that haunts other people's nightmares, you have nothing to fear." Then he sent me back to bed. That was it.

That's where Taybor stepped in. She was someone I could talk to. I didn't have to hide anything from her. There was no judgment. She was a good friend and we had a lot in common. We trained together in battle and had attended most of the same schools. We both had eclectic taste in music, and both played the guitar and piano. Most of my down time was spent with her.

Today we were headed back to Italy for our last year of high school. I would miss Seattle and the family, but we'd be back soon. This time for good.

Luckily, Taybor attended school with me so she would be on this flight as well. Flying with her always made these long trips a lot less tedious.

"Hey, Zi," Taybor said as she shoved her carry-on into an overhead bin. "Ass or crotch buddy?" she asked as she stood by me waiting to take her window seat. I was seated in the aisle.

"Crotch," I responded with a smile. That was a running joke when we flew. She always took the window seat, so when she had to get by that was her way of chiding me about whether she would scoot through facing me or facing away. She plopped down in her seat next to mine.

Taybor perpetually looked like she had overslept. She was a very pretty girl, tall, lean, and muscular with dark brown hair and bright blue eyes. Her clothes were usually casual by choice. Today she wore a purple flannel shirt over a white tank and very tattered blue jeans.

"Fucking planes, if I never seen one again..." She shook her head and exhaled deeply, blowing a strand of hair out of her face.

"I know what you mean." We had always attended schools abroad, so we flew frequently. We had been flying together since the age of nine.

We were sitting in the first-class emergency-exit row. I picked up the aircraft safety card and began to read. "Federal regulations require that a customer select a non-exit seat if he or she cannot or does not wish to perform the following functions: locate the emergency exit, recognize the emergency exit opening mechanism, comprehend the instructions for operating the emergency exit, operate the emergency exit." I stopped and looked at Taybor. "I don't know, Tay, it sounds like a lot of responsibility, maybe I should let the stewardess know we aren't up for it."

"Speak for yourself, loser." She shot me a grin, "I like the exit isle. More leg room." She stretched her legs all the way out. Then she added in a lower voice, "Anyway, some world ruler you're gonna be!" She winked.

I never felt homesick when I was with Taybor.

CHAPTER TWO

Bergamo -La Città dei Mille

School started two days later. I stood in front of my mirror the morning classes began. I was thankful that this school didn't require uniforms, though they did however require business dress every Friday, and that sucked. They said it prepared us for the real world. Today was Monday, and I wore a Homestruck t-shirt and jeans, taking a few extra minutes to scrutinize my reflection before heading out the door. You see yourself every day, so it's easy to not realize how much you have changed during an adolescent growth spurt.

I was several inches taller than the previous school year, standing at 6'2". I flexed my right arm in the mirror and noticed that the soft muscles of childhood had been replaced with the solid, lanky build of a man, the tendons and veins showing prominently under the tan skin of my arms and hands. My face had thinned out and hardened, accentuating the curve of my cheekbones, making my face look sharper, older. My blue eyes peered out from beneath thick, dark eyelashes. Not bad. I shrugged as I turned away from the mirror. I pushed a hand through my dark brown hair, thick with natural waves I could thank my parents for, as they both had curls. Unlike my parents, I had blue eyes, inherited from my maternal grandfather.

Class size at Bergamo Prep School was small, and students were distinguished. My first class of the morning was world religion. We rarely had a classmate that we didn't know from past years of our very exclusive, very expensive private education. That added to the tedium of the school year.

Today, as I walked through the halls, everyone's thoughts were consumed with the trivial drama of a new addition to the small student body here at Bergamo. It took so little to work them all up. I'd seen the new face repeatedly in thought after thought from every angle. Just an ordinary human girl. The excitement over her arrival was tiresomely predictable. Half the males were already imagining themselves in love with her just because she was something new to look at. I tried hard to tune them out this morning.

As I walked into class, a head of auburn hair caught my eye. Underneath the red mane was a pale-skinned, blue-eyed girl. She was sitting at a desk in the back corner of the room, looking around indifferently. She was beautiful. I took the seat next to her. Once I was settled, I turned to her and smiled. Everyone always complimented my smile. I got it from my father.

"Hey, I'm Azaiah," I said a bit too casually.

She raised her chin and flashed a brief grin back. "Mikaela."

"Means, who is God," I responded, thinking it a cleaver icebreaker. I liked to look up the origin and meaning of names. A kind of weird hobby, I guess.

"Huh?" Mikaela looked puzzled.

"That's the meaning of your name. It's Hebrew," I explained, and then thought about it. "Ok I'm lame, sorry." I winked.

She nodded her head in agreement and then looked away. I guess I blew that one. I had not impressed the new girl.

The instructor came in and class began. "I want to let everyone know that we have a new student joining us." Ms. Giovanni motioned her hand toward Mikaela. "Mike-Lah," she stumbled on the name, "just joined us from France. Make her feel welcomed."

"It's Mikaela." The girl nodded.

"Hey Mike-Lah." Skyler laughed. She was a pretty dark-skinned girl sitting in the row across from Mikaela.

"I apologize," offered Ms. Giovanni. "I have a niece named Brisbane, everyone always pronounces it Bris-BAYNE but it's really pronounced Bris'bn, and I know how mad she gets when people mispronounce it." She hmphed. "Almost as mad as I get when I think about the fact that my sister named her Bris'bn."

"What school did you last attend Mikaela?" the teacher questioned, changing the subject. Because of the school exclusivity the teachers were genuinely interested in where we came from and what our lineage might be.

"Until today, I was homeschooled," Mikaela answered.

"Homeschooled kids are freaks." Skyler attempted to share a hushed joke with those that sat nearby, but her voice had a natural tendency to carry and the dig echoed throughout the room. Mikaela didn't acknowledge Skyler even though it was evident she had heard.

"She's probably weirdly religious or something." Marcus snickered back to Skyler.

Mikaela looked toward the group of taunting teens, rolled her eyes, and with a mocking grin and a thick southern accent she whispered, "Yes, and on the eighth day god created the AK-47 so man could kill dinosaurs…and the homosexuals." Then she winked at Marcus. "Amen."

"Wow," I said under my breath. I couldn't hold back how impressed I was at such a bold retort on day one at a new school.

"But don't worry, I went to rehab, I'm totally normal now." She smiled sweetly, but in a demented, crazy way.

The first day back at school was always a blur. A stressful, surreal blur. I had lived my whole life in Seattle, Washington, until at the age of nine when my dad began shipping me off every fall to boarding school. Now here I was once again in the middle of nowhere.

By the time I got to see an American movie it was already on DVD. Too far from civilization to even have a McDonalds, but at least Italy did have good coffee. The town had at least fourteen Renaissance churches, a town hall, and a library. The library had more historic and religious books than the Smithsonian, but nothing current or modern. I mean how many books do you need on the Renaissance period, the Modern Era, Golden Age, and WWII? It's not like the outcome is ever going to change, even if it's written by a different author. History is just that, we know the ending.

The worst part was that each year it was the same damn classmates, their families having attended these private schools for generations.

Later in the day I caught up with Mikaela. "Hey, I'm sorry about those clichés in class, but I'm not one of them."

"Clichés?" She looked at me puzzled.

"People who once were human, but for whom unlimited money and need for attention has corrupted entirely," I said, proud of myself for not relating with my immature classmates.

"Hmm, bet you are really proud of yourself for putting that complex thought together. How many of them have you dated?" Mikaela shot back.

"Wow, that was brutal," I said with eyebrows raised.

"Years cultivating the bitch gene I guess." She answered a bit softer.

"No cure yet, huh?" I chided.

"We can always hope." She bantered back, her voice softening even more. I could feel a mood shift. Maybe I wasn't the enemy. "You've been to a lot of schools, huh?" she asked.

"Yeah," I answered, weary of where she was going with the conversation. I was totally braced for another insult.

"That must be nice. I've only ever lived in one place." She said wistfully.

"I'm from Washington State, but I've been to a lot of these exclusive schools. Maybe my dad thinks it's easier this way since my mom died giving birth to me."

"I only have my dad too, my mom died when I was four." She empathized.

"How did it happen?"

"Fire." Mikaela stammered.

"Wow, I'm sorry, that was an awful question." Way to bring a conversation straight to a dead end.

"Look, I appreciate the company, but I don't feel like being a charity case today." She shrugged me off.

"No, I— Now, that's fairly rude and not true at all." I was taken aback by Mikaela's sharp edge. "Perhaps it's because we haven't been properly introduced."

"I'm Azaiah Frasier." I offered her my hand, but she didn't take it. Instead, she took a deep breath of excitement.

"Wait, you're the Azaiah Frasier?" She had a look of amazement on her face.

"Yeah." I smiled; a bit too impressed with myself.

"Oh my gosh, you mean you're *THE* Azaiah Frasier?" she exclaimed again.

"You've heard of me?" I asked, perplexed.

"Hah." She giggled sarcastically then suddenly her face turned serious, "No. Of course I never heard of you. It's my first day at this school."

I couldn't help but chuckle with fascination. "Do you know where you are going?"

"Rarely," she answered.

As we turned the corner, we ran smack into a group of kids.

"Scusa." I smiled and nodded their way. I was fluent in Italian.

"Azaiah, you should keep better company," Miranda said, her voice full of fake concern. "I heard she's from a mental institution. She burned her mama up in a fire."

"Oh, bullshit," I blurted.

"Azaiah, may I speak with you for a moment?" Miranda asked, pulling me off to the side.

"What is wrong with you Azaiah?" Miranda's voice was full of syrupy concern.

"I'm just not sure why you all are so hell bent on alienating her, she's just a new kid, she's not Hitler. You shouldn't be putting someone down just because you don't know them," I challenged.

"And you know her Azaiah? Is that what you're saying?" she said through glaring eyes.

I opened my mouth but couldn't find more words to say. I swallowed hard trying not to become angry. Classmates rushed by us. "Well, I'm trying to," I finally replied as I pulled my arm away from her grip and headed back toward Mikaela.

"Let's go outside and get some fresh air," I offered.

"Be careful, Azaiah." Miranda laughed hysterically.

Mikaela took my hand. "Come on, Azaiah, I don't need the last laugh. I've been laughing at their dumb asses the entire day." She pulled me down the hall and out the door, immediately letting go of my hand as soon as we were out of sight. "Those are your friends?" She turned to me accusingly.

"I don't know. The older I get the less I like people. You think you know someone and then one day it hits you like a bag of bricks …these people are douchebags, why did I ever think I liked them? And evil takes a human form in Miranda Jones." I continued to ramble. "Nothing is ever as it seems." I shook my head and then smiled, changing the subject. "Do you like movies?"

Mikaela nodded with a shrug. "I'm more of a reader, but yea, they are okay."

I continued, "Take the movie The Village for instance. It's all a set up…a-turn-of-the-century small village whose inhabitants are trapped and terrorized by violent monsters that live in the surrounding woods. When in actuality it is present day and the children of the village are in fact being lied to by a group of people, their parents, who are playing the part of the monsters in order to preserve the myth and keep the villagers in check. This shocker came straight out of left field. What if that is what real life is like…our life? Nothing is as it seems."

Mikaela paused and stared at me. I suddenly became extremely embarrassed. I wasn't sure why I had babbled on like that. Then she smirked. "Jeez, I can't believe you told me the ending to the movie!"

"You've never seen it?"

"No!"

"You really were homeschooled, weren't you?" I laughed.

Mikaela shrugged, then asked very seriously, "What are you doing here? Why are you following me around?"

"Oh, I don't know. You kind of led me out here when you grabbed my hand." I reacted innocently.

"I mean before that?"

"I just came out to make sure you were okay."

"What for?" she shot off defensively.

"I don't know." Shrugging. "Are you okay?"

"Yeah." She seemed embarrassed.

"Okay. Good."

"You can go now that you've done your good deed of the day." Her words were filled with defiance.

"What?" I asked.

"Just go away." She exhaled.

I stood there dumbfounded, not quite sure if she was serious or not.

"Go away!" She said even louder, in an angrier tone.

"No," I replied calmly.

"Yes." If looks could kill, I'd be toast.

"No." I answered holding my ground.

"Go!" She pushed.

"No!" I held my ground.

"Jackass." Her lips were pouty and pink, and despite the words that were coming out of them I wanted to kiss those lips more than anything.

"Look, I'm sorry about those jerks. They are an entitled bunch of pricks." I tried to bring a truce of sorts to the table.

"Is being a prick a bad thing?" I was focused on her squinty blue eyes as she spoke with such attitude. I couldn't read her thoughts and it was frustrating, but I knew this was for show. She was the bullied new kid and she was acting like she didn't need anyone.

"Yes. Well, I don't know. Guess I never really thought about it." I answered.

"Yeah, me neither." A wiry half grin briefly crossed her face. "And I should know better by now.

People my age always hate me, no matter where I go."

"Well, they are idiots."

"What do you care anyway?" She shook her head. "I'll guess you've never been on the outside looking in, have you?" Then she swirled around and stormed off.

C H A P T E R T H R E E

Going Down

I dropped my head when I saw Mikaela enter the cafeteria that afternoon. I was sure, in that instant, our eyes had met. She looked away and glanced around the room curiously.

"That new girl is staring at you; do you know her?" Taybor grunted in my ear.

"I don't know. Does she look pissed?" I couldn't help but ask.

"No," she said, sounding confused by my question. "Should she be?"

"I don't think she likes me," I confided. "She thought I was a total tool this morning in world religion. I think her word of choice was jackass."

"Hmm." Taybor shrugged, stifling a laugh, but her interest was piqued. "But she's still staring at you."

"Stop looking at her," I hissed, elbowing her gently in the ribs. She snorted but looked away. I raised my head enough to make sure that Taybor did actually look away, intending violence if she resisted.

After school that day Mikaela invited herself to hang out at dinner with Taybor and I. She walked up to our table, laid her books down and pulled up a chair.

"Hello," Mikaela said quietly in a silky, pleasant-sounding voice.

I looked up, stunned that she was speaking to us. Her hair was dripping wet from the rain, tousled, but even so, she looked like she had just stepped out of a fashion magazine. Her stunning face was welcoming and open, a slight smile on her flawless lips. Her blue eyes scanned the room carefully.

"My name is Mikaela Moreau," she continued, turning to Taybor. "I didn't have a chance to introduce myself to you this morning."

Taybor shot her a quick "Hey, I'm Taybor," with a slight lift of the chin, then continued reading her book. "You two know each other?" Taybor cut her eyes at me.

"I'm semi familiar with the school bodyguard slash twenty-first century philosopher." Mikaela smiled.

"I never know whether you're insulting me or complimenting me," I shot back.

"Yeah." She nodded.

"Heh." Taybor grunted, sounding annoyed and impatient with Mikaela's and my conversation.

"You know? If it makes any difference, um...I like you. You're funny." I looked her straight in her eyes.

Now Taybor's eyes were really cutting my way. It was almost uncomfortable. "You may not think so later," she countered cryptically.

"Pfft, okay, uh, you can't complain about not having any friends and then make a guy work this hard trying to be one. Unless you actually do think I'm a jackass, and in that case, I'll just leave you be."

"Leave? Run tell your friends about the headcase." She shrugged innocently.

"Do you really think I'm that kind of guy?" My eyebrows shot up.

"No." She looked down and shook her head.

"Okay. Good."

"I guess I should go study." She was uncomfortable. It didn't help that Taybor was looking at us like we were some sideshow conundrum that she just couldn't figure out.

"You, uh, read those chapters in Escape from Freedom?" I didn't want her to leave.

"Yeah, I've read it twice before." She smiled.

"Oh, it's good, isn't it?"

"Yeah."

"You ever read any Burroughs?" I kept the conversation going.

"No."

"Augusten Burroughs? No?" I continued to question. "Running with Scissors. Great stuff. I didn't know whether to fall off my chair laughing or run away screaming in horror when I read it!"

"That's not on the required reading list." She shrugged.

"You only read books on the required reading list?"

"Um, I don't only read required books. All the books they make you read are, pretty boring."

"Yeah, usually I've already read them anyway."

Taybor made it obvious that she did not appreciate the intrusion by candidly ignoring Mikaela and only conversing with me, completely disregarding Mikaela's existence. For this reason, I tried extra hard to make Mikaela feel welcome and attempted to lighten the conversation.

"Now, where you sit in the cafeteria is crucial on your position in life from here on." I nodded, my voice dripping with sincerity. "You've got everybody here positioning themselves for who they are going to be in life. You got your awkward freshmen who are just trying to fit in. There, that table is your typical stuck-up old mone."

I pointed "They are the entitled new money." I then looked in the direction of a bunch of kids with laptops and beanies, "That group is the web.com I.T. my parents got out before everything went belly-up rich geeks, then there's the scholarship kids who study constantly to keep their entitlements."

I nodded toward a group of questionably dressed girls hanging around the 'old money' table. "Those are the slutty girls who are looking for a rich husband. They wear their shirts too tight and their skirts too short." I shrugged. "I guess some guys like that sort of thing. To the right of us are the Asian nerds, next table over are the cool Asians." I didn't usually act this judgmental, and rarely ever talked about anybody in a gossiping way. I wasn't sure why I was showing off for this girl.

Taybor laid down her book, crossed her arms over her chest, and watched intently with squinted eyes as I continued. "In the back of the room are the sad abandoned rich kids who eat their feelings, and those are the girls who don't eat anything." I looked around the room satisfied with myself.

"Then there is the table with the greatest people you will ever meet, that's me…and Taybor of course. Even though you couldn't tell it right now, she's awesome." I winked at Taybor, she shook her head at me. "Then there's the worst table of all. The snobs. Don't be fooled, because they may seem like your typical selfish, two-faced, judgmental, assholes, but in reality, they are so much worse than that. And I really, should point out that you are the new kid in a school that is very non-accepting of new kids, so really, I have you at a disadvantage. You are in no position to pass up friends. So, we accept you at the table of awesomeness." I leaned back in my chair. "You're welcome." I smiled smugly. Mikaela giggled briefly.

"Why didn't they just keep homeschooling you?" Taybor shot Mikaela a question.

"My dad wanted me to get socialized." She rolled her eyes. "Like I'm a rancorous puppy or something."

"And he sent you here for that!? Oh, you'll get socialized, all right. Rich kids are the worst," I retorted smugly.

"Aren't you rich too?" Mikaela cut her eyes at me.

"Well, maybe I was generalizing a bit." I admitted.

Our conversation continued until the warning bell and we all dispersed to our study halls or dorms.

Turned out Mikaela had a brain to go along with the rest of the package. I was always thrilled to find another teenager that could hold a conversation about something other than pop culture. Trust me, we are a rare breed. More importantly, I guess she didn't hate me after all.

The other kids continued to give Mikaela a hard time. I tried to soften the blow when I could. She mostly ignored them in a stoic I don't give a fuck kind of way. I didn't buy it, the cruelty had to bother her.

During the semester Mikaela and I became fast friends, and then more. I could tell Taybor didn't care for Mikaela either, I just wasn't sure why. Mikaela was always overly friendly to Taybor. Part of me wanted to confront Taybor to find out what her problem was, but I thought doing that might cause more issues than it was worth. Taybor never responded well to a challenge.

I always wondered why Taybor never had a boyfriend. Maybe she was just too mean and most boys our age were scared of her? She was a beautiful girl, and she carried herself with a sense of confidence that I would have found extremely sexy if I were any other person my age. So, what if she was lacking a sense of style, she was pretty enough that she could have worn a bath towel and made it a fashion statement. It seemed excessive for her to have both looks and exceptional intelligence.

However, as far as I could tell, life worked that way most of the time. I guess none of that was helping Taybor with her love life at this point. No, I didn't really believe that. The inaccessibility must have been completely her doing. I couldn't imagine any door that wouldn't be opened by that amount of beauty and confidence.

Well, figuring out the opposite sex had puzzled greater men than me for thousands of years, I surely wasn't going to solve that mystery today.

I had a couple of classes with Mikaela, literature was one that we shared. Two months into the year Mikaela continued to be the target of Miranda and her clones. The cruelty was never ending.

One day things got really weird after lit class. We were all gathered around the bank of lockers when Miranda, out of the blue, said to the blond hair, blue-eyed girl standing next to her, "Um, my father says he's not paying good money for my schooling for me to be in the same class with the likes of Mikaela Moreau. It isn't right that those of us privileged with pure lineage be diluted and forced to attend class with people like her."

"Miranda, shut up," I said angrily. She looked shocked that I had spoken to her like that.

Miranda shook her head sadly. "See what she's doing to you, Azaiah? That girl's going to bring you nothing but bad."

Mikaela was glaring at Miranda, clutching her books so tightly that her knuckles were white.

"What are you talking about? Just grow up," I shot back.

"She is an evil, nasty female. You really should listen, Azaiah. I'm telling you this for your own good."

"*Stop it Miranda.*" I chastised her, but it didn't faze her.

"One day you will remember this conversation. You will regret the day you turned your back on your real friends."

"I'm telling you, stop it now!" I demanded.

"She's just not one of us. Its unnatural." Miranda kept going.

"I don't know what you're thinking or why you are doing this, but you need to stop," I was getting angry.

"Save us all from the likes of her. Her daddy probably sent her here to find a wealthy husband." Miranda turned to Mikaela. "She's here for a MRS degree, not a HS diploma" She began opening and closing her index and second finger like scissors. "I bet she spreads her legs every night for you trying to get the golden seed. Punch out the golden ticket and laugh all the way to the bank as she cashes the child support checks."

"*SHUT UP!*" Mikaela screamed.

The ground shook and all of the books from the open lockers fell to the ground. A window broke and the rumbling was drowned out by screaming teenagers. An earthquake?

"She did it!" Miranda pointed at Mikaela as tears streamed down her face. "It was her! She broke the window, she is evil!"

"That's ridiculous!" I said, getting my bearings as everything settled. I ran over to Mikaela, "You all right?"

"What the hell was that?" Taybor walked up behind me. I shrugged. "Earthquake maybe."

* * *

Mikaela went home with her father that weekend. He kept a home just a few hours' drive from the school. That Saturday morning, I decided to take the train to her home and surprise her. For some reason I thought it might cheer her up. It seemed like a great idea until I was standing on the doorstep of the modest villa working my nerve up to knock. Before I had the chance, Mikaela opened the door just enough to poke her head out.

"What are you doing here?" It was obvious that this wasn't a welcome surprise.

"I came to visit you." I paused, slightly embarrassed. "Surprise." I smiled.

From behind Mikaela I heard a man's voice. "Do we have a guest?"

"No," Mikaela answered back. "He's leaving."

"He?" The voice was closer. Mikaela was brushed aside with a gasp as Mikala's father appeared in front of me.

"Hello sir." I extended my hand.

"Manners? That's nice." He came off as a fierce gentleman. He had the most intriguing green eyes. He was dressed in snazzy business-like attire despite it being Saturday. He had an urbane personal style, like he navigated to his own compass.

"I go to school with your daughter. I'm Azaiah Frazier. Pleasure to make your acquaintance." I introduced myself as we shared a firm handshake.

"You Caleb Frazier's boy?" He was direct. I was good at reading people. His style was the real thing. His charisma was a deeply embedded thing. He was one of the few that would survive the true test of a man's character, his dress, character, manner would not change if he was in a room full of people or alone in the middle of nowhere. None of the fake alpha machismo crap. He wouldn't be caught dead cutting in line or stealing cabs from other people at the end of the night.

"Yes, sir. You know my father?" I answered, continuing to size him up.

"Mikaela, why don't you ask your friend in for tea?" He exuded emotional maturity, mental sharpness, knowledge, and worldliness.

Mikaela leaned in toward me and in a hushed tone sternly said, "Tell him you can't stay."

I beamed and said, "I'd love to. Thank you, sir."

"Mr. Frazier, make yourself comfortable. I'm Damian. Charmed, I'm sure." He was calm and imperturbable.

"Oh, I...I'm sorry about showing up uninvited."

"No problem at all. It's so rarely that we get visitors. Mikaela has a tendency to keep to herself. Kids her age are usually so immature." He cultivated insight and intuition.

"Don't be a snob," Mikaela snapped.

"And it's not my fault that I have a predilection for good breeding, reasonable intelligence, and passable personal hygiene." He exhibited boldness, chutzpah.

I couldn't help but laugh at his bluntness. He wasn't wrong.

"So... Mikaela, why don't you play something for our guest on the piano?" As he spoke, I noticed that the inner half of each of his eyebrows slanted sharply downward, creating a mischievous look or even a slight scowl.

"Because this is not some eighteenth-century novel, Dad." Mikaela looked exasperated.

"Then why don't you go make us some tea while your gentleman friend and I get acquainted?" His mouth was small and narrow, conveying reservation.

"Again, wrong century." She huffed.

"Well, then, would it disturb either of you if I ran my fingers across the ivories?" Damian seemed to stare directly at me, taking me in.

"I love music," I shrugged.

"Oh, a young man of good tastes. Mikaela, I could get to like this friend of yours." He seemed to see far deeper into me than just what was on the surface. It was a bit unnerving.

"So how do you know my father?" I asked.

"Oh, I don't really. Just through associates." He played piano beautifully while we conversed.

"School called," Mikaela whispered. "Put me on probation while they investigate the bullying fiasco."

"That's crazy. That was not your fault," I said back in a hushed voice. The piano music filled the room.

"Aw, voice of reason in a crowd of simple minds." Mikala's father's voice carried over the music. *How did he hear us?*

"I mean, no one called *my* father," I said with a tinge of anger.

"Well, your father is Caleb Frasier, Mikaela doesn't have that luxury," he said without judgment or malice. "In any event, I'll sort it out with the school. Yet, I understand your indignation, Azaiah. They mention probation. Probation. Heh. That implies a source of authority, and what is that source? A bank account? A family name? A bunch of sexually frustrated rich men who spend twelve hours a day in a boardroom. Miniscule minds and voluminous backsides."

"Dad, please stop it." Mikaela was flushed with embarrassment.

I could tell she was uncomfortable, so I made an excuse to head back to the school shortly after my arrival. Her father was a welcoming gentleman, it was odd how different Mikaela was around him.

After I said I stood on the front porch looking around. I could hear faint voices coming from an open window next to where I stood.

"What did you do? We agreed to let you attend that school, but no friendships!" he reprimanded.

"Could you not at least let me pretend to be normal for a while?" She sounded deflated. "What else do you suggest I do?"

"You just remember why we are here!" His voice dripped with authority. It was as if he were a general and she was his soldier. "That little incident was the end of it! This is just the beginning of what will cumulate your life's work. That boy is a danger to you. I wouldn't invite him here again if I were you."

I could tell Mikaela was sobbing, "Oh, I wouldn't worry. I'm sure he won't be back."

I walked away from Mikala's house confused by the strange behavior of her father. Especially puzzled by the conversation I had eavesdropped in on. Nevertheless, by the end of the first semester Mikaela and I were an exclusive item. Taybor barely tolerated Mikaela, and only for my sake. Taybor and I were going away to college in Seattle, and she made no secret of the fact that she was happy to be leaving Italy. Mikaela still had another year of high school at Bergamo Prep. Taybor was also unquestionably happy about that.

My father attended my graduation, and when I introduced him to Mikaela, he also seemed skeptical of her. This didn't surprise me, as he and my mother were equally cynical of most new people in my life. Not that there had been many. They were both carrying around a lot of past baggage though. It was understandable.

Taybor and I spent the summer together as per our usual. I had planned to go back to Italy to visit Mikaela in August before school started in the fall. My father strongly disapproved of the trip.

"Dad, why are you trying to keep Mikaela away from me?" I felt like I was far too old to even need to ask for permission, but that is how it was, in my family. If Caleb did not approve, I wasn't allowed to do it.

"You've been different since you met that girl."

"How would you know? I was in Italy; you were in Washington, or who knows where!"

"Taybor said there was a party tonight. You should be at that party Azaiah...with Taybor and your other friends, kicking up your heels with your real friends, with the kids who belong—I mean, the kids you grew up with." He stopped and continued with, "What, you don't like your old friends anymore?"

"Of course, I do." I shook my head. I knew this discussion was over. "I'm not much up for a party tonight, Dad. I'm going to my room."

"Oh, well, that's a shame. I'm sure they would all love to see you."

I decided to give it one more shot. "Why won't you let me see her? Do you really think keeping us apart is the best thing for me?" I was defeated, dejected, and miserable.

"That girl is no good. Not good for you."

"You are wrong. I know Mikaela. I know her like I know myself." I needed to see her. I had an odd feeling lately, like I could feel her slipping away into some place where I couldn't reach her. Desperation was setting in.

"My fight is not with you, son. It's not. Never has been. It's just that girl, with her seductive quirkiness, and you being motherless and all." My father shook his head, he was clearly irritated. "I'm on your side, son. Please, but for your own good, you should really listen to me."

"I don't want to listen to you *this time*. Why can't you trust me to be an adult? That's what I am Dad, an adult."

"No! You do not know anything about what you are. How important you are. This girl, this relationship is nothing in the scheme of how important you are."

"I'm sick of listening to you say that! What does that even mean?" The frustration was no longer containable. "No matter what you do, no matter what you make me do. No matter how long you keep her away from me. I am still here for her. I will always be here for her. So, what does that tell you? I love her, and that's the most powerful feeling in all the realms. It is as alive as you or me. Isn't it, Dad? Didn't you once risk everything for love?"

"No son. I lost everything for love," my father answered sternly.

"Everybody has to deal with shit in their lives, Dad. You can't protect me from everything"

"Au contraire, dear boy, that is what I have to do. Everything depends on it. What are you so angry about? You want to be a normal human. What do you think that is? Humans don't have powers to just change things whenever they like. Being human is feeling bad, it's feeling pissed off. It's feeling scared and not being able to do anything about it until you don't feel that way anymore, until you can see your way out of it." Caleb raked his hand through his thick, wavy hair. He looked very young, but I could see purple half-moons shading the fragile area beneath his eyes. "And I do this because I care about you! That's what normal people do, people who love each other—when one of them is acting like a spoiled brat you call it out. I'm scared for you. If something happens to you, it's not just your fate at stake—the world, everyone is doomed."

"That's a bit dramatic, Dad, don't you think? Love's a risk for anybody."

"I'm not worried about a little heartbreak here, son. I don't mean that, I'm concerned about you being hurt. I'm more worried about you being killed."

"Jeez, Dad. *Kill me?* Really?" The statement was startling.

"I know you haven't come to realize your full role in this war. I know you don't understand. There have been so many dark angels, we have been fighting alongside mortals for centuries, every war, every side.

Just because we are supernatural does not make us any smarter than the mortals. However, son, you are the greatest dark angel. I NEED us to be smart. I need to save you from yourself."

"THERE IS NO WAR, DAD! You know, what I can't figure out? You drag me to church every Sunday as a child to learn about God, my enemy. Then you tell me not to believe any of it. I've never seen anything to make me believe either side."

"Mm-hm. Your point?" Caleb shot back.

"Revelations 20:10: And the devil, who deceived them, was thrown into the lake of burning sulfur, where the beast and the false prophet had been thrown. They will be tormented day and night, forever and ever. This tells us that when he—who is he?

You? Me?" I was being dramatic to push my point home. "When he is cast into Hell, he will not be the ruler. He will be one of those souls tormented with fire, right alongside all the angels who followed him in rebellion against God, and right alongside every human who does not accept Christ's death on the cross as full payment for his or her sins. Why send me to church to learn of my fate only to hold me hostage and not allow me to enjoy my short human existence? Should I be born only to live a life of torture. Should I never have any happiness, not even a taste? What is the point of my life?"

"Son, sometimes you just have to trust others to be smarter than you."

I was done. I spun on my heel and stomped out of the room.

"Kira, I don't think it's the archangels we have to protect him from anymore—I think it's that girl," Caleb said coolly.

Chapter Four

I Don't Love You, But I Always Will

Taybor openly disliked Mikaela and took any chance to let me know it. One afternoon we were having lunch and Taybor asked, "So, how often do you and Mikaela get to talk to each other? The time difference must be a real cock block?"

"We Skype pretty much every day. I usually chat with her on my laptop at night. I fall asleep talking to her before she heads off to class for the day." I answered in between bites of my salad. I was used to Taybor's directness.

"Ah, that's the new way of romance! Gotta love technology." Her voice was dripping with sarcasm.

"And when I wake up the screen is usually frozen, and Mikaela's face is in some funny position like..." I screwed up my face and held the pose.

"When you guys Skype, do you, you know...do you go a little wild. Push the limits of imagination?" She smiled mockingly.

"You're being vulgar, aren't you!" I nodded, already knowing the answer.

"No, I'm not being vulgar. I'm just pursuing research for my undergraduate degree in sociology. Long-distance relationships used to be tied to letter writing, then phone calls, then emails, but these days you can do almost anything real-time in the virtual world. I am asking on a hypothetical level." Taybor shrugged nonchalantly, playing it off.

"So now you're a sociology major?" I looked at her skeptically.

"Yeah." She nodded. "For instance, sex of the future, okay, and I'm totally serious now, it's gonna be just like attaching something to your genitals and watching each other's experience virtually. You'll be having virtual intercourse with anyone of your choice. You will be able to program in all your preferences."

"Ok, I'm following you, that might be enjoyable—or sick and perverse depending on the person. The attachment would definitely be gross." I made a face consistent with being disgusted.

"Come on. You think so?" Taybor looked at me seriously.

"I mean, why not? More and more of our experiences are already taking place in the virtual world. Meetings, medical appointments, interviews, basically anything can be done virtually." I shrugged.

"Technology is going to replace us all." Taybor was always quite the philosopher. She definitely kept me on my toes.

"Not me. The world will always need lawyers. It'll never happen," I said with all of the arrogance I could muster.

"Your ego is so big, Azaiah!" Taybor shrugged. "I think it's only a question about *WHEN* it's going to happen. People can already do all sorts of things today online that in the past they needed an attorney for." Then she turned the conversation back to where we had left off. "So, I guess Mikaela is doing her job, *Mister the world cannot live without me.*"

"What does that mean?" I asked seriously.

"Well, the secret that women learn early on is to always make your man feel like you cannot live without him. Like he is the smartest, most desirable person in the universe. Let him show you how to play Madden, hold a bat, throw a punch, be better than you, smarter than you, even when he's not." I could no longer tell if Taybor was drawing me into an argument or if she was just making her usual confrontational, devils advocate, type of conversation. I remained silent and let her continue. "Oh, okay. Like when we are practicing battle and you never beat me and I saw it was messing with your head, so I let you win that time."

"Last time I won we were, like, eight?!" I answered confused.

"Yes, that time. You could never really beat me. I let you win." She slammed her palm onto the table to drive home her point.

"So, the entire foundation of our relationship is a lie?" I gasped.

"You needed a confidence boost, so I did you a solid. Probably why you are so damn arrogant today." Taybor hmphed. "Azaiah, just admit it, you are the typical closet tough guy. You would love to settle in with a trophy wife who adores you and follows you around like a lost puppy."

"A guy can dream." I smiled, not confirming or denying the allegation.

Taybor changed her demeanor and voice, mimicking a dumb blond stereotype. "So, are you like the super smart senior that got like a perfect score on the SATs?"

"Oh yes that was me." I laughed, playing along.

"So, you're going to be a lawyer when you grow up?" Her voice took on a sexy drawl that I had never heard before.

"Well, I hope to." I laid my fork down, interested in where this was going.

"So, like how much money does a lawyer make in a year?" She asked totally embracing her sex kitten role play.

"I'm not sure, but probably enough to be comfortable." I couldn't help but smile. This discussion had actually taken an entertaining turn.

"Does comfortable include owning a yacht?" Taybor was in full role play, making goo-goo eyes and poking out her chest.

"Well maybe." I shrugged. "Sure, yeah, why not."

"Wow! I never met anyone that was going to be a lawyer before." She gasped with totally credible excitement.

"Really?"

She shook her head, pouty-lipped and doe-eyed. "You must be really smart."

"Well, you know." I turned my palms up in an I was born this way gesture.

"Okay, so since you are so smart answer this question for me." She was totally into this persona and I was finding it completely comical.

"I'll do my best." I smiled.

"What does IDK stand for when people text me?" She quizzed.

"I don't know." I answered confidently.

"Ugh. Nobody does!" She whined. "Well you are still probably very, very smart," and then she leaned over and whispered in a very sexy Marilyn Monroe impression, "and I bet you have a gigantic penis too."

"Damn, why am I finding myself so attracted to you right now?" I broke out in open laughter.

"Wow!" Taybor said, displaying teasing disappointment. "Virgins are dropping like flies, girls giving up their virginity in the restroom or the back seat of a mustang. Why is our generation so easy? People our age spend weekends staring into their phones perusing hook-up sites, making connections, and relishing in easy, frequent, and casual sex. We are too accepting of non-committed relationships. There is a pandemonium of one-night bed-hopping because guys are attracted to girls like that, and girls have major self-esteem issues. Girls with substance are discarded because their breasts aren't large enough!"

* * *

Taybor and I were both able to live at our parent's homes during our freshman year at the university. I was glad for that. When Mikaela graduated things changed. She had applied and been accepted into the University of Washington, to be with me. My dad wanted me to remain at home, but I insisted on taking an apartment closer to campus since Mikaela would be dorming there. Usually what my dad wanted he got, but this time I didn't back down. With Kira's support my dad eventually caved, and I was able to move into a one-bedroom apartment of my own.

When Mikaela arrived in Washington, I picked her up and drove her to my apartment. She and I had been intimate a few times when we were in Italy, but opportunities were few and far between. I was hoping that would change now that she was here.

As soon as I cut the engine I was around the car and at her door, opening it a bit too anxiously. Without giving her a chance to move, I scooped her up so that she was cradled in my arms. My lips found hers as I kicked the door shut behind us. I carried her into the building. We were laughing, and before we knew it we were inside my home. I was lightheaded with anticipation and had to remind myself to breathe. I was nervous, but excited to have Mikaela there.

She seemed as thrilled as I was that we had tonight to concentrate on being together. I set her gently down and wrapped both my arms around her, refusing to allow any space between us. I continued to kiss her for several minutes, standing in the entryway. Her mouth was just as eager and accepting on mine. I began to feel guardedly optimistic. Perhaps this would not be as awkward as I had expected it to be.

"Welcome to Washington babe, I'm really glad you're here. I've missed you so much," I said, my eyes warm with desire for her. She looked even more stunning than when I'd last seen her, and I immediately felt self-conscious at the jeans and t-shirt I'd put on. I missed her so much I could have wept right then. The angle of her cheek bones, the freshly styled hair, her smooth skin. That night she wore a perfume I'd never smelled on her before, some combination of peach and lavender scents. I felt myself getting into trouble, mentally and physically, as I thought about her naked body. I hadn't dated any other women in the time we'd been apart, and I was very attracted to her.

"Your apartment is really nice," she answered, glancing around.

"Thank you." I remembered the charm bracelet I had gotten her as a graduation gift. "I have something for you."

"Oh?" She sounded surprised.

"It's in my bedroom. Shall I go get it or do you want to come with?" I asked, hoping. It was one way of quickly getting from point A to point B.

"Sure," she agreed. I was feeling quite underhanded as I enfolded my fingers through hers and pulled her along after me.

She sat down on my bed as I pulled the bracelet out of my dresser drawer.

I plopped down on the edge of the bed next to her and handed her the box. I was excited to see her reaction to it. The bracelet included several charms commemorating our two years together. The Eiffel Tower, where we trudged up all 704 steps. A gondola to memorialize our weekend in Venice. A tennis shoe that made me laugh remembering the time she lost one of her shoes down the side of a cliff along the Amalfi coast.

She seemed delighted with it. I placed it on her wrist, and she threw her arms around my neck, causing me to fall backward onto the bed, gravity pulling her down on top of me. I quickly encircled her waist and gently held her there.

My heart thumped quickly. I couldn't believe how awkward it felt to be on the bed with her. We were both out of our element. I didn't have the faintest idea how to be seductive. Her lips were gentle against mine, but I could tell her mind was elsewhere. Maybe my imagination was getting the best of me. Nerves and all.

My hands were slightly shaky as I unlocked my arms from around her waist. My fingers slid down her side to the hem of her shirt and I began to lift. Her lips froze, and I could almost hear the click in her head as she put together my motives. She pushed me away at once, her face heavily disapproving.

Of course, it was going to be just exactly as awkward as I thought. The blood began to burn in my face with embarrassment.

"No! We...I can't," Mikaela said suddenly.

"Why?" I asked, dejected. I didn't know what to make of it.

"Because—" Her words broke off. "Because I'm just not ready."

"Ok," I answered.

Then before I realized what had happened, she'd lightly patted my crotch area. I couldn't feel it very much beneath my jeans, but my heart leapt into my throat and I felt a jolt of electricity for a split second.

"I'm sorry, I just got nervous. I feel awful that I said that. Of course, I am ready." Now her voice was seductive and sultry. "I hope I can make it up to you somehow." It was as if her entire attitude toward the topic took a 360-degree turn. She was insatiable. I had created a monster. Luckily, I didn't mind in the least.

I swallowed hard as my heart sped up. "Mikaela, you are so beautiful right now."

I could feel her hand touching my leg, rubbing my thigh as she slowly moved it further up my leg. She paused for second as she unbuttoned my jeans before sliding her hand into my boxers, taking a firm hold. A soft moan escaped my lips as I opened my legs slightly, giving her better access. I began to slowly move my hips as her hand stroked me while her lips engulfed mine. I slipped my fingers under her skirt and began rubbing her sensitive spot through her silk panties. I could feel the wetness of her as she worked anxiously, tugging my jeans and boxers off.

I could have exploded from her touch alone. As I pulled her shirt over her head my fingers brushed against her breast, her nipples immediately stiffening. I began to moan through short breaths as she took me into her mouth and placed her hands on my buttocks, thrusting me forward, deeper into her warm mouth. This continued until I was on the verge of losing it. I flipped her over, spreading her legs once again, and this time I slid my finger through the side of her panties and into her, warm and wet with desire. I slowly moved my fingers in and out, feeling her from inside. I had to have her. I wrestled her panties off and tossed them aside as I sucked on her erect nipples. She took me greedily, pushing faster to meet my thrusts. We both climaxed then fell asleep contently in each other's arms.

Things with Mikaela progressed slowly but steadily over the following months. She eventually moved in with me, although it wasn't official, and she still kept her dorm room. The sex became gradually more adventurous, though certainly not extreme by modern standards. It was usually in the missionary position, with more evolving foreplay. She was turned on by the feeling of being controlled and degraded, and not in the sexy sort of way. Still probably the kinkiest things we did were mild on the overall S&M scorecard. It felt nice, but we didn't push it very far. We were having fun and we cared about each other immensely.

The problem was not Mikaela and me. The closer we became the more distant all my other relationships became. The euphoria of young love had changed me, and my family did not want to allow me the freedom to grow up and have mature adult relationships.

Taybor was the most difficult. Why couldn't she understand that she was special to me too, no matter how much time elapsed between visits. Our compelling connection was the result of shared roots during the formative years. As childhood friends we experienced all the wonderful, horrible, boring, and embarrassing moments that helped to make us who we were today. Nothing could replace that bond. My relationship with Mikaela wasn't a substitute for Taybor, it was completely different and apart from that.

It felt as if our dynamics had metastasized into something toxic and ugly. The sting of this cut me deeply. There were times that I could see no reason to continue trying, but I missed her so much when we were apart.

As kids, Taybor and I fought. It's a fact of family life that siblings fight, and we were like siblings. We got angry with each other for stealing toys, borrowing hoodies, or crossing invisible boundaries in the back seat of the car. We tolerated the normal amount of negativity in our relationship, and we knew that the arguments would always end in resolution. No matter how contentious our relationship was at times we still felt pulled to one another. This time it was not clear how it would play out. I always thought family was forever, but I suppose it isn't always, and sometimes you have to say goodbye.

Chapter Five

Life Goes On ... Or Does it?

A few months after Mikaela's arrival, Taybor and I were enjoying an afternoon in the park while Mikaela was in class. We rarely got to see each other anymore.

"So, how'd you get out of being sequestered for the afternoon?" Taybor joked.

"Please, Tay, don't do that. It really bothers me," I said, shaking my head.

"What does?" She dug through her backpack burrowing for snacks.

"That you and Mikaela are so ready to kill each other all the time!" I grumbled. "It makes me crazy. Why can't you both just be civilized toward each other?"

"Is *she* ready to kill *me*?" Taybor asked with eyebrows raised and a wiry smile, undisturbed by my anger.

"Not as much as you seem to be ready to do her in!" I realized I was becoming annoyed. "At least you could try and be somewhat mature about this. Do you care that it hurts me that I can't have you both in my life?"

Taybor mumbled, her voice dripping with sarcasm, "I'm sure she's ready and willing to share."

"Ugh!" I glared at Taybor, practically fuming. She could be

absolutely infuriating.

Taybor was quiet for a few uncomfortable minutes before eventually moving over and sitting down beside me, draping her arm around my shoulders. I jerked my body, causing her arm to tumble off me.

"Sorry," she said quietly. "I'll try to behave myself."

I didn't respond.

"You just aren't yourself anymore Zi," she stated. "My best friend doesn't exist any longer, and I just cannot be around that girl."

We faced each other for an endless moment. I was searching her expression for any kind of surrender.

"Is this goodbye then, Taybor?" I asked, pushing the point further than I meant to or really wanted to.

She blinked rapidly, her stern expression melting in surprise. "*What?* We can't be friends anymore unless I'm all warm and cuddly, puppies and kittens with Mikaela?" She was openly pissed now. "Listen, Azaiah, there is something off about her. Everyone who loves you has told you this. You just refuse to see it," Taybor pleaded, trying with everything she had to keep her composure.

I shook my head and laughed dryly, lacking all humor.

"Yet you chose her over us." She sounded more broken than angry when she said this. I was not expecting her reaction. She was suddenly on her feet, gathering her belongings.

"Taybor!" I stood, starting to protest, but fell silent when I realized that her entire body was quivering with rage. She glared at me. I froze in place, too shocked by how awry this conversation had gone to remember how to move. I stood too.

"*Does she know about you?*" Taybor stopped and hissed through her teeth. It was more of an accusation than a question.

"Of course not." I shook my head, surprised.

"I don't believe you. If you haven't told her, she still knows.

Somehow, she knows," Taybor said accusingly.

"If she did know I would have figured that out by now. Stop overreacting Taybor!" I demanded.

"Well, when you, or better yet, one of us ends up with eternal death over that bitch of a girlfriend of yours, you just remember, that's on your head." Taybor scowled. "I guess the weapon that will bring down the king of kings is soft and wet and located between the thighs of a tramp." Her words cracked like the snap of a whip.

I recoiled and slapped her. I didn't mean to and regretted it immediately. It hurt me so much more than it did her, I know that for sure.

She grabbed her jacket, leaving the rest of her things. I didn't move as she walked past me glaring the entire time.

I wasn't sure why Taybor was willing to wreck our relationship for life. Was a friend as interchangeable as a new toy for an old one, wasn't there more to our friendship than that? Was I that insignificant to her? *Was she to me?* Did I really have to leave her behind to move forward with Mikaela?

CHAPTER SIX

The Demand to be Loved ...
the Greatest of all Arrogant Presumptions

About a month after our argument I sent Taybor a text. *I miss you.*

Taybor's reply: *Yea I miss you too. A lot. Doesn't change anything.*

* * *

I never mentioned the argument with Taybor to Mikaela or my father. Mikaela could see that I was hurting about something though. She was constantly by my side and extremely attentive.

Once Mikaela started staying at my place she didn't want to go out as much, which cut everyone else out of the picture almost completely. Mikaela and I spent most of our time exclusively together. I felt like Taybor and my father didn't want me to grow up and lead a normal adult life anyway, so I didn't mind avoiding them in lieu of alone time with Mikaela.

CHAPTER SEVEN

Fatherly Advice

One evening my father came by to check on me. Mikaela bowed out, taking the opportunity to go to the coffee shop down the street to study.

"I wanted to talk to you about something," he said.

"I'm listening," I answered stiffly.

"You know Taybor has been a very, very good friend to you."

"*I know that,*" I acknowledged a bit defensively.

"Don't you miss her at all?" he asked, becoming frustrated but trying to remain calm.

My throat suddenly felt swollen. I had to clear it before I answered. "Yes, I do miss her," I admitted, looking down. "I miss her a lot."

"Then why is it so difficult to apologize?"

"With Taybor there is no compromise," I said slowly, cowardly, hoping he didn't know what I had done. "We have a stalemate about my relationship with Mikaela."

"Why do you think that is?" he questioned. However, I knew he felt the same way that Taybor did. I wished he would just get to the point and this could be over.

"She doesn't trust her, I guess." I shrugged.

"Well, Son, maybe she's right. And maybe there's more to Taybor than that," he added.

"Dad, I don't know what you are talking about. Plus, Taybor won't even answer my calls. Lord knows I have tried," I argued.

"Isn't Mikaela up for a little healthy competition?" My father's voice was sarcastic now.

I leveled a dark look at him. "*There is no competition.*"

"I'm positive that she would rather be just friends than nothing." He patted me on the shoulder. How had he turned this into an *I dumped Taybor* scenario? Taybor and I have always been just friends. Sister and brother-type friends, but still only friends. "Dad, quit being weird. I'm pretty sure Taybor doesn't want to be friends at all anymore." The words burned in my throat. "Where'd you get that crazy idea, anyway? The quilter's bee gossip tree?" I attempted to lighten the mood. Epic failure.

"I've been in love before too, son. True love," he said thoughtfully. "What I see between you and Mikaela is not real love." He looked self-conscious now. "I am worried about Taybor *and you*." I winced, at that. "You were always so happy spending time with her." He sighed.

"I'm happy now," I argued, but the contrast between my words and tone of my voice broke through the tension and was easily recognized by both my father and me.

"Okay." He looked at me wearily. "Just try to work things out with Taybor, son."

"I'll try." I promised, and I meant it.

However, Taybor refused to speak with me. It broke my heart, but I didn't blame her. We weren't even practicing our battle arts together anymore. *I had made a grievous error.* I had a huge hole in my chest that Taybor's friendship used to fill.

Eventually my time with Mikaela wasn't enough to fill that hole. Life felt shallow, unfulfilling. The emptiness that Taybor's absence had left hung heavy in my heart. I was hurting and empty and there was nothing I could do to fix it. It was true, immortals do feel pain stronger than humans do. Time does not heal our scars as easily.

Chapter Eight

Honor Thy father

I completed my second year of pre-law at the university. The summer following my sophomore year of college Adrian showed up. Adrian had been an archangel but decided to cross sides. It rarely happened, and when it did the situation caused a great deal of turmoil in the realms. I barely thought about my alter ego as the prophesized antichrist. Other than the powers I possessed, which I rarely used except in battle practice, I felt totally average. I guess my father had done an excellent job in providing me balance in my life.

Mikaela had no idea about me, of course. On rare occasions we visited my father's home, but we usually spent our days at my apartment. Today was one of those uncommon occasions that I was summoned by my father.

"Azaiah, this is Adrian." My father introduced me to an attractive young man with tight brown curls and chocolate brown eyes. He appeared to be around my age, tall and long-limbed with a lot of muscle. He reminded me of a bodybuilder who had been stretched out like taffy. He was at least 6'4" and had so much muscle it seemed like flexibility might be compromised because of pure mass. I knew he was an angel. We could usually get a vibe about that. Adrian shook my hand quietly without saying a word or making eye contact.

My father was concerned about the fallout behind Adrian's cross over and wanted me to be aware of the potential for retaliations. I listened closely even if I didn't take it as seriously as he did. I knew that he felt very stern about my security. I had never been attacked, at least not since birth. Its human nature to put your guard down when so much time had passed without the proposed threat actually occurring. The threats didn't seem real to me anymore.

Mikaela was sitting in the living room with Kira when Adrian and my father walked me out. I noticed Adrian's eyes cut across the room to Mikaela. Their gaze not only lingered, but locked. Both of their eyes grew wide with acknowledgement and surprise of the other. Adrian stopped mid-step.

Mikaela jumped up and nervously said, "Oh, I'm so happy you are finished Azaiah. I'm starving."

My father never missed anything, and he certainly didn't miss Adrian and Mikaela's eye contact drama fest.

"What's going on, Adrian?" he demanded, turning toward Mikaela.

"Mikaela?" Adrian questioned, looking directly at her.

Mikaela began slowly shaking her head, a shadow of fear crossing her face. Kira made a move and was immediately behind Mikaela, ready to react on whatever was happening. My father stood defensively by Adrian's side. Kira and Caleb were like two halves of a well-oiled battle machine, always anticipating the other's move before it had even been made. Thousands of years together apparently gave a person good instinct about the other.

"What's going on?" My father's voice boomed.

"Sh-She's an arch—"Adrian stammered, obviously not wanting to be the target of my father's fury, in a don't shoot the messenger kind of way. *"Archangel!"* He exhaled, pulling himself together.

Simultaneously Kira grabbed Mikaela by the arms and my father moved within striking distance in front of Mikaela. Things were happening so quickly. *What the hell was going on here?* I moved swiftly to a protective position between Mikaela and my father.

"*Stop!*" I yelled with more authority than I had ever thought possible, especially in the presence of my father. The house shook.

"Azaiah, I know this is difficult to understand, but if she's an archangel she's not here for any reason other than to do you harm," my father explained, not hiding his anger.

Mikaela's head was shaking aggressively. "I would never," she insisted.

"Mikaela, are you an angel?" I queried, confused.

"Yes, but I wasn't supposed to tell anyone," she answered openly.

"Why are you here?" I was becoming annoyed. I just needed to know what was going on.

"School. They send some of us down for human school. It's part of our training," she answered, dripping with blamelessness.

"Do you have a mission?" my father demanded.

"Mission?" She looked at us blankly. "I don't have a mission."

Then as if she had fallen in stride with a great acting role, "*Are you people insane?* I didn't know you were an angel, Azaiah. That is all. You didn't tell me about you being an angel either!" She cried defensively, tears filling her eyes and overflowing.

She was right, I had not told her about myself. Could this possibly be mere coincidence?

"Azaiah, she cannot be trusted," my father said slowly, mechanically, as if I may have trouble understanding. "It's unsafe. We have to kill her."

"*WHAT? KILL HER!*" I said, stunned, obviously not understanding the full magnitude of what was happening. "*YOU WILL NOT!*"

"Azaiah, step away!" My father's voice roared.

"Father, to kill her you will have to go through me first!" I stood defiantly in front of Mikaela. My father's face went crimson red.

"Kira, take her." My father restrained me. I had never been so angry in my entire life. I was also afraid for Mikaela. My mind was spinning. I raised my hand and felt the power flow from it, like an extension of myself. It was as natural as stretching. Kira flew across the room.

"Stay!" I yelled. Kira froze, unable to move. "Father please don't make me fight you!" I pleaded.

"Zi, don't do this," my father said as he slowly walked toward me with his hands up in the air. "Some things cannot be undone."

"Don't make me choose father... Because it will be her." I pointed at Mikaela. "I am begging you, don't do this!" I pleaded, but my pleas fell on deaf ears.

Mikaela had been knocked down and was sitting on the ground between Caleb and Kira.

"Come here, Mikaela," I commanded. She stood and swiftly moved to my side.

My father made a move for her. I sent a blast of energy his way. He was thrown against the wall but was back up in a flash.

"Please, Dad, don't make me do this," I implored. "Please stop fighting against me." I was shaking with anger, with the pain of what I was doing. I was ashamed but couldn't stop. They would kill Mikaela without a doubt and without a second thought.

Dad moved toward Mikaela again, sending an energy force my way. I held my hand up deflecting it without effort. I then sent another blast of energy at him. His body was propelled across the room, pinning him up against the wall, rendering him confined.

I wouldn't be able to put my father down for any length of time. This could go on all day, but I needed to get out of the house and get Mikaela to safety. I swooped around behind Kira, grabbed her and assumed a very convincing and threatening stance.

"Dad, don't make me give her eternal death," I said, standing behind Kira. "I'm taking Mikaela and we are leaving. *Do not follow us.*" I had Kira by her arms. She was no match for me, still weakened by my initial blast. I was much stronger than either of them, even both of them together.

Outside of the house I threw Mikaela into the passenger side of the car. "I'm sorry, Kira. I would have never hurt you." I whispered, kissing her on the forehead and letting her go. I was physically sickened by my actions.

"Azaiah, don't do this!" she begged, tears streaking her cheeks. I had never seen her cry. I jumped into the car and sped away.

Chapter Nine

Betrayal and Other Daily Dinner Topics

"Okay, Mikaela! Talk!" I demanded firmly.

"Who are *you*, Azaiah?" She acted lost, confused. I wasn't buying it.

"Don't screw around Mikaela, you know who I am!" I yelled.

My accusation was met with stark silence, then in an instant her face turned from lost and innocent to hard and cold. My heart sank. I was driving too fast as I exited onto the ramp merging us onto the open highway. I began to decelerate as Mikaela pulled out what looked like an antique letter opener. I wasn't sure what she was doing until she lifted it above her head and thrust it toward me. I grabbed her arm in midair with my right hand which caused me to jerk the steering wheel with the left. The car swerved and flipped twice, landing upright in a field.

For a brief moment the knife landed on my lap. It burned like fire. Then as the car flipped again it was gone. The car accident didn't faze either Mikaela or me, since we were both indestructible—at least as far as human terms. The car was totaled. She kicked the door several times until it opened then jumped out of the car in an attempt to escape, but I was faster. She had somehow recovered the knife and thrust it yet again toward me. I was able to grab her wrist and held tightly, restraining her easily, squeezing her hand, forcing her to drop the knife.

"Why, Mikaela?" I asked, feeling beaten and betrayed.

A single stray tear ran down her cheek. "Because it is written, Azaiah. You *are* the antichrist," she answered without guilt or any hint of foul play.

"So, this was all an act?" I asked, disgusted by the thought.

"It was much more than an act. It meant saving everyone, everything." Her voice broke in defeat. "You have to be stopped! Someone has to be successful in this mission. The fate of everyone and everything depends on it," she repeated, broken, hopeless.

"I am a *mission*?" I asked, shaking my head. "I must be stopped from doing what exactly?" My heart ached. Why couldn't I have been born a normal human? I had no desire to rule anything or battle anyone, least of all the god of man. My father had been right all along, and I had betrayed him.

"Annihilating the realms as we know them. Bringing on the holy war that will bring down the walls of all the realms. Chaos will follow you, Azaiah. You can never be king." She held fast to her belief that I was the nemesis of all that was good.

"Funny thing is I never wanted to be *king*," I said reflectively, more to myself than to her. I was crushed. "Why didn't I know about you? I should have felt something if you are an angel?" I suddenly questioned. I always felt the presence of angels. Then the thought hit me. "That's *your* special gift, huh? That's why they sent you." I grinned ironically, shaking my head. "You had so many opportunities to kill me, why didn't you strike when you had the chance?'

"He could always have another son. We needed the entire hornets' nest to fall." She began to pray aloud to the deity. A prayer of sorrow that she had failed her mission to kill the demon son of Satan. Tears streamed down both of our cheeks, clearly for different reasons.

"You were hoping I would turn on my father? Kill him?" I shook my head. "I loved you, Mikaela. It's unfathomable how heartless you have to be to do something like this. For so long. I pushed everyone away. I chose you over all of them!" I flinched at the memories that flashed before me, all the things that had happened since I had met Mikaela. A lifetime of relationships ruined.

"The sacrifice of one to save billions," she stated coldly, looking straight through me, chin held high in acceptance of her fate. "This isn't about me. This is about you. You want me gone? Then you're going to have to man up and make it happen." Her words stung like a grenade. "You needed me to help you realize who you really are? Show yourself, Azaiah, show your true self."

I was livid. I never asked for any of this. She stepped closer, so close I could smell the perspiration on her skin, the sweetness on her breath. She grabbed my wrists. When I tried to pull away, she didn't relent, but I was stronger and broke free from her grip.

Her breath caressed my face as I placed my hand on her shoulder with more trepidation in my heart than I had ever known. I gently kissed her on the forehead. Tears flowed as I looked Mikaela in the eyes and gave the girl, I loved, eternal death.

My hand fell away. I closed my eyes, as she burst into flames. *What the hell did I just do?*

Chapter Ten

Ties That Bind

I spent a lot of time alone after that day with Mikaela. My dad knew what happened after I left; I had no doubt about that. He always knew everything about me. He may have even been there when I took Mikaela down.

But he respected the fact that I was in mourning and he gave me some time before he began calling. I never answered. I didn't deserve his love or clemency, or Kira's. I was so very humiliated by my behavior. I was embarrassed for being played a fool. I had nothing to say to either of them. Saying sorry would never be adequate.

I went back to school and studied at the library, but otherwise stayed home. There wasn't much to my life. I couldn't even cross over and talk to my mom. No way could I face her after what I had done. About six weeks into the self-imposed great depression there was a knock at my door. I was lying on the couch watching television. I quickly muted the volume and stayed quiet, hoping whomever it was would go away.

"Azaiah," I heard a female call from the other side of the door. *KNOCK. KNOCK.* "Open the goddamn door Azaiah, I know you are in there!" I recognized Taybor's voice.

Damnit, I thought to myself. I wasn't ready to face her yet. I continued to sit, cowering silently into my sofa.

"Azaiah, if you don't answer this door, I swear I am going to get the manager to do a welfare check on you. How embarrassing would that be?" Taybor threatened. "Especially since I know you are home! I can feel your presence, remember?"

"It would be pretty embarrassing," I mumbled quietly to myself, tossing the remote aside and getting up.

KNOCK. KNOCK. KNOCK. I walked slowly to the door, running every terrible scenario that could possibly occur through my mind.

I opened the door just as she had begun another succession of knocks. I stood face to face with Taybor. She looked beautiful, as always. Dressed down per her usual in synthetic black spandex workout clothes and a black leather jacket. A knot tightened in the pit of my stomach as I stood watching her, waiting for a reaction. Our eyes locked for several uncomfortable moments while she let me sweat it out.

Then suddenly as if I had only just seen her yesterday and everything were normal, she said, "Come on Zi, let's go battle. I haven't had a decent spar in months!" She smiled, pushing past me, letting herself in.

I stepped aside as she passed. She walked across the room and plopped down on the couch.

"Reality TV! *REALLY ZI*? Is that what you are doing with yourself these days?" She acted appalled as she clicked the remote, turning the television off.

I sat down beside her on the couch. "Tay, I don't know what to say—" I started, but she cut me off.

"I know, you're a big jerk and you're so sorry and blah, blah, blah. OK," she said. "Forgiven. Now didn't it feel good to get that out of the way ... off your chest ... whatever?" Taybor stood up and grabbed my hand, pulling me up off the couch. "Now get ready to battle!" she ordered.

I used the momentum of her helping me up to pull her in for a hug. She embraced me back. We stood there for an awkward moment wrapped in each other's arms. Then Taybor leaned back and said, "It's ok, you don't need to be that concerned, I won't hurt you. I'm out of practice too. I told you I haven't had any competition since the last time we fought..." Then she winked and smiled. "Fought on the battlefield that is."

"Ok, I'll go. You look like the goddamn Unabomber in all those stealthy black clothes, like you're getting ready to blow some shit up. I'm probably gonna open my door and the FBI will be there waiting with the SWAT team ready to take us down." I smiled at her, thinking to myself how sexy she looked, as I went to change.

"They wouldn't have a chance." She grinned confidently.

"Agreed."

I got dressed and Taybor drove us to the practice arena where we trained. I removed my street clothes and slowly rambled into battle position. Taybor abruptly jumped to her feet and shed her coat and hat, releasing her long tresses of hair. Dark brown and shiny, it spilled around her shoulders. She was, in fact, without a doubt, very beautiful. She was also cut like an Olympic athlete. An Olympic athlete equipped with an arsenal of battle moves that would bring the most experienced warriors to their knees. *Just NOT this warrior*, I thought with a confident grin.

As I turned around and walked to take my starting position Taybor charged across the room. Unexpectedly, I was face to face with her. She planted her heel directly into my gut, knocking the breath out of me.

"So, that's how you want to play?" I asked, recovering quickly with a smile. "OK."

She did a spin move and kicked me again, following up with a flurry of punches. I went down temporarily. Swiftly, I recovered, recoiling back to my feet. I managed to get her into a chokehold. I was sure that she was to the point of submission when she got her feet planted firmly and quickly flipped me over her shoulder. She then turned and kicked me in the testicles as I landed. I curled up in the fetal position, groaning.

"DAMN," I moaned as she stood dominantly over me. *OK, I guess she really wanted a fight!* Sweat trickled off my forehead, dripping on the mat beneath me as I propelled myself back into standing position. Once on my feet I waved my fingers, telling her to come on back.

I eventually got her onto the ground, but somehow, she flipped around and was able to restrain me with an elbow to the throat.

"Go ahead and feel free to cry if you need to." She laughed and brought her knee square up into my groin. I fell over onto my side. "You fight like a little girl. Have you had enough, sweetie pie?" she teased.

"*Not. Even. Close!*" I answered, punctuating each word. I lifted my hand and breathed. "Stay!" Abruptly she was frozen in place as I shot a force field of energy her way.

"Bam, babe, you're dead," I said getting up to my feet, taking the time to gain my composure and catch my breath. I took my place as champion, standing face to face with her as I released the force field. She fell forward.

"You cheat!" she yelled, jumping up and punching me hard in the chest.

"Sorry, I am out of practice. You were kicking my ass, I had to do something." I smiled. "It was self-preservation, you might have killed me."

"Well, I wouldn't go that far. But I was givin' you a proper ass whoopin' that's for sure." She laughed, but I could tell she was pissed. Use of my powers was considered cheating unless we were specifically practicing control techniques.

We put our street clothes back on and headed out into the night. I took her hand and linked my fingers with hers. "I love you, Tay."

"I love you too, Zi," she said back. Her words of unrelenting and unconditional love would be forever pressed into my heart.

Chapter Eleven

Forgiveness

Taybor showed back up at my house the next night to pick me up for another round of battle practice. I hadn't been able to replace my car since it had been wrecked, because I hadn't spoken to my father. No job, no significant money, no car. It hadn't been that much of an inconvenience since my apartment was walking distance to the university. Being in a college neighborhood there were many restaurants and stores in the general the vicinity.

Instead of turning off at the exit where the practice field was, Taybor continued straight.

"Where we going, Tay?" I asked.

"To see Caleb and Kira," she said flatly. "Enough is enough, Zi."

I wasn't angry, but my chest did tighten up a bit at the thought. I had to face the consequences of my actions eventually. It might as well be now.

"Do they know we are coming?" I asked.

"Don't worry, Zi, they will be thrilled to see you." She grabbed my hand. "They both love you very much. We all do."

I knew that. I also knew that I didn't even have to ask for forgiveness from either of them, as it had already been granted. I was just attempting to avoid having to re-live the memory of what I had done. I would forever beat myself up over that day. They on the other hand would never mention it again.

My father smiled then hugged me tight when he opened the door and saw me standing there.

"Come in, Son," he said, stepping aside clearing the way.

As I stepped in, I saw Kira standing across the room also smiling at me.

"We missed you, Azaiah," she said walking over and taking me into her arms. Relief washed over me.

"I'm sorry for—" I started to say, but my father cut me off.

"Azaiah, we all make mistakes. The thing is, most twenty-one-year old's don't have the heavens raining down attempting to kill them." He paused. "I'm a lot older than you son, and I still make mistakes."

"You don't have to try and make me feel better," I interjected.

"You don't think I make mistakes? Oh, I've made mistakes. Big ones!" He squeezed my shoulder. "For instance, getting your mother killed is quite the recent fubar. If I would have just left her alone and stayed away, she would still be here with you. But instead I was selfish and couldn't...didn't...and...it almost got you both killed." He looked sad remembering my mother. That always happened when she came up in conversation.

Kira spoke up in an attempt to change the mood of the conversation as it had suddenly become very melancholy. "The men in this family are forever nearly killing me. I'm used to it." She looked at my father then took my hand. "It was nothing. You are like a son to me boy. Don't ever forget that."

Kira looked back at my father. "I've been through so much worse with your father. If you didn't know this, he can be a bit cocky and arrogant on the battlefield, and that's almost gotten us all killed a time or two." She smiled at him with a wry grin.

"Almost doesn't count Kira," my dad said flatly, raising his eyebrows at her with a snarky smile.

CHAPTER TWELVE

A Love Worth Waiting For

Taybor and I spent several nights a week training. The other nights we were back to our old selves, watching movies, finding local artist or independent musicians to go see, or just hanging out talking. I don't know why I didn't see how unhappy I really was with Mikaela. Now that I was truly happy again with Taybor and had my family back in my life it was clear as day to me.

One night it was late and Taybor and I were on a DVD binge at my place. Pizza, beer, and gladiator movies, what could be better? On nights like these we would get tipsy, act silly and watch movies as late as we could stay up. We usually fell asleep on the floor in front of the television.

We were watching *Gladiator* when one of Taybor's favorite parts came on. We had seen these movies so many times we acted out the best parts. We turned to each other and began to speak in unison with the actors on the TV.

"My name is Maximus Decimus Meridius,
Commander of the Armies of the North,
General of the Felix Legions,
loyal servant to the true emperor, Marcus Aurelius.

We would laugh so hard when we nailed it perfectly.

"Well, I do agree that part is very dramatic, making it, I'd say top three scenes, but my favorite scene, without a doubt, number one!" I insisted, going into a gladiator pose and stepping into the role fully as I dramatically held the remove in a sword like fashion, *"Are You Not Entertained? Are You Not Entertained? Is this not why you are here?"* Then I pretended to spat on the ground and throw my invisible sword into the crowd. Taybor laughed hysterically.

We fell in a fit of laughter, ending up lying next to each other. I turned on my side facing her. She followed suit.

"Tay, why do you think we never—" I stopped mid-sentence, feeling the beer buzz and wondering if I wanted to go through with what I started to say.

She lay on her side and stared at me, her elbow resting on the carpet and her cheek resting on her fist.

"I mean...why didn't we ever move past friendship?" I pushed through and it just spilled out.

She shrugged. "Maybe you had bad taste in women when you were younger?"

Ouch, I thought, then smiled. "Isn't that the truth!"

"Also, probably because I thought, *why would you ever love me?* It just doesn't make sense, Azaiah," she whispered with a tinge of gloom in her voice. "You're a god! I am just a plain girl, nothing special."

"God." I hmphed sarcastically. "Are you crazy?" I said, rubbing the palm of my hand down her cheek. "You are beautiful and smart and a super bad-ass. And I'm an idiot." I paused. "I am so attracted to you and I want to kiss you right now more than I've ever wanted anything in my life. I'm just afraid of losing our friendship if it turns out you don't like me that way—" Taybor cut me off by planting her mouth directly onto mine. Chills went down my spine as our lips melted together into a long, deep kiss.

We lay there kissing for what seemed like hours. I wasn't sure whether I should attempt to take it to the next level, even though I wanted to badly. I had been painfully aroused the entire time. There was no hiding it, I was positive that Taybor was very aware of this.

"Do you want to make love to me, Zi?" Taybor asked, sitting up suddenly. She was on top of me in the throes of making out.

"So bad it physically hurts," I stammered. She slid her t-shirt off over her head revealing a black sports bra. Then she slid that off as well. I couldn't believe how beautiful she looked. I smiled. "You are gorgeous, Tay."

"You're not so bad yourself, Zi." She answered by pulling the t-shirt off over my head. I drew her back down to me and kissed her. I could feel her nipples hard against my chest.

I flipped us over, putting me on top, continuing to kiss her deeply. She moaned with pleasure. Her hands were working hard to get my sweats off without interrupting what I was doing. I used one leg to push the other pant leg off and swiftly my sweats were in a ball at our feet, leaving me only in my boxer briefs.

"You still have too many clothes on, Tay," I said, removing her pajama pants and exposing a black pair of bikini panties. Damn she was sensual. I liked the way they looked on her and I was in no hurry to remove them. Her excitement was evident. As my kisses advanced to her neck my fingers explored her body. She was beginning to tense and was moaning freely. I took her mouth with mine as she freely expressed her pleasure, my mouth stifling her moans of ecstasy.

Touching her and watching her response to my touches, caresses, and kisses had me more excited than I had ever been, even with full-on sex. I wanted her desperately. My body ached to the point of pain.

"Tay, I want you. Is that ok?" I asked, moving my kisses down her neck.

"Zi, I've never-" She stopped. I knew she hadn't had a boyfriend and she wasn't the "type" for casual sex, so she didn't have to say any more.

"I'll be gentle baby. I swear on my heart I would never hurt you again." I swore it and meant it. "Are you sure you want to? We don't have to do this."

"Zi! I want to!" She pulled me closer, and her voice dripping with desire she said, "I *really* want to."

She lifted her hips slightly as I slipped her panties off. Her body was striking. Lean, muscular, and smooth. Her skin was pale, and in the low light she looked like porcelain. As I took her, I felt like a criminal defiling a sacred temple. She took a deep breath and I didn't feel her breathe again for several moments. I was concerned that I had hurt her. I stopped and waited. She felt so good. Finally, she exhaled.

"Are you alright?" I asked, holding still.

"Yes," she exhaled. But I watched a tear run down her cheek.

"Should I stop?" I asked, startled.

"No, Zi, Keep going," she insisted.

"Does it hurt?" I asked with concern. Mikaela was not a virgin, and she was the only girl I had been with, so I wasn't sure what to do to make this enjoyable for Taybor.

"A little. But it also feels really amazing." She smiled. As I slowly continued, she would make faint noises occasionally followed by irregular breathing. I hoped it was from pleasure. Then she began to shudder. I wasn't sure how much longer I could hold out.

"Tay, I can't hold out much longer." She had a glow of pleasure about her face. "Is that ok?" I had to slow down to ask her that question or it would have been too late.

"Ohhh!" She groaned loudly as I thrust deeply into her. I was in a place that was unresponsive to anything outside of my pleasure at that moment. I could feel her body shaking. She pulled me into her and held me there tightly against her.

"Holy crap, Zi! What the hell was that?" She was breathless.

I looked at her startled. "What do you mean?"

"I thought I was going to come out of my skin!" She breathed heavily. "If that's what sex is like I'm not sure what the heck I was holding out for." She laughed.

"You were holding out for me," I said firmly, pulling her close. She was right, sex with her was a spiritual experience. Maybe she felt the same.

She lifted my chin, raising my head and looking into my eyes. "Zi, I love you."

"I love you too, Tay," I said with so much emotion that my heart could have exploded.

"Now, can we do it again?" She laughed.

Chapter Thirteen

I Choose You

It was our senior year at the University of Washington. I would be attending Harvard Law the following year and I wanted Taybor to go with me, so for that reason and the fact that I loved her heart, soul, and body, I decided to propose. Once I knew I would be proposing I spent six weeks looking for the perfect ring. I wanted something unique like her. Then as if all the previous steps weren't difficult enough, I had to figure out the proposal.

The story of how I proposed would be told and retold to friends, family, and strangers for the rest of our lives, so I felt absolutely no pressure to get it right.

The weekend before our graduation ceremony Taybor and I had a date to go see a local indie musician that we both really liked. He was performing at a brew house downtown, which we loved. Therefore, the venue and ambience seemed on point.

Taybor looked magnificent in skinny black jeans and a yellow tank, dark hair flowing over her shoulders. We took our seats at the front of the stage and I ordered a couple rounds of our favorite craft beer. We watched the performance, laughing and conversing per our usual routine.

As the artist was wrapping up, he announced that he had an original song that he was going to close with. The song was written by someone in the audience tonight. I awed and looked around the room like everyone else. Then he began to play the song he had written for me and Taybor.

As the last lyrics were sung, I knelt on one knee in front of her and opened the ring box.

She said, "YES!"

Chapter Fourteen

I Do

Taybor wanted a winter wedding so we set a date. December rolled around, semester break. We flew back to Washington to hold the ceremony with our family and friends in attendance. Taybor had flown back a week before me to tie up loose ends before the ceremony. I had missed her and would be happy to be back together.

Before she left, she held me tightly and whispered, "I guess if you don't show up I'll know that you made your escape." The sentence ended with a nervous laugh.

"Are you kidding me? I've been waiting for this my entire life. I'm not going anywhere! Ever." I kissed her and pulled her close. I'm not sure what had transpired between our friendship days and relationship days that caused her to be slightly insecure in our relationship. I didn't like it. It made me question whether I was doing something wrong to make her feel apprehensive. However, for the life of me I couldn't figure anything out.

I know that she was excited about the wedding and had spent a good amount of time planning and coordinating from across the country. It was exhausting just listening to her talk about flowers, lights, food, and all the other small details that would have never crossed my mind.

The big day arrived, and we took a limo to the resort. The two miles of driveway on the way to the hall were covered in fresh snowfall and wrapped in thousands of clear lights. It looked like a winter wonderland, just as Taybor had hoped. Kira met my father and me as we exited the limousine. A low-pressure system had moved in, keeping the car exhaust from dissipating, it was so thick you could taste it.

"Well, don't you boys look dashing?" she asked straightening my father's tie. As we distanced ourselves from the parking lot the air cleared of auto pollution and became cold, crisp, and clean as it mixed with a faint tinge of smoke from nearby wood-burning stoves.

Kira gave me a big hug. "I wish your mother could have been here for this. For both you and Caleb." She said, "You know I didn't actually know her, but she had to be one very special lady to have been blessed with two fine men like you and your father." She had a proud look on her face. "I love you like you were my own, Azaiah. I am very happy for you today."

"I love you too, Kira." I gave her a kiss. "And thank you for taking care of Dad." I winked at her and flashed her a heartfelt smile. She took Caleb by the arm and they went inside to sit down. We had decided to forgo the best man and bridesmaids because of the distance between us and everyone else, while we were away at school.

I was in the groom's quarters for only a few minutes before I was escorted to the front of the room for the start of the ceremony. A friend of Taybor's was doting on me, straightening my suit and tie and adjusting my boutonniere.

"Is that really necessary? I'm going to look homely standing next to her no matter what you do to my suit," I said. She giggled and led me to the altar.

Thankfully the music started. A sudden fanfare trilled through the air, the cue that the wedding was starting. It floated down the aisle and out into the reception area. I concentrated on the door in anticipation of seeing Taybor in her top-secret wedding gown.

Then the wedding march began. It was familiar. I smiled. She had chosen to walk down the aisle to the tune of 'To Make You Feel My Love' performed on the piano and violin, surrounded by a deluge of accompaniments. It was a beautiful choice.

Then she appeared. Her dark chestnut hair was piled up in a soft crown on top of her head. Taybor was so beautiful it made me weak. She wore a white dress that flowed down her slender body like a waterfall, her back and arms covered in lace.

I thought to myself, *Like I said earlier, no one will be looking at me today. Not while she's in the room anyway.* My throat was thick with emotion and pride.

She clung tightly to her father. Sebastian held the hand of the arm that was pretzeled through his. I could hear the murmurs and rustling of the audience as she came into view. She blushed. The smile grew wider on my face and I could feel the tears burn behind my eyes. What did I do to deserve Taybor?

She looked up, her eyes met mine and locked into place. A tear gently escaped down my cheek and I discreetly brushed it away. All I could see was her face. There was only us in the room, in the entire state, on the whole planet, in the universe. Her eyes were a moist, fiery blue. As she zeroed in on my awed gaze she broke into a breathtaking smile of happiness.

The march was too slow, but thankfully the aisle was very short. At long last she was by my side. She held out her hand. Sebastian took my hand and, in a tradition as old as the universe, placed my hand into his daughter's.

Our vows were simple, lacking all religious grandeur. In that moment, as the justice of the peace said his part, my world, which had been upside down for so long, now seemed to settle into its correct axis. I didn't realize that she was crying until it was time to say the obligatory words. For some reason her tears triggered a wave of raw emotion from me.

"I do." She succeeded choking them out in a nearly incomprehensible whisper.

"I do," I vowed loud and clear.

We were declared husband and wife. I reached to cradle her face, carefully, as if it were as fragile as the blue petals that filled her bouquet. I tried to grasp through the film of stinging tears that nearly blinded me the surreal fact that this astonishing person was mine.

I kissed her tenderly, lovingly. I forgot the audience, the place, the time, only remembering that I loved her, and she loved me, and we were finally together ... forever.

The crowd erupted into applause and we turned our bodies to face our friends and family. I couldn't look away from her face long enough to even acknowledge them.

After the ceremony was over, we took a limousine to the reception where we joined our friends and family. It was a great party. Taybor and I were both so very happy. She had picked an eclectic mix of music that fit our upbeat and sarcastic personalities. It was a wonderful night. The best of my life.

CHAPTER FIFTEEN

Power

I graduated from Harvard Law early and with honors. However, my direction was always going to be politics. After a couple years working with a major Seattle law firm in the international treaties' division, getting experience with local politics and working on several election campaigns, my own career in politics took off and I was elected to the Washington State Senate.

On the 4th of November, at the age of thirty-five, I stood on stage in Seattle with my wife, Taybor, and my father, Caleb, while the media announced the American electorate for the presidency.

"Although most polls have already predicted that Azaiah Frasier was slotted to win the election, few predicted the extent of the victory. Having fought such a hard-primary contest against Spencer and Matsui, this simply turned out to be a much less rigorous match than was expected." The crowded stadium erupted in cheers. The announcer paused then continued. *"Frasier achieved 386 Electoral College votes, the highest of any candidate, even topping President Clinton in 1996, who took 379 Electoral College votes."*

Confetti flew, music played, the crowd went wild. There were simultaneous chants that grew in strength. *"Frasier for change! Frasier for change!"*

I thought to myself, *Change is coming. Big change.*

THE END

The Greatest Bastard series continues with **The Book of Azaiah.** Chloe and Caleb's son Azaiah, the prophesized antichrist, has just been elected the first openly apatheist American president. All the while he is trying to ward off the longstanding threat of the Last War. This cumulates with an epic battle between good and evil that eventually leads to the end times. During the apocalypse, Azaiah, being half-human appears to be a champion of mankind and easily wins over scores of followers. Despite being anti-god and anti-religion, he is on the ground, living with humans, protecting them from various apocalyptic assaults from the heavens.

As multiple catastrophes unfold there are still many devout Christians who end up with Azaiah during these tumultuous times. It is difficult, even for the most dedicated and faithful of Christians to dislike Azaiah as they see him selflessly fighting to protect humankind and what is left of their planet.

Acknowledgements:

Thank you to all the groups and individuals who offer to beta reader for new authors. It's very easy to get so close to our work that we don't see the holes in it. Also thank you to my dear husband & family you are a tremendous part of any successes I have—from giving me "time away" to create and finish my book—to doing errands for me so I could stay focused.